MY FAVORITES

BEN BOVA

MY FAVORITES

A COLLECTION OF SHORT STORIES

**BLACK
STONE**

PUBLISHING

Copyright © 2020 by Ben Bova
Published in 2020 by Blackstone Publishing
Cover and design by Kathryn Galloway English
Book design by Amy Craig

The characters and events in this book are fictitious.
Any similarity to real persons, living or dead, is coincidental
and not intended by the author.

Printed in the United States of America

First edition: 2020
ISBN 978-1-09-400092-3
Fiction / Science Fiction / General

1 3 5 7 9 10 8 6 4 2

CIP data for this book is available
from the Library of Congress

Blackstone Publishing
31 Mistletoe Rd.
Ashland, OR 97520

www.BlackstonePublishing.com

To Rashida, the light of my life

And for the little, little span
The dead are borne in mind,
Seek not to question other than
The books I leave behind.

—Rudyard Kipling

CONTENTS

FOREWORD

A dullard once asked Dizzy Gillespie his opinion of Charlie Parker. With admirable economy, Diz said, "No him: no me." Full disclosure: that describes my professional relationship to Ben Bova. As editor of *Analog*, in 1972 he bought my very first submission to any market—a miracle!—but far more important, he rejected the next thirteen stories I sent him, every time with a standard form rejection to which he'd added a single brief sentence by hand. Those thirteen sentences formed a complete course in how to write commercial fiction, and have made it possible for me to earn a living scribbling for nearly half a century.

But that doesn't explain why I'm here recommending this book. It's because my gratitude made me take a very close look at Ben's own fiction—with the result that to this day, he is one of my favorite living writers in our genre. Every Ben Bova story I've ever read has been a trifecta: it taught me something interesting about science, and something important about us, the people science happens to, and also, something illuminating about the nature and practice of heroism. And made it look easy.

This book is a perfect example: a majority of these stories are old favorites of mine too, yarns that penetrated the fog of my own thoughts deeply enough, decades ago, that today I recognized them within a few paragraphs, and reread them with great pleasure. In another forty-odd years, I'm confident you will too.

—Spider Robinson

INTRODUCTION

I can hear you muttering, "Another anthology? Why?"

After all, I've written more than a hundred works of short fiction, and nearly 150 novels, anthologies, and books of nonfiction. Why another anthology?

Because the stories I write are like my children. I want them to see the light of day, to sparkle in the sunshine, to please the men and women who read them.

Is that too much to ask? I hope not.

So here are fourteen stories. From among all the short fiction I've written, these are my favorites.

I wish that they please you.

Ben Bova

Naples, Florida

2019

"MONSTER SLAYER"

They say that there are only three (or maybe seven) basic themes to all fiction. Take your pick.

Which one is the theme of "Monster Slayer"? Darned if I know. Harry Twelvetoes's story didn't come to me in a flash, complete, all neatly categorized and set to be put into words. Most of the creative process for his story was buried deep in my subconscious and only came to the surface as I worked on the tale, day by day, scene by scene, sentence by sentence.

I don't think this story can be neatly fitted into one of those academicians's categories. I think of it as Harry's story, uniquely the tale of an individual man trying to find his place in the world.

And succeeding—although he never realizes he has.

MONSTER SLAYER

This is the way the legend began.

He was called Harry Twelvetoes because, like all the men in his family, he was born with six toes on each foot. The white doctor who worked at the clinic on the reservation said the extra toes should be removed right away, so his parents allowed the whites to cut the toes off, even though his great-uncle Cloud Eagle pointed out that Harry's father, and his father's fathers as far back as anyone could remember, had gone through life perfectly well with twelve toes on their feet.

His secret tribal name, of course, was something that no white was ever told. Even in his wildest drunken sprees Harry never spoke it. The truth is, he was embarrassed by it. For the family had named him Monster Slayer, a heavy burden to lay across the shoulders of a little boy, or even the strong young man he grew up to be.

On the day that the white laws said he was old enough to take a job, his great-uncle Cloud Eagle told him to leave the reservation and seek his path in the world beyond.

"Why should I leave?" Harry asked his great-uncle.

Cloud Eagle closed his sad eyes for a moment, then said to Harry, "Look around you, nephew."

Harry looked and saw the tribal lands as he had always seen them, brown desert dotted with mesquite and cactus, steep bluffs worn and furrowed as great-uncle's face, turquoise-blue sky and blazing Father Sun baking the land. Yet there was no denying that the land was changing. Off in the distance stood the green fields of the new farms and the tiny dark shapes of the square houses the whites were building. And there were gray rain clouds rising over the mountains.

Refugees were pouring into the high desert. The greenhouse warming that gutted the farms of the whites with drought also brought rains that were filling the dry arroyos of the tribal lands and making flowers bloom. The desert would be gone one day, the white scientists predicted, turned green and bountiful. So the whites were moving into the reservation.

"This land has been ours since the time of First Man and First Woman," great-uncle said. "But now the whites are swarming in. There is no stopping them. Soon there will be no place of our own left to us. Go. Find your way in the world beyond. It is your destiny."

Reluctantly, Harry left the reservation and his family.

In the noisy, hurried world of the whites, jobs were easy to find, but *good* jobs were not. With so many cities flooded by the greenhouse warming, they were frantically building new housing, whole new villages and towns. Harry got a job with a construction firm in Colorado, where the government was putting up huge tracts of developments for the hordes of refugees from the drowned coastal cities. He started as a lowly laborer, but soon enough worked himself up to a pretty handy worker, a jack of all trades.

He drank most of his pay, although he always sent some of it back to his parents.

One cold, blustery morning, when Harry's head was thundering so badly from a hangover that even the icy wind felt good to him, his supervisor called him over to her heated hut.

"You're gonna kill yourself with this drinking, Harry," said the supervisor, not unkindly.

Harry said nothing. He simply looked past the supervisor's short-bobbed blondish hair to the calendar tacked to the corkboard. The picture showed San Francisco the way it looked before the floods and the rioting.

"You listening to me?" the supervisor asked, more sharply. "This morning you nearly ran the backhoe into the excavation pit, for chrissake."

"I stopped in plenty time," Harry mumbled.

The supervisor just shook her head and told Harry to get back to work. Harry knew from the hard expression on the woman's face that his days with this crew were numbered.

Sure enough, at the shape-up a few mornings later, the super took Harry aside and said, "Harry, you Indians have a reputation for being good at high steel work."

Harry's head was thundering again. He drank as much as any two men, but he had enough pride to show up on the job no matter how bad he felt. Can't slay monsters laying in bed, he would tell himself, forcing himself to his feet and out to work.

Besides, no work, no money. And no money, no beer. No whiskey. No girls who danced on your lap or stripped off their clothes to the rhythm of synthesizer music.

Harry knew that it was the Mohawks back East who were once famous for their steelwork on skyscrapers, but he said nothing to the supervisor except, "That's what I heard too."

"Must be in your blood, huh?" said the super, squinting at Harry from under her hard hat.

Harry nodded, even though it made his head feel as if some old medicine man was inside there thumping on a drum.

"I got a cousin who needs high steel workers," the super told him. "Over in Greater Denver. He's willing to train newbies. Interested?"

Harry shuffled his feet a little. It was really cold, this early in the morning.

"Well?" the super demanded. "You interested or not?"

"I guess I'm interested," Harry said. It was better than getting fired outright.

As he left the construction site, with the name and number of the super's cousin in his cold-numbed fist, he could hear a few of the other workers snickering.

"There goes old Twelvetoes."

"He'll need all twelve to hold onto those girders up in the wind."

They started making bets on how soon Harry would kill himself.

But Harry became a very good high steel worker, scrambling along the steel girders that formed the skeletons of the new high-rise towers. He cut down on the drinking: alcohol and altitude didn't mix. He traveled from Greater Denver to Las Vegas and all the way down to Texas, where the Gulf of Mexico had swallowed up Galveston and half of Houston.

When he'd been a little boy, his great-uncle had often told Harry that he was destined to do great things. "What great things?" Harry would ask. "You'll see," his great-uncle would say. "You'll know when you find it."

"But what is it?" Harry would insist. "What great things will I do?"

Cloud Eagle replied, "Every man has his own right path, Harry. When you find yours, your life will be in harmony, and you'll achieve greatness."

Before he left his childhood home to find his way in the white world, his great-uncle gave Harry a totem, a tiny black carving of a spider.

"The spider has wisdom," he told Harry. "Listen to the wisdom of the spider whenever you have a problem."

Harry shrugged and stuffed the little piece of obsidian into the pocket of his jeans. Then he took the bus that led out of the reservation.

As a grown, hard-fisted man, Harry hardly ever thought of those silly ideas. He didn't have time to think about them when he was working fifty, sixty, seventy stories high with nothing between him and the ground except thin air that blew in gusts strong enough to knock a man off his feet if he wasn't careful.

He didn't think about his great-uncle's prophecy when he went roaring through the bars and girlie joints over weekends. He didn't think about anything when he got so drunk that he fell down and slept like a dead man.

But he kept the spider totem. More than once his pockets had been emptied while he slept in a drunken stupor, but no one ever took the spider from him.

And sometimes the spider did speak to him. It usually

happened when he was good and drunk. In a thin, scratchy voice, the spider would say, "No more drinking tonight, Harry. You've had enough. Sleep all through tomorrow, be ready for work on Monday."

Most of the time he listened to the totem's whispers. Sometimes he didn't, and those times almost always worked out badly. Like the time in New Houston when three Japanese engineers beat the hell out of him in the alley behind the cathouse. They didn't rob him, though. And when Harry came to, in a mess of his own blood and vomit and garbage, the spider was wise enough to refrain from saying, "I told you not to get them angry."

He bounced from job to job, always learning new tricks of the trades, never finding the true path that would bring him peace and harmony. The days blurred into an unending sameness: crawl out of bed, clamber along the girders of a new high-rise, wait for the end of the week. The nights were a blur, too: beer, booze, women he hardly ever saw more than once.

Now and then Harry wondered where he was going. "There's more to life than this," the spider whispered to him in his sleep. "Yeah, sure," Harry whispered back. "But what? How do I find it?"

One night while Harry was working on the big Atlanta Renewal Project, the high steel crew threw a going-away party for Jesse Ali, the best welder in the gang.

"So, where's Jesse going?" Harry asked a buddy, beer in hand.

The buddy took a swig of his own beer, then laughed. "He's got a good job, Harry. Great job. It's out of this world." Then he laughed as if he'd made a joke.

"But where is it? Are they hiring?"

"Go ask him," the buddy said.

Harry wormed his way through the gang clustered at the bar and finally made it to Jesse's side.

"Gonna miss you, Jess," he said. Shouted, actually, over the noise of the raucous crowd.

Ali smiled brightly. "Christ, Harry, that's the longest sentence you ever said to me, man."

Harry looked down at the steel-tipped toes of his brogans. He had never been much for conversation, yet his curiosity about Jesse's new job was butting its head against his natural reticence. But the spider in his pocket whispered, "Ask him. Don't be afraid. Ask him."

Harry summoned up his courage. "So, where you goin'?"

Ali's grin got wider. He pointed a long, skinny finger straight up in the air.

Harry said nothing, but the puzzlement must have shown clearly on his face.

"In space, man," Ali explained. "They're building a great big habitat in orbit. Miles long. It'll take years to finish. I'll be able to retire by the time the job's done."

Harry digested that information. "It'll take that long?"

The black man laughed. "Nah. But the pay's that good."

"They lookin' for people?"

With a nod, Ali said, "Yeah. You hafta go through a couple months' training first. Half pay."

"Okay."

"No beer up there, Harry. No gravity, either. I don't think you'd like it."

"Maybe," said Harry.

"No bars. No strip joints."

"They got women, though, don't they?"

"Like Yablonski," said Ali, naming one of the crew who was tougher than any two of the guys.

Harry nodded. "I seen worse."

Ali threw his head back and roared with laughter. Harry drifted away, had a few more beers, then walked slowly through the magnolia-scented evening back to the barracks where most of the construction crew was housed.

Before he drifted to sleep, the spider urged him, "Go apply for the job. What do you have to lose?"

It was tough, every step of the way. The woman behind the desk where Harry applied for a position with the space construction outfit clearly didn't like him. She frowned at him and she scowled at her computer screen when his dossier came up. But she passed him on to a man who sat in a private cubicle and had pictures of his wife and kids pinned to the partitions.

"We are an equal opportunity employer," he said, with a brittle smile on his face.

Then he waited for Harry to say something. But Harry didn't know what he should say, so he remained silent.

The man's smile faded. "You'll be living for months at a time in zero gravity, you know," he said. "It effects your bones, your heart. You might not be fit to work again when you return to Earth."

Harry just shrugged, thinking that these whites were trying to scare him.

They put him through a whole day of physical examinations. Then two days of tests. Not like tests in school; they were interested in his physical stamina and his knowledge of welding and construction techniques.

They hired Harry, after warning him that he had to endure

two months of training at half the pay he would start making if he finished the training okay. Half pay was still a little more than Harry was making on the Atlanta Renewal Project. He signed on the dotted line.

So Harry flew to Hunstville, Alabama, in a company tilt-rotor plane. They gave him a private room, all to himself, in a seedy-looking six-story apartment building on the edge of what had once been a big base for the space agency, before the government sold it off to private interests.

His training was intense. Like being in the army, almost, although all Harry knew about being in the army was what he'd heard from other construction workers. The deal was, they told you something once. You either got it or you flunked out. No second chances.

"Up there in orbit," the instructors would hammer home, time and again, "there won't be a second chance. You screw up, you're dead. And probably a lot of other people get killed too."

Harry began to understand why there was no beer up there. Nor was there any at the training center. He missed it, missed the comfort of a night out with the gang, missed the laughs and the eventual oblivion where nobody could bother him, and everything was dark and quiet and peaceful and even the spider kept silent.

The first time they put him in the water tank, Harry nearly freaked. It was *deep*, like maybe as deep as his apartment building was high. He was zipped into a white spacesuit, like a mummy with a bubble helmet on top, and there were three or four guys swimming around him in trunks and scuba gear. But to a man who grew up in the desert, this much water was scary.

"We use the buoyancy tank to simulate the microgravity

you'll experience in orbit," the instructor told the class. "You will practice construction techniques in the tank."

So he sank into the water for the first time, almost petrified with fear. The spider told Harry, "This is an ordeal you must pass. Be brave. Show no fear."

For days on end, Harry suited up and sank into the deep, clear water to work on make-believe pieces of the structure he'd be building up in space. Each day started with fear, but he battled against it and tried to do the work they wanted him to do. The fear never went away, but Harry completed every task they gave him.

When his two months of training ended, the man in charge of the operation called Harry into his office. He was an Asian of some sort; Chinese, Japanese, maybe Korean.

"To tell you the truth, Harry," he said, "I didn't think you'd make it. You have a reputation for being a carouser, you know."

Harry said nothing. The pictures on the man's wall, behind his desk, were all of rockets taking off on pillars of flame and smoke.

The man broke into a reluctant smile. "But you passed every test we threw at you." He got to his feet and stretched his hand out over his desk. "Congratulations, Harry. You're one of us now."

Harry took his proffered hand. He left the office feeling pretty good about himself. He thought about going off the base and finding a nice friendly bar someplace. But as he dug his hand into his pants pocket and felt the obsidian spider there, he decided against it. That night, as he was drowsing off to sleep, the spider told him, "Now you face the biggest test of all."

Launching off the earth was like nothing Harry had ever even dreamed of. The Clippership rocket was a squat cone; its shape reminded Harry of a big teepee made of gleaming metal.

Inside, the circular passenger compartment was decked out like an airliner's, with six short rows of padded reclinable chairs, each of them occupied by a worker riding up to orbit. There was even a pair of flight attendants, one man and one woman.

As he clicked the safety harness over his shoulders and lap, Harry expected they would be blasted off the ground like a bullet fired from a thirty-aught. It wasn't that bad, though in some ways it was worse. The rockets lit off with a roar that rattled Harry deep inside his bones. He felt pressed down into his seat while the land outside the little round window three seats away tilted and then seemed to fly away.

The roaring and rattling wouldn't stop. For the flash of a moment, Harry wondered if this was the demon he was supposed to slay, a dragon made of metal and plastic with the fiery breath of its rockets pushing it off the earth.

And then it all ended. The noise and shaking suddenly cut off, and Harry felt his stomach drop away. For an instant Harry felt himself falling, dropping off into nothingness. Then he took a breath and saw that his arms had floated up from the seat's armrests. Zero G. The instructors always called it microgravity, but to Harry it was zero G. And it felt good.

At the school they had tried to scare him about zero G with stories of how you get sick and heave and get so dizzy you can't move your head without feeling like it's going to burst. Harry didn't feel any of that. He felt as if he were floating in the water tank again, but this was better, much better. There wasn't any water. He couldn't help grinning. This is great, he said to himself.

But not everybody felt so good. Looking around, Harry saw plenty of gray faces, even some green. Somebody behind him was gagging. Then somebody upchucked. The smell made

Harry queasy. Another passenger retched, up front. Then another. It was like a contagious bug; the sound and stench were getting to everyone in the passenger compartment. Harry took the retch bag from the seat pocket in front of him and held it over his mouth and nose. Its cold, sterile smell was better than the reek of vomit that was filling the compartment. There was nothing Harry could do about the noise except to tell himself that these were whites who were so weak. He wasn't going to sink to their level.

"You'll get used to it," the male flight attendant said, grinning at them from up at the front of the compartment. "It might take a day or so, but you'll get accustomed to zero G."

Harry was already accustomed to it. The smell, though, was something else. The flight attendants turned up the air blowers and handed out fresh retch bags, floating through the aisles as if they were swimming in air. Harry noticed they had filters in their nostrils; *that's how they handle the stink*, he thought.

He couldn't see much of anything as the ship approached the construction site, although he felt the slight thump when they docked. The flight attendants had told everybody to stay in their seats and keep buckled in until they gave the word that it was okay to get up. Harry waited quietly and watched his arms floating a good five centimeters off the armrests of his chair. It took a conscious effort to force them down onto the rests.

When they finally told everybody to get up, Harry clicked the release on his harness and pushed to his feet. And sailed right up into the overhead, banging his head with a thump. Everybody laughed. Harry did too, to hide his embarrassment.

He didn't really see the construction site for three whole days. They shuffled the newcomers through a windowless access tunnel, then down a long sloping corridor and into what looked like a processing center, where clerks checked in each new arrival and assigned them to living quarters. Harry saw that there were no chairs anywhere in sight. Tables and desks were chest high, and everybody stood up, with their feet in little loops that were fastened to the floor. *That's how they keep from banging their heads on the ceiling*, Harry figured.

Their living quarters were about the size of anemic telephone booths, little more than a closet with a mesh sleeping bag tacked to one wall.

"We sleep standing up?" Harry asked the guy who was showing them the facilities.

The guy smirked at him. "Standing up, on your head, sideways, or inside out. Makes no difference in zero G."

Harry nodded. *I should have known that*, he said to himself. *They told us about it back at the training base.*

Three days of orientation, learning how to move and walk and eat and even crap in zero G. Harry thought that maybe the bosses were also using the three days to see who got accustomed to zero G well enough to be allowed to work, and who they'd have to send home.

Harry loved zero G. He got a kick out of propelling himself down a corridor like a human torpedo, just flicking his fingertips against the walls every few meters as he sailed along. He never got dizzy, never got disoriented. The food tasted pretty bland, but he hadn't come up here for the food. He laughed the first time he sat on the toilet and realized he had to buckle up the seat belt or he'd take off like a slow, lumbering rocket.

He slept okay, except he kept waking up every hour or so. The second day, during the routine medical exam, the doc asked him if he found it uncomfortable to sleep with a headband. Before Harry could answer, though, the doctor said, "Oh, that's right. You're probably used to wearing a headband, aren't you?"

Harry grunted. When he got back to his cubicle, he checked out the orientation video on the computer built into the compartment's wall. The headband was to keep your head from nodding back and forth in your sleep. In microgravity, the video explained, blood pumping through the arteries in your neck made your head bob up and down while you slept, unless you attached the headband to the wall. Harry slept through the night from then on.

Their crew supervisor was a pugnacious little Irishman with thinning red hair and fire in his eye. After their three days' orientation, he called the dozen newcomers to a big, metal-walled enclosure with a high ceiling ribbed with steel girders. The place looked like an empty airplane hangar to Harry.

"You know many people have killed themselves on this project so far?" he snarled at the assembled newbies.

"Eighteen," he answered his own question. "Eighteen assholes who didn't follow procedures. Dead. One of them took four other guys with him."

Nobody said a word. They just stood in front of the super with their feet secured by floor loops, weaving slightly like long grasses in a gentle breeze.

"You know how many of *my* crew have killed themselves?" he demanded. "None. Zip. Zero. And you know why? I'll tell you. Because I'll rip the lungs out of any jerkoff asshole who goes one millionth of a millimeter off the authorized procedures."

Harry thought the guy was pretty small for such tough talk, but thought, *what the hell, he's just trying to scare us.*

"There's a right way and a wrong way to do anything," the super went on, his face getting splotchy red. "The right way is what I tell you. Anything else is wrong. Anything! Got that?"

A couple of people replied with "Yes, sir," and "Got it." Most just mumbled. Harry said nothing.

"You," the super snapped, pointing at Harry. "Twelvetoes. You got that?"

"I got it," Harry muttered.

"I didn't hear you."

Harry tapped his temple lightly. "It's all right here, chief."

The supervisor glared at him. Harry stood his ground, quiet and impassive. But inwardly he was asking the spider, "Is this the monster I'm gonna slay?"

The spider did not answer.

"All right," the super said at last. "Time for you rookies to see what you're in for."

He led the twelve of them, bobbing like corks in water, out of the hangar and down a long, narrow, tubular corridor. To Harry it seemed more like a tunnel, except that the floor and curving walls were made of what looked like smooth, polished aluminum. Maybe not. He put out a hand and brushed his fingertips against the surface. *Feels more like plastic than metal*, Harry thought.

"Okay, stop here," said the super.

Stopping was easier said than done in zero G. People bumped into one another and jostled around a bit while the super hovered at the head of the group, hands on hips, and glowered at them. Harry, back near the end of the queue, managed to brush against one of the better-looking women, a Hispanic with big, dark eyes and a well-rounded figure.

"Sorry," he muttered to her.

"*Da nada*," she replied, with a smile that might have been shy. Harry read the nametag pinned above her left breast pocket: Marta Santos.

"All right now," the super called to them, tugging a palm-comp from the hip pocket of his coveralls. "Take a look."

He pecked at the handheld, and suddenly the opaque tube became as transparent as glass. Everybody gasped.

They were hanging in the middle of a gigantic spiderwork of curving metal girders, like being inside a dirigible's frame, except that the girders went on and on for miles. And beyond it, Harry saw the immense, curving bulk of Earth, deep blue gleaming ocean, brighter than the purest turquoise. Streams of clouds so white it hurt his eyes to look at them. He blinked, then looked again. He saw long rows of waves flowing across the ocean, and the cloud-etched edge of land, with gray wrinkles of mountains off in the distance. Beyond the flank of the curving world and its thin glowing skin of air was the utterly black emptiness of space.

We're in space! Harry realized. He had known it, in his head, but now he felt it in his guts, where reality lived. *I'm in space*, he said to himself, lost in the wonder of it. *I'm no longer on Earth.*

Abruptly, the tunnel walls went opaque again. The view shut off. An audible sigh of disappointment gusted through the crew.

"That's enough for now," the super said, with a grin that was somewhere between smug and nasty. "Tomorrow you clowns go out there and start earning your pay."

Harry licked his lips in anticipation.

The suits were a pain. The one thing they couldn't prepare you for on Earth was working inside the goddamned spacesuits. Not even the water tank could simulate the zero pressure of vacuum. The suit's torso, arms, and leggings were hard-shell cermet, but the joints and the gloves had to be flexible, which meant they were made of fabric, which meant they ballooned and got stiff, tough to flex and move when you went outside. The gloves were especially stubborn. They had tiny little servomotors on the back that were supposed to amplify your natural muscle power and help you move the fingers. Sometimes that helped, but when it came to handling tools, it was mostly a waste of time.

Harry got used to the clunky gloves, and the new-car smell of his suit. He never quite got used to hanging in the middle of nothing, surrounded by the growing framework of the miles-long habitat with the huge and glowing Earth spread out before his eyes. Sometimes he thought it was below him, sometimes it seemed as if it was hanging overhead. Either way, Harry could gawk at it like a hungry kid looking through a restaurant window, watching it, fascinated, as it slid past, ever-changing, a whole world passing in panoramic review before his staring eyes.

"Stop your goofin', Twelvetoes, and get back to work!" The super's voice grated in Harry's helmet earphones.

Harry grinned sheepishly and nodded inside his helmet. It was awfully easy to get lost in wonder, watching the world turn.

They worked a six-day week. There was no alcohol in the habitat, not even on Sundays. There was a cafeteria, and the crews socialized there. Everybody complained about the soggy sandwiches and bland fruit juices that the food and drink machines dispensed. You didn't have to put money into them; their internal computers docked your pay automatically.

Harry was scanning the menu of available dishes, wishing they'd bring up somebody who knew how to cook with spices, when a woman suggested, "Try the chicken soup. It's not bad."

She introduced herself: Liza Goldman, from the engineering

office. She was slightly taller than Harry, on the skinny side, he thought. But she looked pretty when she smiled. Light brown hair piled up on top of her head. She and Harry carried their trays to one of the chest-high tables. Harry took a swig from the squeeze bulb of soup. It was lukewarm.

Goldman chattered away as if they were old friends. At first Harry wondered why she had picked him to share a meal with, but pretty soon he was enjoying her company enough to try to make conversation. It wasn't easy. Small talk was not one of his skills.

"You'd think they'd be able to keep the hot foods hot," Goldman was saying, "and the cold foods cold. Instead, once they're in the dispensers they all go blah. Entropy, I guess."

Harry wrinkled his brow and heard himself ask, "You know what I wonder about?"

"No. What?"

"How come they got automated systems for life support and computers all over the place, but they still need us construction jocks."

Goldman's brows rose. "To build the habitat. What else?"

"I mean, why don't they have automated machines to do the construction work? Why do we hafta go outside and do it? They could have machines doin' it, couldn't they?"

She smiled at him. "I suppose."

"Like, they have rovers exploring Mars, don't they? All automated. The scientists run them from their station in orbit around Mars, don't they?"

"Teleoperated, yes."

"Then why do they need guys like me up here?"

Goldman gave him a long, thoughtful look. "Because, Harry, you're cheaper than teleoperated equipment."

Harry was surprised. "Cheaper?"

"Sure. You construction people are a lot cheaper than developing teleoperated machinery. And more flexible."

"Not in those damned suits," Harry grumbled.

With an understanding laugh, Goldman said, "Harry, if they spent the money to develop teleoperated equipment, they'd still have to bring people up here to run the machines. And more people to fix them when they break down. You guys are cheaper."

Harry needed to think about that.

Goldman invited him to her quarters. She had an actual room to herself; not a big room, but there was a stand-up desk and a closet with a folding door and a smart screen along one wall and even a sink of her own. Harry saw that her sleeping mesh was pinned to the ceiling. The mesh would stretch enough to accommodate two, he figured.

"What do you miss most, up here?" Goldman asked him.

Without thinking, Harry said, "Beer."

Her eyes went wide with surprise for a moment, then she threw her head back and laughed heartily. Harry realized that he had given her the wrong answer.

She unpinned her hair, and it spread out like a fan, floating weightlessly.

"I don't have beer, Harry, but I've got something just as good. Maybe better."

"Yeah?"

Goldman slid back the closet door and unzipped a faux leather bag hanging inside. She glided back to Harry and held out one hand. He saw there were two gelatin capsules in her palm.

"The guys in the chem lab cook this up," she said. "It's better than beer."

Harry hesitated. He was on-shift in the morning.

"No side effects," Goldman coaxed. "No hangover. It's just a recreational compound. There's no law against it."

He looked into her tawny eyes. She was offering a lot more than a high.

Her smile turned slightly malicious. "I thought you Native Americans were into peyote and junk like that."

Thinking he'd rather have a beer, Harry took the capsule and swallowed it. As it turned out, they didn't need the sleeping bag. They floated in the middle of the room, bumping into a wall now and then, but who the hell cared?

———

The next morning Harry felt fine, better than he had in months. He was grinning and humming to himself as he suited up for work.

Then he noticed the super was suiting up, too, a couple of spaces down the bench.

Catching Harry's puzzled look, the super grumbled, "Mitsuo called in sick. I'm goin' out with you."

It was a long, difficult shift, especially with the super dogging him every half second:

"Be careful with those beams, hotshot! Just 'cause they don't weigh anything doesn't mean they can't squash you like a bug."

Harry nodded inside his helmet and wrestled the big, weightless girder into place so the welders could start on it while the supervisor went into a long harangue about the fact that zero G didn't erase a girder's mass.

"You let it bang into you, and you'll get crushed just like you would down on Earth."

He went on like that for the whole shift. Harry tried to tune him out, wishing he had the powers of meditation that his great-uncle had talked about, back home. But it was impossible to escape the super's screechy voice yammering in his helmet earphones. Little by little, though, Harry began to realize that the super was trying to educate him, trying to teach him how to survive in zero G, giving him tips that the training manuals never mentioned.

Instead of ignoring the little man's insistent voice, Harry started to listen. Hard. The guy knew a lot more about this work than Harry did, and Harry decided he might as well learn, if the super was willing to teach.

By the time they went back inside and began to worm themselves out of the spacesuits, Harry was grinning broadly.

The super scowled at him. "What's so funny?"

Peeling off his sweat-soaked thermal undergarment, Harry shook his head. "Not funny. Just happy."

"Happy? You sure don't smell happy!"

Harry laughed. "Neither do you, chief."

The super grumbled something too low for Harry to catch.

"Thanks, chief," Harry said.

"For what?"

"For all that stuff you were telling me out there. Thanks."

For once, the supervisor was speechless.

———

Days and weeks blurred into months of endless drudgery. Harry worked six days each week, the monotony of handling the big girders broken only by the never-ending thrill of watching the always-changing Earth sliding along below. Now and then the super would give him another impromptu lecture, but once they were inside again, the super never socialized with Harry, nor with any of his crew.

"I don't make friends with the lunks who work for me," he explained gruffly. "I don't want to be your friend. I'm your boss."

Harry thought it over and decided the little guy was right. Most of the others on the crew were counting the days until their contracts were fulfilled and they could go back to Earth and never see the super again. Harry was toying with the idea of signing up for another tour when this one was finished. There was still plenty of work to do on the habitat, and there was talk of other habitats being started.

He spent some of his evenings with Goldman, more of them with the chemists who cooked up the recreational drugs. Goldman had spoken straight: the capsules were better than beer, a great high with no hangovers, no sickness.

He didn't notice that he was actually craving the stuff, at first. Several months went by before Harry realized his insides got jumpy if he went a few days without popping a pill. And the highs seemed flatter. He started taking two at a time and felt better.

Then the morning came when his guts were so fluttery, he wondered if he could crawl out of his sleeping bag. His hands shook noticeably. He called in sick.

"Yeah, the same thing happened to me," Goldman said that evening, as they had dinner in her room. "I had to go to the infirmary and get my system cleaned out."

"They do that?" Harry asked, surprised.

She tilted her head slightly. "They're not supposed to. The regulations say they should report drug use, and the user has to be sent back Earthside for treatment."

He looked at her. "But they didn't send you back."

"No," said Goldman. "The guy I went to kept it quiet and treated me off the record."

Harry could tell from the look on her face that the treatment wasn't for free.

"I don't have anything to pay him with," he said.

Goldman said, "That's okay, Harry. I'll pay him. I got you into this shit, I'll help you get off it."

Harry shook his head. "I can't do that."

"I don't mind," she said. "He's not a bad lay."

"I can't do it."

She grasped both his ears and looked at him so closely that their noses touched. "Harry, sooner or later, you'll have to do something. It doesn't get better all by itself. Addiction always gets worse."

He shook his head again. "I'll beat it on my own."

He stayed away from the pills for nearly a whole week. By the fifth day, though, his supervisor ordered him to go to the infirmary.

"I'm not going to let you kill yourself out there," the super snarled at him. "Or anybody else, either."

"But they'll send me back Earthside," Harry said. Pleaded, really.

"They ought to shoot you out of a mother-humping cannon," the super growled.

"I'll beat it. Give me a chance."

"The way your hands are shaking? The way your eyes look? You think I'm crazy?"

"Please," Harry begged. It was the hardest word he had ever spoken in his whole life.

The super stared at him, his face splotchy red with anger, his eyes smoldering. At last he said, "You work alone. You kill yourself, that's your problem, but I'm not going to let you kill anybody else."

"Okay," Harry agreed.

"And if you don't start shaping up damned soon, you're finished. Understand?"

"Yeah, but—"

"No *buts*. You shape up, or I'll fire your ass back to Earth so fast, they'll hear the sonic boom on Mars."

So Harry got all the solo jobs: setting up packages of tools at the sites where the crew would be working next; hauling emergency tanks of oxygen; plugging in electronics boards in a new section after the crew finished putting it together; spraying heat-reflecting paint on slabs of the habitat's outer skin. He worked slowly, methodically, because his hands were shaking most of the time, and his vision went blurry now and then. He fought for control of his own body inside the confines of his spacesuit, which didn't smell like a new car anymore; it smelled of sweat and piss and teeth-gritting agony.

He spent his nights alone too, in his closet-sized quarters, fighting the need to down a few pills. Just a few. A couple, even; *that's all I need. Maybe just one would do it. Just one, for tonight. Just to get me through the night. I'll be banging my head against the wall if I don't get something to help me.*

But the spider would tell him, "Fight the monster, Harry. Nobody said it would be easy. Fight it."

The rest of the crew gave him odd looks in the mornings when he showed up for work. Harry thought it was because he looked so lousy, but finally, one of the women asked him why the super was picking on him.

"Pickin' on me?" Harry echoed, truly nonplussed.

"He's giving you all the shit jobs, Twelvetoes."

Harry couldn't explain it to her. "I don't mind," he said, trying to make it sound cheerful.

She shook her head. "You're the only Native American on

the crew and you're being kept separate from the rest of us, every shift. You should complain to the committee—"

"I got no complaints," Harry said firmly.

"Then I'll bring it up," she flared.

"Don't do me any favors."

After that he was truly isolated. None of the crew would talk to him. *They think I'm a coward*, Harry said to himself. *They think I'm letting the super shit on me.*

He accepted their disdain. *I've earned it, I guess*, he told the spider. The spider agreed.

When the accident happened, Harry was literally a mile away. The crew was working on the habitat's endcap assembly, where the curving girders came together and had to be welded precisely in place. The supervisor had Harry installing the big, thin, flexible sheets of honeycomb metal that served as a protective shield against micrometeoroid hits. Thin as they were, the bumpers would still absorb the impact of a pebble-sized meteoroid and keep it from puncturing the habitat's skin.

Harry heard yelling in his helmet earphones, then a high-pitched scream. He spun himself around and pushed off as far as his tether would allow. Nothing seemed amiss as far as he could see along the immense curving flank of the habitat. But voices were hollering on the intercom frequency, several at the same time.

Suddenly the earphones went dead silent. Then the controller's voice, pitched high with tension: "EMERGENCY. THIS IS AN EMERGENCY. ALL OUTSIDE PERSONNEL PROCEED TO ENDCAP IMMEDIATELY. REPEAT. EMERGENCY AT ENDCAP."

The endcap, Harry knew, was where the rest of the crew was working.

Without hesitation, without even thinking about it, Harry

pulled himself along his tether until he was at the cleat where it was fastened. He unclipped it and started dashing along the habitat's skin, flicking his gloved fingers from one handhold to the next, his legs stretched out behind him, batting along the curving flank of the massive structure like a silver barracuda.

Voices erupted in his earphones again, but after a few seconds, somebody inside cut off the intercom frequency. *Probably the controller*, Harry thought. As he flew along, he stabbed at the keyboard on the wrist of his suit to switch to the crew's exclusive frequency. The super warned them never to use that frequency unless he told them to, but this was an emergency.

Sure enough, he heard the super's voice rasping, "I'm suiting up; I'll be out there in a few minutes. By the numbers, report in."

As he listened to the others counting off, the shakes suddenly turned Harry's insides to burning acid. He fought back the urge to retch, squeezed his eyes tight shut, clamped his teeth together so hard his jaws hurt. His bowels rumbled. *Don't let me crap in the suit!* he prayed. He missed a handhold and nearly soared out of reach of the next one, but he righted himself and kept racing toward the scene of the accident, whatever it was, blind with pain and fear. When his turn on the roll call came, he gasped out, "Twelvetoes, on my way to endcap."

"Harry! You stay out of this!" the super roared. "We got enough trouble here already!"

Harry shuddered inside his suit and obediently slowed his pace along the handholds. He had to blink several times to clear up his vision, and then he saw, off in the distance, what had happened.

The flitter that was carrying the endcap girders must have misfired its rocket thruster. Girders were strewn all over the place, some of them jammed into the skeleton of the endcap's unfinished structure, others spinning in slow motion out and away from the habitat. Harry couldn't see the flitter itself; probably it was jammed inside the mess of girders sticking out where the endcap was supposed to be.

Edging closer, hand over hand, Harry began to count the spacesuited figures of his crew, some floating inertly at the ends of their tethers, either unconscious or hurt or maybe dead. Four, five. Others were clinging to the smashed-up pile of girders. Seven, eight. Then he saw one spinning away from the habitat, its tether gone, tumbling head over heels into empty space.

Harry clambered along the handholds to a spot where he had delivered emergency oxygen tanks a few days earlier. Fighting down the bile burning in his gut, he yanked one of the tanks loose and straddled it with his legs. The tumbling, flailing figure was dwindling fast, outlined against a spiral sweep of gray clouds spread across the ocean below. A tropical storm, Harry realized. He could even see its eye, almost in the middle of the swirl.

Monster storm, he thought as he opened the oxy tank's valve and went jetting after the drifting figure. But instead of flying straight and true, the tank started spinning wildly, whirling around like an insane pinwheel. Harry hung on like a cowboy clinging to a bucking bronco.

The earphones were absolutely silent, nothing but a background hiss. Harry guessed that the super had blanked all their outgoing calls, keeping the frequency available for himself to give orders. He tried to talk to the super, but he was speaking into a dead microphone.

He's cut me off. He doesn't want me in this, Harry realized.

Then the earphones erupted. "Who the hell is that? Harry, you shithead, is that you? Get your ass back here!"

Harry really wanted to, but he couldn't. He was clinging as hard as he could to the whirling oxy tank, his eyes squeezed tight shut again. The bile was burning up his throat. When he opened his eyes, he saw that he was riding the spinning tank into the eye of the monster storm down on Earth.

He gagged. Then retched. Dry heaves, hot acid bile spattering against the inside of his bubble helmet. *Death'll be easy after this*, Harry thought.

The spacesuited figure of the other worker was closer, though. Close enough to grab, almost. Desperately, Harry fired a few quick squirts of the oxygen, trying to stop his own spinning or at least slow it down some.

It didn't help much, but then he rammed into the other worker and grabbed with both hands. The oxygen tank almost slipped out from between his legs, but Harry clamped hard onto it. His life depended on it. His, and the other guy's.

"Harry? Is that you?"

It was Marta Santos, Harry saw, looking into her helmet. With their helmets touching, Harry could hear her trembling voice, shocked and scared.

"We're going to die, aren't we?"

He had to swallow down acid before he could say, "Hold on."

She clung to him as if they were racing a Harley through heavy traffic. Harry fumbled with the oxy tank's nozzle, trying to get them moving back toward the habitat. At his back the mammoth tropical storm swirled and pulsated like a thing alive, beckoning to Harry, trying to pull him down into its spinning heart.

"For chrissake," the super's voice screeched, "how long does it take to get a rescue flitter going? I got four injured people here and two more streakin' out to friggin' Costa Rica!"

Harry couldn't be certain, but it seemed that the habitat was getting larger. *Maybe we're getting closer to it*, he thought. *At least we're heading in the right direction. I think.*

He couldn't really control the oxygen tank. Every time he opened the valve for another squirt of gas, the damned tank started spinning wildly. Harry heard Marta sobbing as she clung to him. The habitat was whirling around, from Harry's point of view, but it was getting closer.

"Whattaya mean it'll take another ten minutes?" the super's voice snarled. "You're supposed to be a rescue vehicle. Get out there and rescue them!"

Whoever was talking to the super, Harry couldn't hear it. The supervisor had blocked out everything except his own outgoing calls.

"By the time you shitheads get into your friggin' suits, my guys'll be dead!" the super shrieked. Harry wished he could turn off the radio altogether but to do that he'd have to let go of the tank and if he did *that*, he'd probably go flying off the tank completely. So he held on and listened to the super screaming at the rescue team.

The habitat was definitely getting closer. Harry could see spacesuited figures floating near the endcap and the big mess of girders jammed into the skeletal structure there. Some of the girders were still floating loose, tumbling slowly end over end like enormous throwing sticks.

"Harry!"

Marta's shriek of warning came too late. Harry turned his head inside the fishbowl helmet and saw one of those big, massive girders looming off to his left, slightly behind him, swinging down on him like a giant tree falling.

Automatically, Harry opened the oxy tank valve again. It was the only thing he could think to do as the ponderous steel girder swung down on him like the arm of an avenging god. He felt the tank spurt briefly, then the shadow of the girder blotted out everything, and Marta was screaming behind him, and then he could feel his leg crush like a berry bursting between his teeth, and the pain hit so hard that he felt like he was being roasted alive, and he had one last glimpse of the mammoth storm down on Earth before everything went black.

———

When Harry woke, he was pretty sure he was dead. But if this was the next world, he slowly realized, it smelled an awful lot like a hospital. Then he heard the faint, regular beeps of monitors and saw that he *was* in a hospital, or at least, the habitat's infirmary. *Must be the infirmary*, Harry decided, once he recognized that he was floating without support, tethered only by a light cord tied around his waist.

And his left leg was gone.

His leg ended halfway down the thigh. Just a bandaged stump there. His right leg was heavily bandaged too, but it was all there, down to his toes.

Harry Sixtoes now, he said to himself. For the first time since his mother had died, he felt like crying. But he didn't. He felt like screaming or pounding the walls. But he didn't do that either. He just lay there, floating in the middle of the antiseptic white cubicle, and listened to the beeping of the monitors that were keeping watch over him.

He drifted into sleep, and when he awoke the supervisor was standing beside him, feet encased in the floor loops, his wiry body bobbing slightly, the expression on his face grim.

Harry blinked several times. "Hi, chief."

"That was a damned fool thing you did," the super said quietly.

"Yeah. Guess so."

"You saved Marta's life. The frickin' rescue team took half an hour to get outside. She'd a' been gone by then."

"My leg . . ."

The super shook his head. "Mashed to a pulp. No way to save it."

Harry let out a long, weary breath.

"They got therapies back Earthside," the super said. "Stem cells and stuff. Maybe they can grow the leg back again."

"Workman's insurance cover that?"

The super didn't answer for a moment. Then, "We'll take up a collection for you, Harry. I'll raise whatever it takes."

"No," Harry said. "No charity."

"It's not charity, it's—"

"Besides, a guy doesn't need his legs up here. I can get around just as well without it."

"You can't stay here!"

"Why not?" Harry said. "I can still work. I don't need the leg."

"Company rules," the super mumbled.

Harry was about to say, "Fuck the company rules." Instead, he heard himself say, "Change 'em."

The super stared at him.

Hours after the supervisor left, a young doctor in a white jacket came into Harry's cubicle.

"We did a routine tox screen on your blood sample," he said.

Harry said nothing. He knew what was coming.

"You had some pretty fancy stuff in you," said the doctor, smiling.

"Guess so."

The doctor pursed his lips, as if he were trying to come to a decision. At last he said, "Your blood work report is going to get lost, Harry. We'll detox you here before we release you. All off the record."

That's when it hit Harry.

"You're Liza's friend."

"I'm not doing this for Liza. I'm doing it for you. You're a hero, Harry. You saved a life."

"Then I can stay?" Harry asked hopefully.

"Nobody's going to throw you out because of drugs," said the doctor. "And if you can prove you can still work, even with only one leg, I'll recommend you be allowed to stay."

And the legend began. One-legged Harry Twelvetoes. He never returned to Earth. When the habitat was finished, he joined a new crew that worked on the next habitat. And he started working on a dream, as well. As the years turned into decades, and the legend of Harry Twelvetoes spread all across the orbital construction sites, even out to the cities that were being built on the moon, Harry worked on his dream until it started to come true.

He lived long enough to see the start of construction for a habitat for his own people, a man-made world where his tribe could live in their own way, in their own desert environment, safe from encroachment, free to live as they chose to live.

He buried his great-uncle there, and the tribal elders named the habitat after him: Cloud Eagle.

Harry never quite figured out what the monster was that he was supposed to slay. But he knew he had somehow found his path, and he lived a long life in harmony with the great world around him. When his great-grandchildren laid him to rest beside Cloud Eagle, he was at peace.

And his legend lived long after him.

"MUZHESTVO"

Jamie Waterman is the central character (hero?) of my three novels about Mars: *Mars* (published 1992), *Return to Mars* (1999), and *Mars Life* (2008).

Jamie is half Navajo, half Yankee. As the novels evolved while I wrote them, the two worlds of Earth and Mars came to represent the two sides of Jamie's character: the blue world, Earth, and the red world of Mars.

The Anglo and the Navajo.

"Muzhestvo" takes place early in Jamie's career, before he's even selected to make the first mission to Mars. It's a tale about courage and comradeship, about the strange inner workings of the people who want to extend humankind's horizons—and their own.

MUZHESTVO

As they drove along the river, Yuri Zavgorodny gestured with his free hand.

"Like your New Mexico, no?" he asked in his hesitant English.

Jamie Waterman unconsciously rubbed his side. They had taken the stitches out only yesterday, and the incision still felt sore.

"New Mexico," Zavgorodny repeated. "Like this? Yes?"

Jamie almost answered, "No." But the mission administrators had warned them all to be as diplomatic as possible with the Russians—and everyone else.

"Sort of," Jamie murmured.

"Yes?" asked Zavgorodny over the rush of the searing wind blowing through the car windows.

"Yes," said Jamie.

The flat, brown countryside stretching out beyond the river looked nothing like New Mexico. The sky was a washed-out pale blue, the desert bleak and empty in every direction. *This is an old, tired land*, Jamie said to himself as he squinted against the baking hot wind. Used up. Dried out. Nothing like the vivid mountains and bold skies of his home. New Mexico was a new land, raw and magic and mystical. This dull, dusty desert out here is ancient; it's been worn flat by too many armies marching across it.

"Like Mars," said one of the other Russians. His voice was a deep rumble, where Zavgorodny's was reedy, like a snake-charmer's flute. Jamie had been quickly introduced to all four of them but the only name that stuck was Zavgorodny's.

Christ, I hope Mars isn't this dull, Jamie said to himself.

Yesterday Jamie had been at Bethesda Naval Hospital, having the stitches from his appendectomy removed. All the Mars mission trainees had their appendixes taken out. Mission regulations. No sense risking an attack of appendicitis twenty million miles from the nearest hospital. Even though the decisions about who would actually go to Mars had not been made yet, everyone lost their appendix.

"Where are we going?" Jamie asked. "Where are you taking me?"

It was Sunday, supposedly a day of rest even for the men and women who were training to fly to Mars. Especially for a new arrival, jet-lagged and bearing a fresh scar on his belly. But at sunrise the four cosmonauts had roused Jamie from his bed at the hotel and insisted that he come with them.

"Airport," said the deep-voiced cosmonaut on Jamie's left. He was jammed into the back seat, sandwiched between two of the Russians, sweaty body odor pungent despite the sharp scent of strong soap. Two more rode up front, Zavgorodny at the wheel.

Like a gang of Mafia hit men taking me for a ride, Jamie thought. The Russians smiled at one another a lot, grinning as they talked among themselves and hiking their eyebrows significantly.

Something was up. And they were not going to tell the American geologist about it until they were damned good and ready.

They were solidly built men, all four of them. Short and thickset. Like Jamie himself, although the Russians were much lighter in complexion than Jamie's half-Navajo skin.

"Is this official business?" he had asked them when they pounded on his hotel door at the crack of dawn.

"No business," Zavgorodny had replied while the other three grinned broadly. "Pleasure. Fun."

Fun for them, maybe, Jamie grumbled to himself as the car hummed along the concrete of the empty highway. The river curved off to their left. The wind carried the smell of sun-baked dust. The old town of Tyuratam and Leninsk, the new city built for the space engineers and cosmonauts, was miles behind them now.

"Why are we going to an airport?" Jamie asked.

The one on his right side laughed aloud. "For fun. You will see."

"Yes," said the one on his left. "For much fun."

Jamie had been a Mars trainee for little more than six months. This was his first trip to Russia—to Kazakhstan, really—although his schedule had already whisked him to Australia, Alaska, French Guiana, and Spain. There had been endless physical examinations, tests of his reflexes, his strength, his eyesight, his judgment. They had probed his teeth and pronounced them in excellent shape, then sliced his appendix out of him.

And now a quartet of cosmonauts he'd never met before was taking him in the early morning hours of a quiet Sunday for a drive to Outer Nowhere, Kazakhstan.

For much fun.

There had been precious little fun in the training for Mars. A lot of competition among the scientists, since only sixteen would eventually make the flight: sixteen out of more than two hundred trainees. Jamie realized that the competition must be equally fierce among the cosmonauts and astronauts.

"Have you all had your appendixes removed?" he asked.

The grins faded. The cosmonaut beside him answered, "No. Is not necessary. We do not go to Mars."

"You're not going?"

"We are instructors," Zavgorodny said over his shoulder. "We have already been turned down for the flight mission."

Jamie wanted to ask why, but he thought better of it. This was not a pleasant topic of conversation.

"Your appendix?" asked the man on his left. He ran a finger across his throat.

Jamie nodded. "They took the stitches out yesterday." He realized it had actually been Friday in Bethesda and now it was Sunday, but it felt like yesterday.

"You are an American Indian?"

"Half Navajo."

"The other half?"

"Anglo," said Jamie. He saw that the word meant nothing to the Russians. "White. English."

The man sitting up front beside Zavgorodny turned to face him. "When they took out your appendix—you had a medicine man with painted face to rattle gourds over you?"

All four of the Russians burst into uproarious laughter. The car swerved on the empty highway, Zavgorodny laughed so hard.

Jamie made himself grin back at them. "No, I had anesthesia, just as you would."

The Russians chattered among themselves. Jamie got a vision of jokes about Indians, maybe about a red man wanting to go to the red planet. There was no nastiness in it, he felt, just four beer-drinking fliers having some fun with a new acquaintance.

Wish I understood Russian, he said to himself. Wish I knew what these four clowns are up to. Much fun.

Then he remembered that none of these men could even hope to get to Mars anymore. They had been relegated to the role of instructors. He thought to himself, *I've still got a chance to make the mission. Do they hold that against me? Just what in the hell are they planning to do?*

Zavgorodny swung the car off the main highway and down a two-lane dirt road that paralleled a tall wire fence. Jamie could see, far in the distance, hangars and planes parked haphazardly. *So we really are going to an airport*, he realized.

They drove through an unguarded gate and out to a far corner of the sprawling, silent airport where a single small hangar stood all by itself, like an outcast or an afterthought. A high-wing, twin-engine plane sat on squat tricycle landing gear on the concrete apron in front of the hangar. To Jamie it looked like a Russian version of a Twin Otter, a plane he had flown in during his week's stint in Alaska's frigid Brooks Range.

"You like to fly?" Zavgorodny asked as they piled out of the car.

Jamie stretched his arms and back, glad to be no longer squeezed into the car's back seat. It was not even nine o'clock yet, but the sunshine felt hot and good as it baked into his shoulders.

"I enjoy flying," he said. "I don't have a pilot's license, though. I'm not qualified—"

Zavgorodny laughed. "Good thing! We are four pilots. That is three too many."

The four cosmonauts were already wearing one-piece flight suits of faded, well-worn tan. Jamie had pulled on a white short-sleeved knit shirt and a pair of denims when they had roused him from his hotel bed. He followed the others into the sudden, cool darkness of the hangar. It smelled of machine oil and gasoline. Two of the cosmonauts went clattering up a flight of metal stairs to an office perched on the catwalk above.

Zavgorodny beckoned Jamie to a long table where a row of parachute packs sat big and lumpy, with straps spread out like the limp arms of octopi.

"We must all wear parachutes," Zavgorodny said. "Regulations."

"To fly in that?" Jamie jabbed a thumb toward the plane.

"Yes. Military plane. Regulations. Must wear chutes."

Zavgorodny picked up one of the cumbersome chute packs and handed it to Jamie like a laborer passing a sack of cement.

"Where are we flying to?" Jamie asked.

"A surprise," the Russian said. "You will see."

"Much fun," said the other cosmonaut, already buckling the groin straps of his chute.

Much fun for who? Jamie asked silently. But he worked his arms through the shoulder straps of the chute and leaned over to click the groin straps together and pull them tight.

The other two came down the metal steps, boots echoing in the nearly empty hangar. Jamie followed the quartet of cosmonauts out into the baking sunshine toward the plane. A wide metal hatch had been cut into its side. There were no stairs. When he hiked his foot up to the rim of the hatch, Jamie's side twinged with pain. He grabbed the sides of the hatch and pulled himself inside the plane. Without help. Without wincing.

It was like an oven inside. Two rows of bucket seats, bare, unpadded. The two men who had been sitting in the back of the car with Jamie pushed past him and went into the cockpit. The pilot's and copilot's chairs were thick with padding; they looked comfortable.

Zavgorodny gestured Jamie to the seat directly behind the pilot. He sat himself in the opposite seat and pulled the safety harness across his shoulders and thighs. Jamie did the same, making certain the straps were tight. The parachute pack served as a sort of cushion, but it felt awkward to Jamie: like underwear that had gotten twisted.

One by one, the engines coughed, sputtered, then blasted into life. The plane shook like a palsied old man. As the propellers whirred to invisible blurs, Jamie heard all sorts of rattling noises, as if the plane was going to fall apart at any moment. Something creaked, something moaned horribly. The plane rolled forward.

The two pilots had clamped headphones over their heads, but if they were in contact with the control tower, Jamie could not hear a word they spoke over the roar of the engines and the wind blowing fine, sandpapery dust through the cabin. The fourth cosmonaut was sitting behind Jamie. No one had shut the hatch. Twisting around in his seat, Jamie saw that there was no door for the hatch: they were going to fly with it wide open.

The gritty wind roared through as the plane gathered speed down the runway, skidding slightly first one way and then the other.

Awfully long run for a plane this size, Jamie thought. He glanced across at Zavgorodny. The Russian grinned at him.

And then they were off the ground. The sandblasting ended; the wind was clean now. Jamie saw the airport dwindling away out his window, the parked planes and buildings shrinking into toys. The land spread out, brown and dead-dry beneath the cloudless pale-blue sky. The engines settled into a rumbling growl; the wind howled so loudly that Jamie had to lean across the aisle and shout into Zavgorodny's ear:

"So where are we going?"

Zavgorodny shouted back, "To find Muzhestvo."

"Moo . . . what?"

"Muzhestvo!" the cosmonaut yelled louder.

"Where is it? How far away?"

The Russian laughed. "You will see."

They climbed steadily for what seemed like an hour. *Can't be more than ten thousand feet*, Jamie said to himself. It was difficult to judge vertical distances, but they would have to go on oxygen if they flew much beyond ten thousand feet, he thought. It was getting cold. Jamie wished he had brought his windbreaker. *They should have told me*, he complained silently. *They should have warned me.*

The copilot looked back over his shoulder, staring directly at Jamie. He grinned, then put a hand over his mouth and hollered, "Hoo-hoo-hoo!" His version of an Indian war whoop. Jamie kept his face expressionless.

Suddenly, the plane dipped and skidded leftward. Jamie was slammed against the curving skin of the fuselage and almost banged his head against the window. He stared out at the brown landscape beneath him, wrinkled with hills and a single sparkling lake far below, as the plane seemed to hang on its left wingtip and slowly, slowly revolve.

Then it dove and pulled upward, squeezing Jamie down into his seat. The plane climbed awkwardly, waddling in the air, then flipped over onto its back. Jamie felt all weight leave him; he was hanging by his seat harness but weighed practically nothing. It dived again, and weight returned, heavy, crushing, as the plane hurtled toward those brown bare hills, engines screaming, wind whistling through the shaking, rattling cabin.

And then it leveled off, engines purring, everything as normal as a commuter flight.

Zavgorodny was staring at Jamie. The copilot glanced back over his shoulder. And Jamie understood. They were ragging him. He was the new kid on the block, and they were seeing if they could scare him. *Their own little version of the Vomit Comet*, Jamie said to himself. *See if they can make me turn green or get me to puke. Much fun.*

Every tribe has its initiation rites, he realized. He had never been properly initiated as a Navajo; his parents had been too Anglicized to allow it. But it seemed these guys were going to make up for that.

Jamie made himself grin at Zavgorodny. "That was fun," he yelled, hoping that the other three could hear him over the engines and the wind. "I didn't know you could loop an old crate like this."

Zavgorodny bobbed his head up and down. "Not recommended. Maybe the wings come off."

Jamie shrugged inside his seat harness. "What's next?"

"Muzhestvo."

They flew peacefully for another quarter-hour or so, no aerobatics, no conversation. Jamie realized they had made one wide, circling turn and were starting another. He looked out the window. The ground below was flat and empty, as desolate as Mars except for a single narrow road running straight across the brown, barren wasteland.

Zavgorodny unbuckled his safety harness and stood up. He had to crouch slightly because the of the cabin's low overhead as he stepped out into the aisle and back toward the big, wide, still-open hatch.

Jamie turned in his seat and saw that the other cosmonaut was on his feet, too, and standing at the hatch.

Christ, one lurch of this crate and he'll go ass over teakettle out the door!

Zavgorodny stood beside the other Russian with one hand firmly gripping a slim metal rod that ran the length of the cabin's ceiling. They seemed to be chatting, heads close together, nodding as if they were at their favorite bar holding a casual conversation. With ten thousand feet of empty air just one step away.

Zagorodny beckoned to Jamie with his free hand, gesturing him to come up and join them. Jamie felt a cold knot in his stomach. *I don't want to go over there. I don't want to.*

But he found himself unbuckling the seat harness and walking unsteadily toward the two men near the open hatch. The plane bucked slightly, and Jamie grabbed that overhead rod with both fists.

"Parachute range." Zavgorodny pointed out the hatch. "We make practice jumps here."

"Today? Now?"

"Yes."

The other cosmonaut pulled a plastic helmet onto his head. He slid the tinted visor down over his eyes, yelled something in Russian, and jumped out of the plane.

Jamie gripped the overhead rod even tighter.

"Look!" Zavgorodny yelled at him, pointing. "Watch!"

Cautiously, Jamie peered through the gaping hatch. The cosmonaut was falling like a stone, arms and legs outstretched, dwindling into a tiny tan dot against the deeper brown of the land so far below.

"Is much fun," Zavgorodny hollered into Jamie's ear.

Jamie shivered, not merely from the icy wind slicing through his lightweight shirt.

Zavgorodny pushed a helmet into his hands. Jamie stared at it. The plastic was scratched and pitted, its red and white colors almost completely worn off.

"I've never jumped," he said.

"We know."

"But I . . ." He wanted to say that he had just had the stitches removed from his side, that he knew you could break both your legs parachute jumping, that there was absolutely no way they were going to get him to step out of this airplane.

Yet he put the helmet on and strapped it tight under his chin.

"Is easy," Zavgorodny said. "You have done gymnastics. It is on your file. Just land with knees bent and roll over. Easy."

Jamie was shaking. The helmet felt as if weighed three hundred pounds. His left hand was wrapped around that overhead rod in a death grip. His right was fumbling along the parachute harness straps, searching blindly for the D-ring that would release the chute.

Zavgorodny looked quite serious now. The plane was banking slightly, tilting them toward the open, yawning hole in the plane's side. Jamie planted his feet as solidly as he could, glad that he had worn a sturdy pair of boots.

The Russian took Jamie's searching right hand and placed it on the D-ring. The metal felt cold as death.

"Not to worry," Zavgorodny shouted, his voice muffled by Jamie's helmet. "I attach static line to overhead. It opens chute automatically. No problem."

"Yeah." Jamie's voice was shaky. His insides were boiling. He could feel sweat trickling down his ribs even though he felt shivering cold.

"You step out. You count to twenty. Understand? If chute has not opened by then you pull ring. Understand?"

Jamie nodded.

"I will follow behind you. If you die, I will bury you." His grin returned. Jamie felt like puking.

Zavgorodny gave him a probing look. "You want to go back and sit down?"

Every atom in Jamie's being wanted to answer a fervent, "Hell yes!" But he shook his head and took a hesitant, frightened step toward the open hatch.

The Russian reached up and slid the visor over Jamie's eyes. "Count to twenty slowly. I will see you on ground in two minutes. Maybe three."

Jamie swallowed hard and let Zavgorodny position him squarely at the lip of the hatch. The ground looked iron-hard and very, very far below. They were in shadow, the overhead wing was shading them, the propeller too far forward to be any danger. Jamie took that all in with a single wild glance.

A tap on his shoulder. Jamie hesitated a heartbeat, then pushed off with both feet.

Nothing. No motion. No sound except the thrum of wind rushing past. Jamie suddenly felt that he was in a dream, just hanging in emptiness, floating, waiting to wake up safe and somehow disappointed in bed. The plane had disappeared somewhere behind and above him. The ground was miles below, revolving slowly, not getting noticeably closer.

He was spinning, turning lazily as he floated in midair. It was almost pleasant. Fun, nearly. Just hanging in nothingness, separated from the entire world, alone, totally alone and free.

It was as if he had no body, no physical existence at all. Nothing but pure spirit, clean and light as the air itself. He remembered the old legends his grandfather had told him about Navajo heroes who had traveled across the bridge of the rainbow. *Must be like this*, he thought, high above the world, floating, floating. *Like Coyote when he hitched a ride on a comet.*

He realized with a heart-stopping lurch that he had forgotten to count. And his hand had come off the D-ring. He fumbled awkwardly, seeing now that the hard-baked ground was rushing up to smash him, pulverize him, kill him dead, dead, dead.

A gigantic hand grabbed him and nearly snapped his head off. He twisted in midair as new sounds erupted all around him. Like the snapping of a sail, the parachute unfolded and spread above him, leaving Jamie hanging in the straps floating gently down toward the barren ground.

His heart was hammering in his ears, yet he felt disappointed. Like a kid who had gone through the terrors of his first roller coaster ride and now was sad that it had ended. Far down below he could see the tiny figure of a man gathering up a dirty-white parachute.

I did it! Jamie thought. *I made the jump.* He wanted to give out a real Indian victory whoop.

But the sober side of his mind warned, *you've still got to land without breaking your ankles. Or popping that damned incision.*

The ground was really rushing up now. *Relax. Bend your knees. Let your legs absorb the shock.*

He hit hard, rolled over twice, and then felt the hot wind tugging at his billowing chute. Suddenly Zavgorodny was at his side pulling on the cords, and the other cosmonaut was wrapping his arms around the chute itself like a man trying to stuff a ton of wrapping paper back inside a gift box.

Jamie got to his feet shakily. They helped him wriggle out of the chute harness. The plane circled lazily overhead.

"You did hokay," Zavgorodny said, smiling broadly now.

"How'd you get down so fast?" Jamie asked.

"I did free-fall, went past you. You didn't see me? I was like a rocket!"

"Yuri is free-fall champion," said the other cosmonaut, his arms filled with Jamie's parachute.

The plane was coming in to land, flaps down, engines coughing. Its wheels hit the ground and kicked up enormous plumes of dust.

"So now we go to Muzhestvo?" Jamie asked Zavgorodny.

The Russian shook his head. "We have found it already. *Muzhestvo* means in English language *courage*. You have courage, James Waterman. I am glad."

Jamie took a deep breath. "Me too."

"We four," Zavgorodny said, "we will not go to Mars. But some of our friends will. We will not allow anyone who does not show courage to go to Mars."

"How can you . . . ?"

"Others test you for knowledge, for health, for working with necessary equipment. We test for courage. No one without courage goes to Mars. It would make a danger for our fellow cosmonauts."

"Muzhestvo," Jamie said.

Zavgorodny laughed and slapped him on the back and they started walking across the bare, dusty ground toward the waiting plane.

Muzhestvo, Jamie repeated to himself. Their version of a sacred ritual. Like a Navajo purifying rite. *I'm one of them now. I've proved it to them. I've proved it to myself.*

"WE'LL ALWAYS HAVE PARIS"

If all works of fiction can be categorized as a simple conflict of motivation, such as "love vs. duty" or "responsibility vs. freedom," how would you summarize the classic film *Casablanca?*

To me, the underlying power of that film is the conflict in the soul of Richard Blaine, the American owner of Rick's Café Americain, in Casablanca in 1941. Rick is deeply in love with Ilsa, a beautiful Swedish refugee from the Nazis who have conquered Europe from Poland to the English Channel.

But there are other things happening in Europe, a war and human conflicts that dwarf the love of an individual man for a wonderful woman.

Well, you undoubtedly know the movie. It's at the top of every list of Hollywood classics. And you know the heart-wrenching final scene at the airport, where Rick sends Ilsa away, to return to her husband while he—and Capt.

Reynaud—head for the war. Love vs. duty, portrayed as dramatically as you'll ever see it.

But what happened to Rick and Ilsa and Reynaud after the war? Did they ever meet again? Did love triumph after all?

Read on.

WE'LL ALWAYS HAVE PARIS

He had changed from the old days, but of course, going through the war had changed us all.

We French had just liberated Paris from the Nazis, with a bit of help (I must admit) from General Patton's troops. The tumultuous outpouring of relief and gratitude that night was the wildest celebration any of us had ever witnessed.

I hadn't seen Rick during that frantically joyful night, but I knew exactly where to find him. La Belle Aurore had hardly changed. I recognized it from his vivid, pained description: the low ceiling, the checkered tablecloths—frayed now after four years of German occupation. The model of the Eiffel Tower on the bar had been taken away, but the spinet piano still stood in the middle of the floor.

And there he was, sitting on the cushioned bench by the window, drinking champagne again. Somewhere he had found a blue pinstripe double-breasted suit. He looked good in it; trim and debonair. I was still in uniform and felt distinctly shabby.

In the old days, Rick had always seemed older, more knowing than he really was. Now the years of war had made an honest face for him: world-weary, totally aware of human folly, wise with the experience that comes from sorrow.

"Well, well," he said, grinning at me. "Look what the cat dragged in."

"I knew I'd find you here," I said as I strode across the bare wooden floor toward him. Limped, actually; I still had a bit of shrapnel in my left leg.

As I pulled up a chair and sat in it, Rick called to the proprietor, behind the bar, for another bottle.

"You look like hell," he said.

"It was an eventful night. Liberation. Grateful Parisians. Adoring women."

With a nod, Rick muttered, "Any guy in uniform who didn't get laid last night must be a real loser."

I laughed, but then pointed out, "You're not in uniform."

"Very perceptive."

"It's my old police training."

"I'm expecting someone," he said.

"A lady?"

"Uh-huh."

"You can't imagine that she'll be here to—"

"She'll be here," Rick snapped.

Henri put another bottle of champagne on the table, and a fresh glass for me. Rick opened it with a loud pop of the cork and poured for us both.

"I would have thought the Germans had looted all the good wine," I said between sips.

"They left in a hurry," Rick said, without taking his eyes from the doorway.

He is expecting a ghost, I thought. She'd been haunting him all these years, and now he expected her to come through that doorway and smile at him and take up life with him just where they'd left it the day the Germans marched into Paris.

Four years. We had both intended to join De Gaulle's forces when we'd left Casablanca, but once the Americans got into the war, Rick disappeared like a puff of smoke. I ran into him again by sheer chance in London, shortly before D-Day. He was in the uniform of the US Army, a major in their intelligence service, no less.

"I'll buy you a drink in La Belle Aurore," he told me when we'd parted, after a long night of brandy and reminiscences at the Savoy bar. Two weeks later I was back on the soil of France at last, with the Free French army. Now, in August, we were both in Paris once again.

Through the open windows behind him, I could hear music from the street; not martial brass bands, but the whining, wheezing melodies of a concertina. Paris was becoming Paris again.

Abruptly, Rick got to his feet, an expression on his face that I'd never seen before. He looked . . . surprised, almost.

I turned in my chair and swiftly rose to greet her as she walked slowly toward us, smiling warmly, wearing the same blue dress that Rick had described to me so often.

"You're here," she said, looking past me, her smile, her eyes, only for him.

He shrugged almost like a Frenchman. "Where else would I be?"

He came around the table, past me. She kissed him swiftly, lightly on the lips. It was affectionate, but not passionate.

Rick helped her slip onto the bench behind the table and then slid in beside her. I would have expected him to smile at her, but his expression was utterly serious. She said hello to me at last, as Henri brought another glass to the table.

"Well," I said as I sat down, "this is like old times, eh?"

Rick nodded. Ilsa murmured, "Old times."

I saw that there was a plain gold band on her finger. I was certain that Rick noticed it too.

"Perhaps I should be on my way," I said. "You two must have a lot to talk about."

"Oh, no, don't leave," she said, actually reaching across the table toward me. "I . . ." She glanced at Rick. "I can't stay very long, myself."

I looked at Rick.

"It's all right, Louie," he said.

He filled her glass, and we all raised them and clinked. "Here's . . . to Paris," Rick toasted.

"To Paris," Ilsa repeated. I mumbled it too.

Now that I had the chance to study her face, I saw that the war years had changed her, as well. She was still beautiful, with the kind of natural loveliness that other women would kill to possess. Yet where she had been fresh and innocent in the old days, now she looked wearier, warier, more determined.

"I saw Sam last year," she said.

"Oh?"

"In New York. He was playing in a nightclub."

Rick nodded. "Good for Sam. He got home."

Then silence stretched between them until it became embarrassing. These two had so much to say to each other, yet neither of them was speaking. I knew I should go, but they both seemed to want me to remain.

Unable to think of anything else to say, I asked, "How on earth did you ever get into Paris?"

Ilsa smiled a little. "I've been working with the International Red Cross . . . in London."

"And Victor?" Rick asked. There. It was out in the open now.

"He's been in Paris for the past month."

"Still working with the Resistance." It wasn't a question.

"Yes." She took another sip of champagne, then said, "We have a child, you know."

Rick's face twitched into an expression halfway between a smile and a grimace.

"She'll be three in December."

"A Christmas baby," Rick said. "Lucky kid."

Ilsa picked up her glass but put it down again without drinking from it. "Victor and I . . . we thought, well, after the war is over, we'd go back to Prague."

"Sure," said Rick.

"There'll be so much to do," Ilsa went on, almost whispering, almost pleading. "His work won't be finished when the war ends. In a way, it will just be beginning."

"Yes," I said, "that's understandable."

Rick stared into his glass and said nothing.

"What will you do when the war's over?" she asked him.

Rick looked up at her. "I never make plans that far ahead."

Ilsa nodded. "Oh, yes. I see."

"Well," I said, "I'm thinking about going into politics, myself."

With a wry grin, Rick said, "You'd be good at it, Louie. Perfect."

Ilsa took another brief sip of champagne, then said, "I'll have to go now."

He answered, "Yeah, I figured."

"He's my husband, Rick."

"Right. And a great man. We all know that."

Ilsa closed her eyes for a moment. "I wanted to see you, Richard," she said, her tone suddenly different, urgent, the words coming out all in a rush. "I wanted to see that you were all right. That you'd made it through the war all right."

"I'm fine," he said, his voice flat and cold and final. He got up from the bench and helped her come out from behind the table.

She hesitated just a fraction of a second, clinging to his arm for a heartbeat. Then she said, "Goodbye, Rick."

"Goodbye, Ilsa."

I thought there would be tears in her eyes, but they were dry and unwavering. "I'll never see you again, will I?"

"It doesn't look that way."

"It's . . . sad."

He shook his head. "We'll always have Paris. Most poor chumps don't even get that much."

She barely nodded at me, then walked swiftly to the door and was gone.

Rick blew out a gust of air and sat down again.

"Well, that's over." He drained his glass and filled it again.

I'm not a sentimentalist, but my heart went out to him. There was nothing I could say, nothing I could do.

He smiled at me. "Hey, Louie, why the long face?"

I sighed. "I've seen you two leave each other twice now. The first time, you left her. This time, though, she definitely left you. And for good."

"That's right." He was still smiling.

"I should think—"

"It's over, Louie. It was finished a long time ago."

"Really?"

"That night at the airport, I knew it. She was too much of a kid to understand it herself."

"I know something about women, my friend. She was in love with you."

"Was," Rick emphasized. "But what she wanted, I couldn't give her."

"And what was that?"

Rick's smile turned just slightly bitter. "What she's got with Victor. The whole nine yards. Marriage. Kids. A respectable home after the war. I could see it then, that night at the airport. That's why I gave her the kiss-off. She's a life sentence. That's not for me."

I had thought that I was invulnerable when it came to romance. But Rick's admission stunned me.

"Then you really did want to get her out of your life?"

He nodded slowly. "That night at the airport. I figured she had Victor, and they'd make a life for themselves after this crazy war was over. And that's what they'll do."

"But . . . why did you come here? She *expected* to find you here. You both knew . . ."

"I told you. I came here to meet a lady."

"Not Ilsa?"

"Not Ilsa."

"Then who?"

He glanced at his watch. "Figuring that she's always at least ten minutes late, she ought to be coming in right about now."

I turned in my seat and looked toward the door. She came

striding through, tall, glamorous, stylishly dressed. I immediately recognized her, although she'd been little more than a lovesick child when I'd known her in Casablanca.

Rick got to his feet again and went to her. She threw her arms around his neck and kissed him the way a Frenchwoman should.

Leading her to the table, Rick poured a glass of champagne for her. As they touched glasses, he smiled and said, "Here's looking at you, kid."

Yvonne positively glowed.

INTRODUCTION TO

"THE GREAT MOON HOAX, OR, A PRINCESS OF MARS"

When I was a kid, the solar system seemed much more interesting than it looks today.

I mean, we had canals on Mars. Maybe an intelligent civilization there, desperately trying to save themselves from the encroaching drought that was drying out their planet.

And Venus: beneath its pole-to-pole cover of clouds, the planet was probably a Mesozoic jungle, teeming with the local variety of dinosaurs and such.

Alas, our space probes shattered those exciting possibilities. There are no canals on Mars, no dinosaurs on Venus.

Too bad. It was much more exciting before NASA's spacecraft showed us the truth.

But is it the truth?

THE GREAT MOON HOAX, OR, A PRINCESS OF MARS

I leaned back in my desk chair and just plain stared at the triangular screen.

"What do you call this thing?" I asked the Martian.

"It is an interociter," he said. He was half in the tank, as usual.

"Looks like a television set," I said.

"Its principles are akin to your television, but you will note that its picture is in full color, and you can scan events that were recorded in the past."

"We should be watching the president's speech," said Professor Schmidt.

"Why? We know what he's going to say. He's going to tell Congress that he wants to send a man to the moon before 1970."

The Martian shuddered. His name was a collection of hisses and sputters that came out to something pretty close to

Jazzbow. Anyhow, that's what I called him. He didn't seem to mind. Like me, he was a baseball fan.

We were sitting in my Culver City office, watching Ted Williams's last ball game from last year. Now there was a base-ball player. Best damned hitter since Ruth. And as independent as Harry Truman. Told the rest of the world to go to hell when-ever he felt like it. I admired him for that.

I had missed almost the whole season last year; the Martians had taken me to Venus on safari with them. They were always doing little favors like that for me; this interociter device was just the latest one.

"I still think we should be watching President Kennedy," Schmidt insisted.

"We can view it afterward, if you like," said Jazzbow diplo-matically. As I said, he had turned into quite a baseball fan, and we both wanted to see the Splendid Splinter's final home run.

Jazzbow was a typical Martian. Some of the scientists still can't tell one from another, they look so much alike, but I guess that's because they're all cloned rather than conceived sexually. Mars is pretty damned dull that way, you know. Of course, most of the scientists aren't all that smart outside of their own fields of specialization. Take Einstein, for example. Terrific thinker. He believes if we all scrapped our atomic bombs, the world would be at peace. Yah. Sure.

Anyway, Jazzbow is about four feet nine with dark, leath-ery skin, kind of like a football that's been left out in the sun too long. The water from the tank made him look even darker, of course. Powerful barrel chest, but otherwise a real spidery build, arms and legs like pipe stems. Webbed feet, evolved for walk-ing on loose sand. Their hands have five fingers with opposable thumbs, just like ours, but the fingers have so many little bones in them that they're as flexible as an octopus's tentacles.

Martians would look really scary, I guess, if it weren't for their goofy faces. They've got big, sorrowful, limpid eyes with long feminine eyelashes like a camel; their noses are splayed from one cheek to the other; and they've got these wide, lipless mouths stretched into a perpetual silly-looking grin, like a dolphin. No teeth at all. They eat nothing but liquids. Got long tongues, like some insects, which might be great for sex if they had any, but they don't, and, anyway they usually keep their tongues rolled up inside a special pouch in their cheeks so they don't startle any of us earthlings. How they talk with their tongues rolled up is beyond me.

Anyway, Jazzbow was half in the tank, as I said. He needed the water's buoyancy to make himself comfortable in earthly gravity. Otherwise, he'd have to wear his exoskeleton suit, and I couldn't see putting him through that just so we could have a face-to-face with Professor Schmidt.

The professor was fidgeting unhappily in his chair. He didn't give a rat's ass about baseball, but at least he could tell Jazzbow from the other Martians. I guess it's because he was one of the special few who'd known the Martians ever since they had first crash-landed in New Mexico back in '46.

Well, Williams socked his home run, and the Fenway Park fans stood up and cheered for what seemed like an hour and a half, but he never did come out of the dugout to tip his cap for them. *Good for him!* I thought. His own man to the very end. That was his last time on a ball field as a player. I found I had tears in my eyes.

"Now can we see the president?" Schmidt asked, exasperated. Normally, he looked like a young Santa Claus, round and red-cheeked, with a pale, blond beard. He usually was a pretty jolly guy, but just now his responsibilities were starting to get the better of him.

Jazzbow snaked one long, limber arm out of the water and fiddled with the control knobs beneath the inverted triangle of the interociter's screen. JFK came on the screen in full color, in the middle of his speech to the joint session of Congress:

"I believe that this nation should commit itself to achieving the goal, before this decade is out, of landing a man on the moon and returning him safely to the earth. I believe we should go to the moon."

Jazzbow sank down in his water tank until only his big eyes showed, and he started noisily blowing bubbles, his way of showing that he was upset.

Schmidt turned to me. "You're going to have to talk him out of it," he said flatly.

I had not voted for John Kennedy. I had instructed all of my employees to vote against him, although I imagine some of them disobeyed me out of some twisted sense of independence. Now that he was president, though, I felt sorry for the kid. Eisenhower had let things slide pretty badly. The Commies were infiltrating the Middle East and, of course, they had put up the first artificial satellite and just a couple weeks ago had put the first man into space.

Yuri something-or-other. Meanwhile, young Jack Kennedy had let that wacky plan for the reconquest of Cuba go through. I had told the CIA guys that they'd need strong air cover, but they went right ahead and hit the Bay of Pigs without even a Piper Cub over them. Fiasco.

So the new president was trying to get everybody's mind off

all this crap by shooting for the moon. Which would absolutely destroy everything we'd worked so hard to achieve since that first desperate Martian flight here some fifteen years earlier.

I knew that somebody had to talk the president out of this moon business. And of all the handful of people who were in on the Martian secret, I guess that the only one who could really deal with the White House on an eye-to-eye level was me.

"Okay," I said to Schmidt. "But he's going to have to come out here. I'm not going to Washington."

It wasn't that easy. The president of the United States doesn't come traipsing across the country to see an industrial magnate, no matter how many services the magnate has performed for his country. And my biggest service, of course, he didn't know anything about.

To make matters worse, while my people were talking to his people, I found out that the girl I was grooming for stardom turned out to be a snoop from the goddamned Internal Revenue Service. I had had my share of run-ins with the feds, but using a beautiful starlet like Jean was a low blow, even for them. A real crotch shot.

It was Jazzbow who found her out, of course. Jean and I had been getting along very nicely indeed. She was tall and dark-haired and really lovely, with a sweet disposition and the kind of wide-eyed innocence that makes life worthwhile for a nasty old SOB like me. And she loved it, couldn't get enough of whatever I wanted to give her. One of my hobbies was making movies; it was a great way to meet girls. Believe it or not, I'm really very shy. I'm more at home alone in a plane at twenty thousand feet than at some Hollywood cocktail party. But if you own a studio, the girls come flocking.

Okay, so Jean and I are getting along swell. Except that during the period when my staff was dickering with the White House staff, one morning I wake up and she's sitting at the writing desk in my bedroom, going through my drawers. The desk drawers, that is.

I cracked one eye open. There she is, naked as a Greek goddess and even more gorgeous, rummaging through the papers in my drawers. There's nothing in there, of course. I keep all my business papers in a germ tight, fireproof safe back at the office.

But she had found something that fascinated her. She was holding it in front of her, where I couldn't see what was in her hand, her head bent over it for what seemed like ten minutes, her dark hair cascading to her bare shoulders like a river of polished onyx.

Then she glanced up at the mirror and spotted me watching her.

"Do you always search your boyfriends' desks?" I asked. I was pretty pissed off, you know.

"What is this?" She turned, and I saw she was holding one of my safari photos between her forefinger and thumb, like she didn't want to get fingerprints on it.

Damn! I thought. I should've stashed those away with my stag movies.

Jean got up and walked over to the bed. Nice as pie, she sat on the edge and stuck the photo in front of my bleary eyes.

"What is this?" she asked again.

It was a photo of a Martian named Crunchy, the physicist George Gamow, the kid actor James Dean, and me in the dripping dark jungle in front of a brontosaurus I had shot. The Venusian version of a brontosaurus, that is. It looked like a small mountain of mottled leather. I was holding the stun rifle Crunchy had lent me for the safari.

I thought fast. "Oh, this. It's a still from a sci-fi film we started a few years ago. Never finished it, though. The special effects cost too much."

"That's James Dean, isn't it?"

I peered at the photo as if I was trying to remember something that wasn't terribly important. "Yeah, I think so. The kid wanted more money than I wanted to spend on the project. That's what killed it."

"He's been dead for five or six years."

"Has it been that long?" James Dean was alive and having the time of life working with the Martians on Venus. He had left his acting career and his life on Earth far behind him to do better work than the president's Peace Corps could even dream about.

"I didn't know he did a picture for you," she said, her voice dreamy, ethereal. Like every other woman her age, she had a crush on James Dean. That's what drove the poor kid to Venus.

"He didn't," I snapped. "We couldn't agree on terms. Come on back to bed."

She did, but in the middle of it, my damned private phone rang. Only five people on earth knew that number, and one of them wasn't human.

I groped for the phone. "This better be important," I said.

"The female you are with," said Jazzbow's hissing voice, "is a government agent."

Oh, yeah, the Martians are long-distance telepaths too.

So I took Jean for a drive out to the desert in my Bentley convertible. She loved the scenery, thought it was romantic. Or so she said. Me, I looked at that miserable, dry Mohave scrubland

and thought of what it could become: blossoming farms, spacious tracts of housing where people cooped up in the cities could raise their kids, glamorous shopping malls. But about all it was good for now was an Air Force base where guys like Chuck Yeager and Scott Crossfield flew the X-planes and the Martians landed their saucers every now and then. After dark, of course.

"Just look at that sunset," Jean said, almost breathless with excitement, maybe real, maybe pretend. She was an actress, after all.

I had to admit the sunset was pretty. Red and purple glowing brighter than Technicolor.

"Where are we going?" she kept on asking, a little more nervous each time.

"It's a surprise." I had to keep on going until it was good and dark. We had enough UFO sightings as it was, no sense taking a chance on somebody getting a really good look. Or even worse, a photograph.

The stars came out, big and bright and looking close enough to touch. I kept looking for one in particular to detach itself from the sky and land on the road beside us. All that stuff about saucers shining green rays on cars or planes and sucking them up inside themselves is sheer hooey. The Martians don't have anything like that. Wish they did.

Pretty soon I saw it.

"Look!" said Jean. "A falling star!"

I didn't say anything, but a couple of minutes later, the headlights picked up the saucer sitting there by the side of the road, still glowing a little from the heat of its reentry from orbit.

"Don't tell me you've driven me all the way out here to see another movie set," Jean said, sounding disappointed. "This isn't your big surprise, is it?"

"Not quite," I said, pulling up beside the saucer's spindly little ladder.

She was pretty pissed off. Even when two of the Martians came slithering down the ladder, she still thought it was some kind of a movie stunt. They had to move pretty slowly and awkwardly because of the gravity; made me think of the monster movies we made. Jean was definitely not impressed.

"Honestly, Howard, I don't see why—" Then one of the Martians put its snake-fingered hands on her, and she gave a yelp and did what any well-trained movie starlet would do. She fainted.

Jazzbow wasn't in the ship, of course. The Martians wouldn't risk a landing in Culver City to pick him up, not even at night. Nobody but Professor Schmidt and I knew he was in my office suite there. And the other Martians, of course.

So I got Jazzbow on the ship's interociter while his fellow Martians draped the unconscious Jean on one of their couches. Her skirt rucked up nicely, showing off her legs to good advantage.

"They're not going to hurt her any, are they?" I asked Jazzbow.

"Of course not," his image answered from the inverted triangular screen. "I thought you knew us better than that."

"Yeah, I know. You couldn't hurt a fly. But still, she's just a kid . . . "

"They're merely probing her mind to see how much she actually knows. It will only take a few minutes."

I won't go into all the details. The Martians are extremely sensitive about their dealings with other living creatures. Not hurt a fly? Hell, they'd make the Dalai Lama look like a bloodthirsty maniac.

Very gently, like a mother caressing her sleeping baby, three of them touched her face and forehead with those tentacle-like fingers. Probing her mind. Some writer got wind of the technique second or thirdhand and used it on television a few years later. Called it a Velcro mind-melt or something like that.

"We have for you," the ship's science officer told me, "good news and bad news."

His name sounded kind of like Snitch. Properly speaking, every Martian is an it, not a him or a her. But I always thought of them as males.

"The good news," Snitch said to me, "is that this female knew nothing of our existence. She hadn't the faintest suspicion that Martians exist or that you are dealing with them."

"Well, she does now," I grumbled.

"The bad news," he went on, with that silly grin spread across his puss, "is that she is acting as an undercover agent for your Internal Revenue Service—while she's between acting jobs."

Aw, hell.

I talked it over with Jazzbow. Then he talked in Martian with Snitch. Then all three of us talked together. We had evolved a Standard Operating Procedure for situations like this, when somebody stumbled onto our secret. I didn't much like the idea of using it on Jean, but there wasn't much else we could do.

So, reluctantly, I agreed. "Just be damned careful with her," I insisted. "She's not some hick cop who's been startled out of his snooze by one of your cockamamie malfunctioning saucers."

Their saucers were actually pretty reliable, but every once in a while, the atmospheric turbulence at low altitude would get them into trouble. Most of the sightings happened when the damned things wobbled too close to the ground.

Jazzbow and Snitch promised they'd be extra special careful.

Very gently, the Martians selectively erased Jean's memory so that all she remembered the next morning, when she woke up a half a mile from a Mohave gas station, was that she had been abducted by aliens from another world and taken aboard a flying saucer.

The authorities wanted to put her in a nuthouse, of course. But I sent a squad of lawyers to spring her, since she was under contract to my movie studio. The studio assumed responsibility for her, and my lawyers assured the authorities that she was about to star in a major motion picture. The yokels figured it had all been a publicity stunt and turned her loose. I actually did put her into a couple of starring roles, which ended her career with the IRS, although I figured that not even the feds would have had anything to do with Jean after the tabloids headlined her story about being abducted by flying-saucer aliens. I took good care of her, though. I even married her, eventually. That's what comes from hanging around with Martians.

See, the Martians have a very high ethical standard of conduct. They cannot willingly hurt anybody or anything. Wouldn't step on an ant. It's led to some pretty nasty scrapes for us, though. Every now and then, somebody stumbles onto them, and the whole secret's in jeopardy. They could wipe the person's brain clean, but that would turn the poor sucker into a zombie. So they selectively erase only the smallest possible part of the sucker's memory.

And they always leave the memory of being taken into a flying saucer. They tell me they have to. That's part of their moral code too. They're constantly testing us—the whole human race, that is—to see if we're ready to receive alien visitors from another world. And to date, the human race as a whole has consistently flunked every test.

Sure, a handful of very special people know about them.

I'm pretty damned proud to be among that handful, let me tell you. But the rest of the human race, the man in the street, the news reporters and preachers and even the average university professor—they either ridicule the very idea that there could be any kind of life at all on another world or they get scared to death of the possibility. Take a look at the movies we make!

"Your people are sadly xenophobic," Jazzbow told me more than once, his big liquid eyes looking melancholy despite that dumbbell clown's grin splitting his face.

I remembered Orson Welles' broadcast of The War of the Worlds back in '38. People got hysterical when they thought Martians had landed in New Jersey, although why anybody would want to invade New Jersey is beyond me. Here I had real Martians zipping all over the place, and they were gentle as butterflies. But no one would believe that; the average guy would blast away with his twelve-gauge first and ask where they came from afterward.

So I had to convince the president that if he sent astronauts to the moon, it would have catastrophic results.

Well, my people and Kennedy's people finally got the details ironed out, and we agreed to meet at Edwards Air Force Base, out in the Mohave. Totally secret meeting. JFK was giving a speech in LA that evening at the Beverly Wilshire. I sent a company helicopter to pick him up there and fly him over to Edwards. Just him and two of his aides. Not even his Secret Service bodyguards; he didn't care much for having those guys lurking around him, anyway. Cut down on his love life too much.

We agreed to meet in Hangar Nine, the place where the first Martian crew was stashed back in '46, pretty battered from their crash landing. That's when I first found out about them. I was asked by Professor Schmidt, who looked like a very agitated young Santa Claus back then, to truck in as many refrigeration units as my company could lay its hands on. Schmidt wanted to keep the Martians comfortable, and since their planet is so cold, he figured they needed *mucho* refrigeration. That was before he found out that the Martians spend about half their energy budget at home just trying to stay reasonably warm. They loved Southern California! Especially the swimming pools.

Anyway, there I am waiting for the president in good old Hangar Nine, which had been so top secret since '46 that not even the base commander's been allowed inside. We'd partitioned it and decked it out with nice furniture and all the modern conveniences.

I noticed that Jazzbow had recently had an interociter installed. Inside the main living area, we had put up a big water tank for Jazzbow and his fellow Martians, of course. The place kind of resembled a movie set: nice modern furnishings, but if you looked past the ten-foot-high partitions that served as walls you saw the bare metal support beams crisscrossing up in the shadows of the ceiling.

Jazzbow came in from Culver City in the same limo that brought Professor Schmidt. As soon as he got into the hangar, he unhooked his exoskeleton and dived into the water tank. Schmidt started pacing nervously back and forth on the Persian carpeting I had put in. He was really wound up tight: letting the president in on this secret was an enormous risk. Not for us, so much as for the Martians.

It was just about midnight when we heard the throbbing-motor sound of a helicopter in the distance. I walked out into the open and saw the stars glittering like diamonds all across the desert sky. How many of them are inhabited? I wondered. How many critters out there are looking at our sun and wondering if there's any intelligent life there?

Is there any intelligent life in the White House? That was the big question as far as I was concerned.

Jack Kennedy looked tired. No, worse than that, he looked troubled. Beaten down. Like a man who had the weight of the world on his shoulders. Which he did. Elected by a paper-thin majority, he was having hell's own time getting Congress to vote for his programs. Tax relief, increased defense spending, civil rights — they were all dead in the water, stymied by a Congress that wouldn't do spit for him. And now I was going to pile another ton and a half on top of all that.

"Mr. President," I said as he walked through the chilly desert night from the helicopter toward the hangar door. I sort of stood at attention: for the office, not the man, you understand. Remember, I voted for Nixon.

He nodded at me and made a weary smile and stuck out his hand the way every politician does. I let him shake my hand, making a mental note to excuse myself and go to the washroom as soon as decently possible.

As we had agreed, he left his two aides at the hangar door and accompanied me inside all by himself. He kind of shuddered.

"It's cold out there, isn't it?" he said.

He was wearing a summer-weight suit. I had an old windbreaker over my shirt and slacks.

"We've got the heat going inside," I said, gesturing him through the door in the first partition. I led him into the living area and to the big carpeted central room where the water tank was. Schmidt followed behind us so close I could almost feel his breath on my neck. It gave me that crawly feeling I get when I realize how many millions of germs are floating through the air all the time.

"Odd place for a swimming tank," the president said as soon as we entered the central room.

"It's not as odd as you think," I said. Jazzbow had ducked low, out of sight for the time being.

My people had arranged two big sofas and a scattering of comfortable armchairs around a coffee table on which they had set up a fair-sized bar. Bottles of every description, even champagne in its own ice bucket.

"What'll you have?" I asked. We had decided that, with just the three of us humans present, I would be the bartender.

Both the president and Schmidt asked for scotch. I made the drinks big, knowing they would both need them.

"Now, what's this all about?" Kennedy asked after his first sip of the booze. "Why all this secrecy and urgency?"

I turned to Schmidt, but he seemed to be petrified. So absolutely frozen that he couldn't even open his mouth or pick up his drink. He just stared at the president, overwhelmed by the enormity of what we had to do.

So I said, "Mr. President, you have to stop this moon program."

He blinked his baggy eyes. Then he grinned. "Do I?"

"Yessir."

"Why?"

"Because it will hurt the Martians."

"The Martians, you said?"

"That's right. The Martians," I repeated.

Kennedy took another sip of scotch, then put his glass down on the coffee table. "Mr. Hughes, I had heard that you'd gone off the deep end, that you've become a recluse and something of a mental case—"

Schmidt snapped out of his funk. "Mr. President, he's telling you the truth. There are Martians."

Kennedy gave him a "who are you trying to kid" look. "Professor Schmidt, I know you're a highly respected astronomer, but if you expect me to believe there are living creatures on Mars, you're going to have to show me some evidence."

On that cue, Jazzbow came slithering out of the water tank. The president's eyes goggled as old Jazzie made his painful way, dripping on the rug, to one of the armchairs and half collapsed into it.

"Mr. President," I said, "may I introduce Jazzbow of Mars. Jazzbow, President Kennedy."

The president just kept on staring. Jazzbow extended his right hand, that perpetual clown's grin smeared across his face. With his jaw hanging open, Kennedy took it in his hand. And flinched.

"I assure you," Jazzbow said, not letting go of the president's hand, "that I am truly from Mars."

Kennedy nodded. He believed it. He had to. Martians can make you see the truth of things. Goes with their telepathic abilities, I guess.

Schmidt explained the situation. How the Martians had built their canals once they realized that their world was dying. How they tried to bring water from the polar ice caps to their cities and farmlands. It worked, for a few centuries, but eventually even that wasn't enough to save the Martians from slow but certain extinction.

They were great engineers, great thinkers. Their technology was roughly a century or so ahead of ours. They had invented the electric lightbulb, for example, during the time of our French and Indian War.

By the time they realized that Mars was going to dry up and wither away despite all their efforts, they had developed a rudimentary form of spaceflight. Desperate, they thought that maybe they could bring natural resources from other worlds in the solar system to revive their dying planet. They knew that Venus was, beneath its clouds, a teeming Mesozoic jungle. Plenty of water there, if they could cart it back to Mars.

They couldn't. Their first attempts at spaceflight ended in disasters. Of the first five saucers they sent toward Venus, three of them blew up on takeoff, one veered off course and was never heard from again, and the fifth crash-landed in New Mexico—which is a helluva long way from Venus.

Fortunately, their saucer crash-landed near a small astronomical station in the desert. A young graduate student—who eventually became Professor Schmidt—was the first to find them. The Martians inside the saucer were pretty banged up, but three of them were still alive. Even more fortunately, humans had something that the Martians desperately needed: the raw materials and manufacturing capabilities to mass-produce flying saucers for them. That's where I had come in, as a tycoon of the aviation industry.

President Kennedy found his voice. "Do you mean to tell me that the existence of Martians—living, breathing, intelligent Martians—has been kept a secret since 1946? More than fifteen years?"

"It's been touch-and-go on several occasions," said Schmidt. "But, yes, we've managed to keep the secret pretty well."

"Pretty well?" Kennedy seemed disturbed, agitated. "The Central Intelligence Agency doesn't know anything about this, for Christ's sake!" Then he caught himself, and added, "Or, if they do, they haven't told me about it."

"We have tried very hard to keep this a secret from all the politicians of every stripe," Schmidt said.

"I can see not telling Eisenhower," said the president. "Probably would've given old Ike a fatal heart attack." He grinned. "I wonder what Harry Truman would've done with the information."

"We were tempted to tell President Truman, but—"

"That's all water over the dam," I said, trying to get them back onto the subject. "We're here to get you to call off this Project Apollo business."

"But why?" asked the president. "We could use Martian spacecraft and plant the American flag on the moon tomorrow morning!"

"No," whispered Jazzbow. Schmidt and I knew that when a Martian whispers, it's a sign that he's scared shitless.

"Why not?" Kennedy snapped.

"Because you'll destroy the Martians," said Schmidt, with real iron in his voice.

"I don't understand."

Jazzbow turned those big luminous eyes on the president. "May I explain it to you . . . the Martian way?"

I'll say this for Jack Kennedy. The boy had guts. It was obvious that the basic human xenophobia was strong inside him. When Jazzbow had first touched his hand, Kennedy had almost jumped out of his skin. But he met the Martian's gaze and, not knowing what would come next, solemnly nodded his acceptance.

Jazzbow reached out his snaky arm toward Kennedy's face. I saw beads of sweat break out on the president's brow, but he sat still and let the Martian's tentacle-like fingers touch his forehead and temple.

It was like jumping a car battery. Thoughts flowed from Jazzbow's brain into Kennedy's. I knew what those thoughts were.

It had to do with the Martians' moral sense. The average Martian has an ethical quotient about equal to St. Francis of Assisi. That's the *average* Martian. While they're only a century or so ahead of us technologically, they're light-years ahead of us morally, socially, ethically. There hasn't been a war on Mars in more than a thousand years. There hasn't even been a case of petty theft in centuries. You can walk the avenues of their beautiful, gleaming cities at any time of the day or night in complete safety. And since their planet is so desperately near absolute depletion, they just about worship the smallest blade of grass.

If our brawling, battling human nations discovered the fragile, gentle Martian culture, there would be a catastrophe. The Martians would be swarmed under, shattered, dissolved by a tide of politicians, industrialists, real-estate developers, evangelists wanting to save their souls, drifters, grifters, conmen, thieves petty and grand. To say nothing of military officers driven by xenophobia. It would make the Spanish Conquest of the Americas look like a Boy Scout jamboree.

I could see from the look in Kennedy's eyes that he was getting the message. "*We* would destroy *your* culture?" he asked.

Jazzbow had learned the human way of nodding. "You would not merely destroy our culture, Mr. President. You would kill us. We would die, all of us, very quickly."

"But you have the superior technology . . ."

"We could never use it against you," said Jazzbow. "We would lie down and die rather than deliberately take the life of a paramecium."

Schmidt spoke up. "So you see, Mr. President, why this moon project has got to be called off. We can't allow the human race en masse to learn of the Martians' existence."

"I understand," he murmured.

Schmidt breathed out a heavy sigh of relief. Too soon.

"But I can't stop the Apollo project."

"Can't?" Schmidt gasped.

"Why not?" I asked.

Looking utterly miserable, Kennedy told us, "It would mean the end of my administration. For all practical purposes, at least."

"I don't see—"

"I haven't been able to get a thing through Congress except the moon project. They're stiffing me on everything else: my economics package, my defense buildup, civil rights, everything except the moon program has been stopped dead in Congress. If I give up on the moon, I might as well resign the presidency."

"You are not happy in your work," said Jazzbow.

"No, I'm not," Kennedy admitted, in a low voice. "I never wanted to go into politics. It was my father's idea. Especially after my older brother got killed in the war."

A dismal, gloomy silence descended on us.

"It's all been a sham," the president muttered. "My marriage is a mess, my presidency is a farce, I'm in love with a woman who's married to another man—I wish I could just disappear from the face of the earth."

Which, of course, is exactly what we arranged for him.

It was tricky, believe me. We had to get his blond inamorata to disappear, which wasn't easy, since she was in the public eye just about as much as the president. Then we had to fake his own assassination, so we could get him safely out of the way. At first, he was pretty reluctant about it all, but then the Berlin Wall went up, and the media blamed him for it and he agreed that he wanted out—permanently. We were all set to pull it off when the

Cuban Missile Crisis hit the fan and we had to put everything on hold for more than a month. By the time we had calmed that mess down, he was more than ready to leave this earth. So we arranged the thing for Dallas.

We didn't dare tell Lyndon Johnson about the Martians, of course. He would've wanted to go to Mars and annex the whole damned planet. To Texas, most likely. And we didn't have to tell Nixon; he was happy to kill the Apollo program—after taking as much credit for the first lunar landing as the media would give him.

The toughest part was hoodwinking the astronomers and planetary scientists and the engineers who built spacecraft probes of the planets. It took all of Schmidt's ingenuity and the Martians' technical skills to get the various Mariner and Pioneer probes jiggered so that they would show a barren dry Venus devastated by a runaway greenhouse effect instead of the lush Mesozoic jungle that really exists beneath those clouds. I had to pull every string I knew, behind the scenes, to get the geniuses at JPL to send their two Viking landers to the Martian equivalents of Death Valley and the Atacama Desert in Chile. They missed the cities and the canals completely.

Schmidt used his international connections too. I didn't much like working with Commies, but I've got to admit the two Russian scientists I met were okay guys.

And it worked. Sightings of the canals on Mars went down to zero once our faked Mariner 6 pictures were published. Astronomy students looking at Mars for the first time through a telescope thought they were victims of eyestrain! They knew there were no canals there, so they didn't dare claim they saw any.

So that's how we got to the moon and then stopped going. We set up the Apollo program so that a small number of

Americans could plant the flag and their footprints on the moon and then forget about it. The Martians studiously avoided the whole area during the four years that we were sending missions up there. It all worked out very well, if I say so myself.

I worked harder than I ever had before in my life to get the media to downplay the space program and make it a dull, no-news affair. The man in the street, the average xenophobic Joe Six-Pack, forgot about the glories of space exploration soon enough. It tore at my guts to do it, but that's what had to be done.

So now we're using the resources of the planet Venus to replenish Mars. Schmidt has a tiny group of astronomers who've been hiding the facts of the solar system from the rest of the profession since the late forties. With the Martians' help, they're continuing to fake the pictures and data sent from NASA's space probes.

The rest of the world thinks that Mars is a barren, lifeless desert and Venus is a bone-dry hothouse beneath its perpetual cloud cover, and space in general is pretty much a bore. Meanwhile, with the help of Jazzbow and a few other Martians, we've started an environmental movement on Earth. Maybe if we can get human beings to see their own planet as a living entity, to think of the other animals and plants on our own planet as fellow residents of this Spaceship Earth rather than resources to be killed or exploited—maybe then we can start to reduce the basic xenophobia in the human psyche.

I won't live long enough to see the human race embrace the Martians as brothers. It will take generations, centuries, before we grow to their level of morality. But maybe we're on the right track now. I hope so.

I keep thinking of what Jack Kennedy said when he finally

agreed to rig Project Apollo the way we did, and to arrange his own and his girlfriend's demises.

"It is a far, far better thing I do, than I have ever done," he quoted.

Thinking of him and Marilyn shacked up in a honeymoon suite on Mars, I realized that the remainder of the quote would have been totally inappropriate: "It is a far, far better rest that I go to, than I have ever known."

But what the hell, who am I to talk? I've fallen in love for the first time. Yeah, I know. I've been married several times, but this time it's real, and I'm going to spend the rest of my life on a tropical island with her, just the two of us alone, far from the madding crowd.

Well, maybe not the whole rest of my life. The Martians know a lot more about medicine than we do. Maybe we'll leave this Pacific island where the Martians found her and go off to Mars and live a couple of centuries or so. I think Amelia would like that.

"INSPIRATION"

John W. Campbell, the towering editorial figure who molded science fiction into the exciting, mind-expanding field of literature that it is today, was fond of comparing science fiction to other forms of writing in this way:

He would spread his long arms wide and declaim, "This is science fiction! It takes in the entire universe, past, present, and future." Then he would hold his thumb and forefinger a scant inch apart and add, "This is all other forms of fiction, restricted to the here and now, or the known past."

"Inspiration" could only be written as a science fiction story. It brings together a teenaged Albert Einstein, the British writer H. G. Wells, and Sir William Thomson—Lord Kelvin, one of the giants among physicists.

And one other person.

INSPIRATION

He was as close to despair as only a lad of seventeen can be.

"But you heard what the professor said," he moaned. "It is all finished. There is nothing left to do."

The lad spoke in German, of course. I had to translate it for Mr. Wells.

Wells shook his head. "I fail to see why such splendid news should upset the boy so."

I said to the youngster, "Our British friend says you should not lose hope. Perhaps the professor is mistaken."

"Mistaken? How could that be? He is a famous. A nobleman! A baron!"

I had to smile. The lad's stubborn disdain for authority figures would become world-famous one day. But it was not in evidence this summer afternoon in AD 1896.

We were sitting in a sidewalk café with a magnificent view

of the Danube and the city of Linz. Delicious odors of cooking sausages and bakery pastries wafted from the kitchen inside. Despite the splendid, warm sunshine, though, I felt chilled and weak, drained of what little strength I had remaining.

"Where is that blasted waitress?" Wells grumbled. "We've been here half an hour, at the least."

"Why not just lean back and enjoy the afternoon, sir?" I suggested tiredly. "This is the best view in all the area."

Herbert George Wells was not a patient man. He had just scored a minor success in Britain with his first novel and had decided to treat himself to a vacation in Austria. He came to that decision under my influence, of course, but he did not yet realize that. At age twenty-nine, he had a lean, hungry look to him that would mellow only gradually with the coming years of prestige and prosperity.

Albert was round-faced and plumpish; still had his baby fat on him, although he had started a moustache as most teen-aged boys did in those days. It was a thin, scraggly, black wisp, nowhere near the full white brush it would become. If all went well with my mission.

It had taken me an enormous amount of maneuvering to get Wells and this teenager to the same place at the same time. The effort had nearly exhausted all my energies. Young Albert had come to see Professor Thomson with his own eyes, of course. Wells had been more difficult; he had wanted to see Salzburg, the birthplace of Mozart. I had taken him instead to Linz, with a thousand assurances that he would find the trip worthwhile.

He complained endlessly about Linz, the city's lack of beauty, the sour smell of its narrow streets, the discomfort of our hotel, the dearth of restaurants where one could get decent food—by which he meant burnt mutton. Not even the city's justly famous Linzertorte pleased him.

"Not as good as a decent trifle," he groused. "Not as good by half."

I, of course, knew several versions of Linz that were even less pleasing, including one in which the city was nothing more than charred, radioactive rubble and the Danube so contaminated that it glowed at night all the way down to the Black Sea. I shuddered at that vision and tried to concentrate on the task at hand.

It had almost required physical force to get Wells to take a walk across the Danube on the ancient stone bridge and up the Postlingberg to this little sidewalk café. He had huffed with anger when we had started out from our hotel at the city's central square, then soon was puffing with exertion as we toiled up the steep hill. I was breathless from the climb also. In later years a tram would make the ascent, but on this particular afternoon, we had been obliged to walk.

He had been mildly surprised to see the teenager trudging up the precipitous street just a few steps ahead of us. Recognizing that unruly crop of dark hair from the audience at Thomson's lecture that morning, Wells had graciously invited Albert to join us for a drink.

"We deserve a beer or two after this blasted climb," he said, eying me unhappily.

Panting from the climb, I translated to Albert, "Mr. Wells . . . invites you . . . to have a refreshment with us."

The youngster was pitifully grateful, although he would order nothing stronger than tea. It was obvious that Thomson's lecture had shattered him badly. So now we sat on uncomfortable cast-iron chairs and waited—they for the drinks they had ordered, me for the inevitable. I let the warm sunshine soak into me and hoped it would rebuild at least some of my strength.

The view was little short of breathtaking: the brooding castle across the river, the Danube itself streaming smoothly and actually blue as it glittered in the sunlight, the lakes beyond the city and the blue-white snow peaks of the Austrian Alps hovering in the distance like ghostly petals of some immense, unworldly flower.

But Wells complained, "That has to be the ugliest castle I have ever seen."

"What did the gentleman say?" Albert asked.

"He is stricken by the sight of the Emperor Fried-rich's castle," I answered sweetly.

"Ah. Yes, it has a certain grandeur to it, doesn't it?"

Wells had all the impatience of a frustrated journalist. "Where is that damnable waitress? Where is our beer?"

"I'll find the waitress," I said, rising uncertainly from my iron-hard chair. As his ostensible tour guide, I had to remain in character for a while longer, no matter how tired I felt. But then I saw what I had been waiting for.

"Look!" I pointed down the steep street. "Here comes the professor himself!"

William Thomson, First Baron Kelvin of Largs, was striding up the pavement with much more bounce and energy than any of us had shown. He was seventy-one, his silver-gray hair thinner than his impressive gray beard, lean almost to the point of looking frail. Yet he climbed the ascent that had made my heart thunder in my ears as if he were strolling amiably across some campus quadrangle.

Wells shot to his feet and leaned across the iron rail of the café. "Good afternoon, your Lordship." For a moment I thought he was going to tug at his forelock.

Kelvin squinted at him. "You were in my audience this morning, were you not?"

"Yes, m'lud. Permit me to introduce myself: I am H.G. Wells."

"Ah. You're a physicist?"

"A writer, sir."

"Journalist?"

"Formerly. Now I am a novelist."

"Really? How keen."

Young Albert and I had also risen to our feet. Wells introduced us properly and invited Kelvin to join us.

"Although I must say," Wells murmured as Kelvin came 'round the railing and took the empty chair at our table, "that the service here leaves quite a bit to be desired."

"Oh, you have to know how to deal with the Teutonic temperament," said Kelvin jovially as we all sat down. He banged the flat of his hand on the table so hard it made us all jump. "Service!" he bellowed. "Service here!"

Miraculously, the waitress appeared from the doorway and trod stubbornly to our table. She looked very unhappy; sullen, in fact. Sallow, pouting face with brooding brown eyes and down-turned mouth. She pushed back a lock of hair that had strayed across her forehead.

"We've been waiting for our beer," Wells said to her. "And now this gentleman has joined us—"

"Permit me, sir," I said. It was my job, after all. In German I asked her to bring us three beers and the tea that Albert had ordered and to do it quickly.

She looked the four of us over as if we were smugglers or criminals of some sort, her eyes lingering briefly on Albert, then turned without a word or even a nod and went back inside the café.

I stole a glance at Albert. His eyes were riveted on Kelvin, his lips parted as if he wanted to speak but could not work up the nerve. He ran a hand nervously through his thick mop of hair. Kelvin seemed perfectly at ease, smiling affably, his hands laced across his stomach just below his beard; he was the man of authority, acknowledged by the world as the leading scientific figure of his generation.

"Can it be really true?" Albert blurted at last. "Have we learned everything of physics that can be learned?"

He spoke in German, of course, the only language he knew. I immediately translated for him, exactly as he asked his question.

Once he understood what Albert was asking, Kelvin nodded his gray old head sagely. "Yes, yes. The young men in the laboratories today are putting the final dots over the *i*s, the final crossings of the *t*s. We've just about finished physics; we know at last all there is to be known."

Albert looked crushed.

Kelvin did not need a translator to understand the youngster's emotion. "If you are thinking of a career in physics, young man, then I heartily advise you to think again. By the time you complete your education, there will be nothing left for you to do."

"Nothing?" Wells asked as I translated. "Nothing at all?"

"Oh, add a few decimal places here and there, I suppose. Tidy up a bit, that sort of thing."

Albert had failed his admission test to the Federal Polytechnic in Zurich. He had never been a particularly good student. My goal was to get him to apply again to the Polytechnic and pass the exams.

Visibly screwing up his courage, Albert asked, "But what about the work of Roentgen?"

Once I had translated, Kelvin knit his brows. "Roentgen? Oh, you mean that report about mysterious rays that go through solid walls? X-rays, is it?"

Albert nodded eagerly.

"Stuff and nonsense!" snapped the old man. "Absolute bosh. He may impress a few medical men who know little of science, but his X-rays do not exist. Impossible! German daydreaming."

Albert looked at me with his whole life trembling in his piteous eyes. I interpreted:

"The professor fears that X-rays may be illusory, although he does not as yet have enough evidence to decide, one way or the other."

Albert's face lit up. "Then there is hope! We have not discovered everything as yet!"

I was thinking about how to translate that for Kelvin, when Wells ran out of patience. "Where is that blasted waitress?"

I was grateful for the interruption. "I will find her, sir."

Dragging myself up from the table, I left the three of them, Wells and Kelvin chatting amiably while Albert swiveled his head back and forth, understanding not a word. Every joint in my body ached, and I knew that there was nothing anyone in this world could do to help me. The café was dark inside and smelled of stale beer. The waitress was standing at the bar, speaking rapidly, angrily, to the stout barkeep in a low, venomous tone. The barkeep was polishing glasses with the end of his apron; he looked grim and, once he noticed me, embarrassed.

Three seidels of beer stood on a round tray next to her, with a single glass of tea. The beers were getting warm and flat, the tea cooling, while she blistered the bartender's ears.

I interrupted her viscous monologue. "The gentlemen want their drinks," I said in German.

She whirled on me, her eyes furious. "The gentlemen may have their beers when they get rid of that infernal Jew!"

Taken aback somewhat, I glanced at the barkeep. He turned away from me.

"No use asking him to do it," the waitress hissed. "We do not serve Jews here. I do not serve Jews, and neither will he!"

The café was almost empty this late in the afternoon. In the dim shadows, I could make out only a pair of elderly gentlemen quietly smoking their pipes and a foursome, apparently two married couples, drinking beer. A six-year-old boy knelt at the far end of the bar, laboriously scrubbing the wooden floor.

"If it's too much trouble for you," I said, and started to reach for the tray.

She clutched at my outstretched arm. "No! No Jews will be served here! Never!"

I could have brushed her off. If my strength had not been drained away, I could have broken every bone in her body and the barkeep's too. But I was nearing the end of my tether and I knew it.

"Very well," I said softly. "I will take only the beers."

She glowered at me for a moment, then let her hand drop away. I removed the glass of tea from the tray and left it on the bar. Then I carried the beers out into the warm afternoon sunshine.

As I set the tray on our table, Wells asked, "They have no tea?"

Albert knew better. "They refuse to serve Jews," he guessed. His voice was flat, unemotional, neither surprised nor saddened.

I nodded as I said in English, "Yes, they refuse to serve Jews."

"You're Jewish?" Kelvin asked, reaching for his beer.

The teenager did not need a translation. He replied, "I was

born in Germany. I am now a citizen of Switzerland. I have no religion. But, yes, I am a Jew."

Sitting next to him, I offered him my beer. "No, no," he said with a sorrowful little smile. "It would merely upset them further. I think perhaps I should leave."

"Not quite yet," I said. "I have something that I want to show you." I reached into the inner pocket of my jacket and pulled out the thick sheaf of paper I had been carrying with me since I had started out on this mission. I noticed that my hand trembled slightly.

"What is it?" Albert asked.

I made a little bow of my head in Wells's direction. "This is my translation of Mr. Wells's excellent story, *The Time Machine*."

Wells looked surprised, Albert curious. Kelvin smacked his lips and put his half-drained seidel down.

"Time machine?" asked young Albert.

"What's he talking about?" Kelvin asked.

I explained, "I have taken the liberty of translating Mr. Wells's story about a time machine, in the hope of attracting a German publisher."

Wells said, "You never told me—"

But Kelvin asked, "Time machine? What on earth would a time machine be?"

Wells forced an embarrassed, self-deprecating little smile. "It is merely the subject of a tale I have written, m'lud: a machine that can travel through time. Into the past, you know. Or the, uh, future."

Kelvin fixed him with a beady gaze. "Travel into the past or the future?"

"It is fiction, of course," Wells said apologetically.

"Of course."

Albert seemed fascinated. "But how could a machine travel through time? How do you explain it?"

Looking thoroughly uncomfortable under Kelvin's wilting eye, Wells said hesitantly, "Well, if you consider time as a dimension—"

"A dimension?" asked Kelvin.

"Rather like the three dimensions of space."

"Time as a fourth dimension?"

"Yes. Rather."

Albert nodded eagerly as I translated. "Time as a dimension, yes! Whenever we move through space, we move through time as well, do we not? Space and time! Four dimensions, all bound together!"

Kelvin mumbled something indecipherable and reached for his half-finished beer.

"And one could travel through this dimension?" Albert asked. "Into the past or the future?"

"Utter bilge," Kelvin muttered, slamming his emptied seidel on the table. "Quite impossible."

"It is merely fiction," said Wells, almost whining. "Only an idea I toyed with in order to—"

"Fiction. Of course," said Kelvin, with great finality. Quite abruptly, he pushed himself to his feet. "I'm afraid I must be going. Thank you for the beer."

He left us sitting there and started back down the street, his face flushed. From the way his beard moved, I could see that he was muttering to himself.

"I'm afraid we've offended him," said Wells.

"But how could he become angry over an idea?" Albert wondered. The thought seemed to stun him. "Why should a new idea infuriate a man of science?"

The waitress bustled across the patio to our table. "When is this Jew leaving?" she hissed at me, eyes blazing with fury. "I won't have him stinking up our café any longer!"

Obviously shaken, but with as much dignity as a seventeen-year-old could muster, Albert rose to his feet. "I will leave, Madame. I have imposed on your so-gracious hospitality long enough."

"Wait," I said, grabbing at his jacket sleeve. "Take this with you. Read it. I think you will enjoy it."

He smiled at me, but I could see the sadness that would haunt his eyes forever. "Thank you, sir. You have been most kind to me."

He took the manuscript and left us. I saw him already reading it as he walked slowly down the street toward the bridge back to Linz proper. I hoped he would not trip and break his neck as he ambled down the steep street, his nose stuck in the manuscript.

The waitress watched him too. "Filthy Jew. They're every-where! They get themselves into everything."

"That will be quite enough from you," I said as sternly as I could manage.

She glared at me and headed back for the bar.

Wells looked more puzzled than annoyed, even after I explained what had happened.

"It's their country, after all," he said, with a shrug of his narrow shoulders. "If they don't want to mingle with Jews, there's not much we can do about it, is there?"

I took a sip of my warm, flat beer, not trusting myself to come up with a properly polite response. There was only one timeline in which Albert lived long enough to make an effect on the world. There were dozens where he languished in obscurity or was gassed in one of the death camps.

Wells's expression turned curious. "I didn't know you had translated my story."

"To see if perhaps a German publisher would be interested in it," I lied.

"But you gave the manuscript to that Jewish fellow."

"I have another copy of the translation."

"You do? Why would you—"

My time was almost up, I knew. I had a powerful urge to end the charade. "That young Jewish fellow might change the world, you know."

Wells laughed.

"I mean it," I said. "You think that your story is merely a piece of fiction. Let me tell you, it is much more than that."

"Really?"

"Time travel will become possible one day."

"Don't be ridiculous!" But I could see the sudden astonishment in his eyes. And the memory. It was I who had suggested the idea of time travel to him. We had discussed it for months, back when he had been working for the newspapers. I had kept the idea in the forefront of his imagination until he finally sat down and dashed off his novel.

I hunched closer to him, leaned my elbows wearily on the table. "Suppose Kelvin is wrong? Suppose there is much more to physics than he suspects?"

"How could that be?" Wells asked.

"That lad is reading your story. It will open his eyes to new vistas, new possibilities."

Wells cast a suspicious glance at me. "You're pulling my leg."

I forced a smile. "Not altogether. You would do well to pay attention to what the scientists discover over the coming years.

You could build a career writing about it. You could become known as a prophet if you play your cards properly."

His face took on the strangest expression I had ever seen: he did not want to believe me, and yet he did; he was suspicious, curious, doubtful, and yearning—all at the same time. Above everything else he was ambitious; thirsting for fame. Like every writer, he wanted to have the world acknowledge his genius.

I told him as much as I dared. As the afternoon drifted on and the shadows lengthened, as the sun sank behind the distant mountains and the warmth of day slowly gave way to an uneasy, deepening chill, I gave him carefully veiled hints of the future. A future. The one I wanted him to promote.

Wells could have no conception of the realities of time travel, of course. There was no frame of reference for the infinite branch-ings of the future in his tidy nineteenth-century English mind. He was incapable of imagining the horrors that lay in store. How could he be? Time branches endlessly, and only a few, a precious hand-ful of those branches, manage to avoid utter disaster.

Could I show him his beloved London obliterated by fusion bombs? Or the entire northern hemisphere of Earth depopu-lated by man-made plagues? Or a devastated world turned to a savagery that made his Morlocks seem compassionate?

Could I explain to him the energies involved in time travel or the damage they did to the human body? The fact that time trav-elers were volunteers sent on suicide missions, desperately trying to preserve a timeline that saved at least a portion of the human race? The best future I could offer him was a twentieth century tortured by world wars and genocide. That was the best I could do.

So all I did was hint, as gently and subtly as I could, trying to guide him toward that best of all possible futures, horrible though it would seem to him. I could neither control nor coerce anyone; all I could do was to offer a bit of guidance. Until the radiation dose from my own trip through time finally killed me.

Wells was happily oblivious to my pain. He did not even notice the perspiration that beaded my brow despite the chilling breeze that heralded nightfall.

"You appear to be telling me," he said at last, "that my writings will have some sort of positive effect on the world."

"They already have," I replied, with a genuine smile.

His brows rose.

"That teenaged lad is reading your story. Your concept of time as a dimension has already started his fertile mind working."

"That young student?"

"Will change the world," I said. "For the better."

"Really?"

"Really," I said, trying to sound confident. I knew there were still a thousand pitfalls in young Albert's path. And I would not live long enough to help him past them. Perhaps others would, but there were no guarantees.

I knew that if Albert did not reach his full potential, if he were turned away by the university again or murdered in the coming holocaust, the future I was attempting to preserve would disappear in a global catastrophe that could end the human race forever. My task was to save as much of humanity as I could.

I had accomplished a feeble first step in saving some of humankind, but only a first step. Albert was reading the time-machine tale and starting to think that Kelvin was blind to the real world. But there was so much more to do. So very much more.

We sat there in the deepening shadows of the approaching twilight, Wells and I, each of us wrapped in our own thoughts about the future. Despite his best English self-control, Wells was smiling contentedly. He saw a future in which he would be hailed as a prophet. I hoped it would work out that way. It was an immense task that I had undertaken. I felt tired, gloomy, daunted by the immensity of it all. Worst of all, I would never know if I succeeded or not.

Then the waitress bustled over to our table. "Well, have you finished? Or are you going to stay here all night?"

Even without a translation Wells understood her tone. "Let's go," he said, scraping his chair across the flagstones.

I pushed myself to my feet and threw a few coins on the table. The waitress scooped them up immediately and called into the café, "Come here and scrub down this table! At once!"

The six-year-old boy came trudging across the patio, lugging the heavy wooden pail of water. He stumbled and almost dropped it; water sloshed onto his mother's legs. She grabbed him by the ear and lifted him nearly off his feet. A faint, tortured squeak issued from the boy's gritted teeth.

"Be quiet and your do work properly," she told her son, her voice murderously low. "If I let your father know how lazy you are . . ."

The six-year-old's eyes went wide with terror as his mother let her threat dangle in the air between them.

"Scrub that table good, Adolf," his mother told him. "Get rid of that damned Jew's stink."

I looked down at the boy. His eyes were burning with shame and rage and hatred. *Save as much of the human race as you can*, I told myself. But it was already too late to save him.

"Are you coming?" Wells called to me.

"Yes," I said, tears in my eyes. "It's getting dark, isn't it?"

INTRODUCTION TO
"SCHEHERAZADE AND THE STORYTELLERS"

Two points: One, science fiction isn't confined to stories about the future. Two, science fiction writers are (for the most part) friends, comrades in the sometimes-bitter world of publishing, brothers-in-arms . . . er, make that brothers-in-pens (and sisters, of course).

As the aforementioned John W. Campbell noted, science fiction is not restricted to tales about the future. The past is also part of our territory.

Here is a tale of the storied past, of a cruel sultan and a beautiful, clever young woman—and of a ragged clutch of story-tellers who are loosely based on my science-fiction-writing friends and colleagues.

SCHEHERAZADE AND THE STORYTELLERS

"I need a new story!" exclaimed Scheherazade, her lovely almond eyes betraying a rising terror. "By tonight!"

"Daughter of my heart," said her father, the grand vizier, "I have related to you every tale that I know. Some of them, best beloved, were even true!"

"But, most respected father, I am summoned to the sultan again tonight. If I have not a new tale with which to beguile him, he will cut off my head in the morning!"

The grand vizier chewed his beard and raised his eyes to Allah in supplication. He could not help but notice that the gold leaf adorning the ceiling is his chamber was peeling once more. *I must call the workmen again*, he thought, his heart sinking.

For although the grand vizier and his family resided in a splendid wing of the sultan's magnificent palace, the grand vizier was responsible for the upkeep of his quarters. The sultan was no fool.

"Father!" Scheherazade screeched. "Help me!"

"What can I do?" asked the grand vizier. He expected no answer.

Yet his beautiful, slim-waisted daughter immediately replied, "You must allow me to go to the Street of the Storytellers."

"The daughter of the grand vizier going into the city! Into the bazaar! To the street of those loathsome storytellers? Commoners! Little better than beggars! Never! It is impossible! The sultan would never permit you to leave the palace."

"I could go in disguise," Scheherazade suggested.

"And how could anyone disguise those ravishing eyes of yours, my darling child? How could anyone disguise your angelic grace, your delicate form? No, it is impossible. You must remain in the palace."

Scheherazade threw herself onto the pillows next to her father and sobbed desperately, "Then bid your darling daughter farewell, most noble father. By tomorrow's sun I will be slain."

The grand vizier gazed upon his daughter with true tenderness, even as her sobs turned to shrieks of despair. He tried to think of some way to ease her fears, but he knew that he could never take the risk of smuggling his daughter out of the palace. They would both lose their heads if the sultan discovered it.

Growing weary of his daughter's wailing, the grand vizier suddenly had the flash of an idea. He cried out, "I have it, my best beloved daughter!"

Scheherazade lifted her tear-streaked face.

"If the Prophet—blessed be his name—cannot go to the mountain, then the mountain will come to the Prophet!"

The grand vizier raised his eyes to Allah in thanksgiving for his revelation and he saw once again the peeling gold leaf of the ceiling. His heart hardened with anger against all slipshod workmen, including (of course) storytellers.

———

And so it was arranged that a quartet of burly guards was dispatched that very morning from the sultan's palace to the street of the storytellers, with orders to bring a storyteller to the grand vizier without fail. This they did, although the grand vizier's hopes fell once he beheld the storyteller the guards had dragged in.

He was short and round, round of face and belly, with big, round eyes that seemed about to pop out of his head. His beard was ragged, his clothes tattered and tarnished from long wear. The guards hustled him into the grand vizier's private chamber and threw him roughly onto the mosaic floor before the grand vizier's high-backed, elaborately carved chair of sandalwood inlaid with ivory and filigrees of gold.

For long moments the grand vizier studied the storyteller, who knelt trembling on the patched knees of his pantaloons, his nose pressed to the tiles of the floor. Scheherazade watched from the veiled gallery of the women's quarters, high above, unseen by her father or his visitor.

"You may look upon me," said the grand vizier.

The storyteller raised his head but remained kneeling. His eyes went huge as he took in the splendor of the sumptuously appointed chamber. *Don't you dare look up at the ceiling*, the grand vizier thought.

"You are a storyteller?" he asked, his voice stern.

The storyteller seemed to gather himself and replied with a surprisingly strong voice, "Not merely *a* storyteller, oh mighty one. I am *the* storyteller of storytellers. The best of all those who—"

The grand vizier cut him short with, "Your name?"

"Hari-ibn-Hari, eminence." Without taking a breath, the storyteller continued, "My stories are known throughout the world. As far as distant Cathay and the misty isles of the Celts, my stories are beloved by all men."

"Tell me one," said the grand vizier. "If I like it, you will be rewarded. If not, your tongue will be cut from your boastful throat."

Hari-ibn-Hari clutched at his throat with both hands.

"Well?" demanded the grand vizier. "Where's your story?"

"Now, your puissance?"

"Now."

———

Nearly an hour later, the grand vizier had to admit that Hari-ibn-Hari's tale of the sailor Sinbad was not without merit.

"An interesting fable, storyteller. Have you any others?"

"Hundreds, oh protector of the poor!" exclaimed the storyteller. "Thousands!"

"Very well," said the grand vizier. "Each day you will come to me and relate to me one of your tales."

"Gladly," said Hari-ibn-Hari. But then, his round eyes narrowing slightly, he dared to ask, "And what payment will I receive?"

"Payment?" thundered the grand vizier. "You keep your tongue! That is your reward!"

The storyteller hardly blinked at that. "Blessings upon you, most merciful one. But a storyteller must eat. A storyteller must drink, as well."

The grand vizier thought that perhaps drink was more important than food to this miserable wretch.

"How can I continue to relate my tales to you, oh magnificent one, if I faint from hunger and thirst?"

"You expect payment for your tales?"

"It would seem just."

After a moment's consideration, the grand vizier said magnanimously, "Very well. You will be paid one copper for each story you relate."

"One copper?" squeaked the storyteller, crestfallen. "Only one?"

"Do not presume upon my generosity," the grand vizier warned. "You are not the only storyteller in Baghdad."

Hari-ibn-Hari looked disappointed, but he meekly agreed, "One copper, oh guardian of the people."

———

Six weeks later, Hari-ibn-Hari sat in his miserable little hovel on the Street of the Storytellers and spoke thusly to several other storytellers sitting around him on the packed-earth floor.

"The situation is this, my fellows: the sultan believes that all women are faithless and untrustworthy."

"Many are," muttered Fareed-al-Shaffa, glancing at the only female storyteller among the men, who sat next to him, her face boldly unveiled, her hawk's eyes glittering with unyielding determination.

"Because of the sultan's belief, he takes a new bride to his bed each night and has her beheaded the next morning."

"We know all this," cried the youngest among them, Haroun-el-Ahson, with obvious impatience.

Hari-ibn-Hari glared at the upstart, who was always seeking attention for himself, and continued, "But Scheherazade, daughter of the grand vizier, has survived more than two months now by telling the sultan a beguiling story each night."

"A story stays the sultan's bloody hand?" asked another storyteller, Jamil-abu-Blissa. Lean and learned, he was sharing a hookah water pipe with Fareed-al-Shaffa. Between them, they blew clouds of soft, gray smoke that wafted through the crowded little room.

With a rasping cough, Hari-ibn-Hari explained, "Scheherazade does not finish her story by the time dawn arises. She leaves the sultan in such suspense that he allows her to live to the next night, so he can hear the conclusion of her story."

"I see!" exclaimed the young Haroun-el-Ahson. "Cliffhangers! Very clever of her."

Hari-ibn-Hari frowned at the upstart's vulgar phrase but went on to the heart of the problem.

"I have told the grand vizier every story I can think of," he said, his voice sinking with woe, "and still he demands more."

"Of course. He doesn't want his daughter to be slaughtered."

"Now I must turn to you, my friends and colleagues. Please tell me your stories, new stories, fresh stories. Otherwise the lady Scheherazade will perish." Hari-ibn-Hari did not mention that the grand vizier would take the tongue from his head if his daughter was killed.

Fareed-al-Shaffa raised his hands to Allah and pronounced, "We will be honored to assist a fellow storyteller in such a noble pursuit."

Before Hari-ibn-Hari could express his undying thanks, the bearded, gnomish storyteller who was known throughout the bazaar as the Daemon of the Night, asked coldly, "How much does the sultan pay you for these stories?"

Thus, it came to pass that Hari-ibn-Hari, accompanied by Fareed-al-Shaffa and the gray-bearded Daemon of the Night, knelt before the grand vizier. The workmen refurbishing the golden ceiling of the grand vizier's chamber were dismissed from their scaffolds before the grand vizier demanded, from his chair of authority:

"Why have you asked to meet with me this day?"

The three storytellers, on their knees, glanced questioningly at one another. At length, Hari-ibn-Hari dared to speak.

"Oh, magnificent one, we have provided you with a myriad of stories so that your beautiful and virtuous daughter, on whom Allah has bestowed much grace and wisdom, may continue to delight the sultan."

"May he live in glory," exclaimed Fareed-al-Shaffa in his reedy voice.

The grand vizier eyed them impatiently, waiting for the next slipper to drop.

"We have spared no effort to provide you with new stories, father of all joys," said Hari-ibn-Hari, his voice quaking only slightly. "Almost every storyteller in Baghdad has contributed to the effort."

"What of it?" the grand vizier snapped. "You should be happy to be of such use to me—and my daughter."

"Just so," Hari-ibn-Hari agreed. But then he added, "However, hunger is stalking the Street of the Storytellers. Starvation is on its way."

"Hunger?" the grand vizier snapped. "Starvation?"

Hari-ibn-Hari explained, "We storytellers have bent every thought we have to creating new stories for your lovely daughter—blessings upon her. We don't have time to tell stories in the bazaar anymore—"

"You'd better not!" the grand vizier warned sternly. "The

sultan must hear only new stories, stories that no one else has heard before. Otherwise, he would not be intrigued by them, and my dearly loved daughter would lose her head."

"But, most munificent one," cried Hari-ibn-Hari, "by devoting ourselves completely to your needs, we are neglecting our own. Since we no longer have the time to tell stories in the bazaar, we have no other source of income except the coppers you pay us for our tales."

The grand vizier at last saw where they were heading. "You want more? Outrageous!"

"But, oh far-seeing one, a single copper for each story is not enough to keep us alive!"

Fareed-al-Shaffa added, "We have families to feed. I myself have four wives and many children."

"What is that to me?" the grand vizier shouted. He thought that these pitiful storytellers were just like workmen everywhere, trying to extort higher wages for their meager efforts.

"We cannot continue to give you stories for a single copper apiece," Fareed-al-Shaffa said flatly.

"Then I will have your tongues taken from your throats. How many stories will you be able to tell then?"

The three storytellers went pale. But the Daemon of the Night, small and frail though he was in body, straightened his spine and found the strength to say, "If you do that, most noble one, you will get no more stories, and your daughter will lose her life."

The grand vizier glared angrily at the storytellers. From her hidden post in the veiled gallery, Scheherazade felt her heart sink. *Oh, father!* she begged silently, *be generous. Open your heart.*

At length, the grand vizier muttered darkly, "There are many storytellers in Baghdad. If you three refuse me, I will find others who will gladly serve. And, of course, the three of you will lose your tongues. Consider carefully. Produce stories for me at one copper apiece or be silenced forever."

"Our children will starve!" cried Fareed-al-Shaffa.

"Our wives will have to take to the streets to feed themselves," wailed Hari-ibn-Hari.

The Daemon of the Night said nothing.

"That is your choice," said the grand vizier, as cold and unyielding as a steel blade. "Stories at one copper apiece, or I go to other storytellers. And you lose your tongues."

"But magnificent one—"

"That is your choice," the grand vizier repeated sternly. "You have until noon tomorrow to decide."

———

It was a gloomy trio of storytellers who wended their way back to the bazaar that day.

"He is unyielding," Fareed-al-Shaffa said. "Too bad. I have been thinking of a new story about a band of thieves and a young adventurer. I think I'll call him Ali Baba."

"That's a silly name," Hari-ibn-Hari rejoined. "Who could take seriously a story where the hero's name is so silly?"

"I don't think the name is silly," Fareed-al-Shaffa maintained. "I rather like it."

As they turned in to the Street of the Storytellers, with ragged, lean, and hungry men at every door pleading with passersby to listen to their tales, the Daemon of the Night said softly, "Arguing over a name is not going to solve our problem. By tomorrow noon we could lose our tongues."

Hari-ibn-Hari touched reflexively at his throat. "But to continue to sell our tales for one single copper is driving us into starvation."

"We will starve much faster if our tongues are cut out," said Fareed-al-Shaffa.

The others nodded unhappily as they plodded up the street and stopped at al-Shaffa's hovel.

"Come in and have coffee with me," he said to his companions. "We must think of a way out of this problem."

All four of Fareed-al-Shaffa's wives were home, and all four of them asked the storyteller how they were expected to feed their many children if he did not bring in more coins.

"Begone," he commanded them—after they had served the coffee. "Back to the women's quarters."

The women's quarters was nothing more than a squalid room in the rear of the hovel, teeming with noisy children.

Once the women had left, the three storytellers squatted on the threadbare carpet and sipped at their coffee cups.

"Suppose this carpet could fly," mused Hari-ibn-Hari.

Fareed-al-Shaffa humphed. "Suppose a genie appeared and gave us riches beyond imagining."

The Daemon of the Night fixed them both with a somber gaze. "Suppose you both stop toying with new story ideas and turn your attention to our problem."

"Starve from low wages or lose our tongues," sighed Hari-ibn-Hari.

"And once our tongues have been cut out, the grand vizier goes to other storytellers to take our place," said the Daemon of the Night.

Fareed-al-Shaffa said slowly, "The grand vizier assumes the other storytellers will be too terrified by our example to refuse his starvation wage."

"He's right," Hari-ibn-Hari said bitterly.

"Is he?" mused Fareed. "Perhaps not."

"What do you mean?" his two companions asked in unison.

Stroking his beard thoughtfully, Fareed-al-Shaffa said, "What if all the storytellers refused to work for a single copper per tale?"

Hari-ibn-Hari asked cynically, "Would they refuse before or after our tongues have been taken out?"

"Before, of course."

The Daemon of the Night stared at his fellow storyteller. "Are you suggesting what I think you're suggesting?"

"I am."

Hari-ibn-Hari gaped at the two of them. "No, it would never work. It's impossible!"

"Is it?" asked Fareed-al-Shaffa. "Perhaps not."

———

The next morning, the three bleary-eyed storytellers were brought before the grand vizier. Once again Scheherazade watched and listened from her veiled gallery. She herself was bleary-eyed as well, having spent all night telling the sultan the tale of Ala-al-Din and his magic lamp. As usual, she had left the tale unfinished as the dawn brightened the sky.

This night she must finish the tale and begin another. But she had no other to tell! Her father had to get the storytellers to bring her fresh material. If not, she would lose her head with tomorrow's dawn.

"Well?" demanded the grand vizier as the three storytellers knelt trembling before him. "What is your decision?"

The three of them had chosen the Daemon of the Night to

be their spokesperson. But as he gazed up at the fierce countenance of the grand vizier, his voice choked in his throat.

Fareed-al-Shaffa nudged him, gently at first, then more firmly.

At last the Daemon said, "Oh, magnificent one, we cannot continue to supply your stories for a miserable one copper per tale."

"Then you will lose your tongues!"

"And your daughter will lose her head, most considerate of fathers."

"Bah! There are plenty of other storytellers in Baghdad. I'll have a new story for my daughter before the sun goes down."

Before the Daemon of the Night could reply, Fareed-al-Shaffa spoke thusly, "Not so, sir. No storyteller will work for you for a single copper per tale."

"Nonsense!" snapped the grand vizier.

"It is true," said the Daemon of the Night. "All the storytellers have agreed. We have sworn a mighty oath. None of us will give you a story unless you raise your rates."

"Extortion!" cried the grand vizier.

Hari-ibn-Hari found his voice. "If you take our tongues, oh most merciful of men, none of the other storytellers will deal with you at all."

Before the astounded grand vizier could reply to that, Fareed-al-Shaffa explained, "We have formed a guild, your magnificence, a storyteller's guild. What you do to one of us, you do to us all."

"You can't do that!" the grand vizier sputtered.

"It is done," said the Daemon of the Night. He said it softly, almost in a whisper, but with great finality.

The grand vizier sat on his chair of authority getting redder and redder in the face, his chest heaving, his fists clenching. He looked like a volcano about to erupt.

When, from the veiled gallery above them, Scheherazade cried out, "I think it's wonderful! A storyteller's guild. And you created it just for me!"

The three storytellers raised their widening eyes to the balcony of the gallery, where they could make out the slim and graceful form of a young woman, suitably gowned and veiled, who stepped forth for them all to see. The grand vizier twisted around in his chair and nearly choked with fury.

"Father," Scheherazade called sweetly, "is it not wonderful that the storytellers have banded together so that they can provide stories for me to tell the sultan night after night?"

The grand vizier started to reply once, twice, three times. Each time, no words escaped his lips. The three storytellers knelt before him, staring up at the gallery where Scheherazade stood openly before them—suitably gowned and veiled.

Before the grand vizier could find his voice, Scheherazade said, "I welcome you, storytellers, and your guild. The grand vizier, the most munificent of fathers, will gladly pay you ten coppers for each story you relate to me. May you bring me a thousand of them!"

Before the grand vizier could figure how much a thousand stories would cost, at ten coppers per story, Fareed-al-Shaffa smiled up at Scheherazade and murmured, "A thousand and one, oh gracious one."

———

The grand vizier was unhappy with the new arrangement, although he had to admit that the storyteller's newly founded guild provided stories that kept the sultan bemused and his daughter alive.

The storytellers were pleased, of course. Not only did they keep their tongues in their heads and earn a decent income from their stories, but they shared the subsidiary rights to the stories with the grand vizier once Scheherazade had told them to the sultan, and they could then be related to the general public.

Ten coppers per story was extortionate, in the grand vizier's opinion, but the storyteller's guild agreed to share the income from the stories once they were told in the bazaar. There was even talk of an invention from far-off Cathay, where stories could be printed on vellum and sold throughout the kingdom. The grand vizier consoled himself with the thought that if sales were good enough, the income could pay for regilding his ceiling.

The sultan eventually learned of the arrangement, of course. Being no fool, he demanded that he be cut in on the profits. Reluctantly, the grand vizier complied.

Scheherazade was the happiest of all. She kept telling stories to the sultan until he relented of his murderous ways and eventually married her, much to the joy of all Baghdad.

She thought of the storyteller's guild as her own personal creation and called it Scheherazade's Fables and Wonders Association.

That slightly ponderous name was soon abbreviated to SFWA[1].

---

1 SFWA is also the abbreviated form of the Science Fiction Writers Association, the professional organization of science fiction and fantasy writers. The coincidence between that organization's title and Scheherazade's association is purely . . . well, intentional.

INTRODUCTION TO

"THE SUPERSONIC ZEPPELIN"

I worked in the aerospace industry for a number of years, and this story is a slightly exaggerated spoof of how major projects get initiated and somehow acquire a life of their own.

The characters herein are also slightly exaggerated portraits of some of the people I worked with. *Slightly* exaggerated.

The Busemann biplane concept is real, by the way. I've always believed that good science fiction should be based as solidly as possible on real science.

THE SUPERSONIC ZEPPELIN

Let's see now. How did it all begin?

A bunch of the boys were whooping it up in the Malamute Saloon—no, that's not right; actually, it started in the cafeteria of the Anson Aerospace plant in Phoenix.

Okay, then, how about:

There are strange things done in the midnight sun by the men who moil for gold—well, yeah, but it was only a little after noon when Bob Wisdom plopped his loaded lunch tray on our table and sat down like a man disgusted with the universe. And anyway, engineers don't moil for gold; they're on salary.

I didn't like the way they all looked down on me, but I certainly didn't let it show. It wasn't just that I was the newbie among them: I wasn't even an engineer, just a recently graduated MBA assigned to work with the Advanced Planning Team, aptly acronymed APT. As far as they were concerned, I was either a useless appendage forced on them, or a snoop from management sent to provide info on which of them should get laid off.

Actually, my assignment was to get these geniuses to come up with a project that we could sell to somebody, anybody. Otherwise, we'd all be hit by the iron ball when the next wave of layoffs started, just before Christmas.

Six shopping weeks left; I knew.

"What's with you, Bob?" Ray Kurtz asked. "You look like you spent the morning sniffing around a manure pile."

Bob Wisdom was tall and lanky, with a round face that was normally cheerful, even in the face of Anson Aerospace's coming wave of cutbacks and layoffs. Today he looked dark and pouchy-eyed.

"Last night I watched a TV documentary about the old SST."

"The *Concorde*?" asked Kurtz. He wore a full bushy beard that made him look more like a dogsled driver than a metallurgical engineer.

"Yeah. They just towed the last one out to the Smithsonian on a barge. A beautiful hunk of flying machine like that riding to its final resting place on a converted garbage scow."

That's engineers for you. Our careers were hanging by a hair, and he's upset over a piece of machinery.

"Beautiful, maybe," said Tommy Rohr. "But it was never a practical commercial airliner. It could never fly efficiently enough to be economically viable."

For an engineer, Rohr was unnervingly accurate in his economic analyses. He'd gotten out of the dot-com boom before it burst. Of the five of us at the lunch table, Tommy was the only one who wasn't worried about losing his job—he had a much more immediate worry: his new trophy wife and her credit cards.

"It's just a damned shame," Wisdom grumbled. "The end of an era."

Kurtz, our bushy-bearded metallurgist, shook his graying head. "The eco-nuts wouldn't let it fly supersonic overpopulated areas. They didn't want sonic booms rattling their neighborhoods. That ruined its chances of being practical."

"The trouble is," Wisdom muttered as he unwrapped a soggy sandwich, "you can build a supersonic aircraft that doesn't produce a sonic boom."

"No sonic boom?" I asked. Like I said, I was the newcomer to the APT group.

Bob Wisdom smiled like a sphinx.

"What's the catch?" asked Richard Grand in his slightly Anglified accent. He'd been born in the Bronx, but he'd won a Rhodes scholarship and came back trying to talk like Sir Stafford Cripps.

The cafeteria was only half filled, but there was still a fair amount of clattering and yammering going on all around us. Outside the picture window I could see it was raining cats and elephants, a real monsoon downpour. Something to do with global warming, I'd been told.

"Catch?" Bob echoed, trying to look hurt. "Why should there be a catch?"

"Because if someone could build a supersonic aircraft that didn't shatter one's eardrums with its sonic boom, old boy, obviously someone could have done it long before this."

"We could do it," Bob said pleasantly. Then he bit it into his sandwich.

"Why aren't we, then?" Kurtz asked, his brows knitting.

Bob shrugged elaborately as he chewed on his ham and five-grain bread.

Rohr waggled a finger at him. "What do you know that we don't? Or is this a gag?"

Bob swallowed and replied, "It's just simple aerodynamics."

"What's the go of it?" Grand asked. He got that phrase from reading a biography of James Clerk Maxwell.

"Well," Bob said, putting down the limp remains of the sandwich, "there's a type of wing that a German aerodynamicist named Adolph Busemann invented back in the 1920s. It's a sort of biplane configuration, actually. The shock waves that cause a sonic boom are canceled out between the two wings."

"No sonic boom?"

"No sonic boom. Instead of flat wings, like normal, you need to wrap the wings around the fuselage, make a ringwing."

"What's a ringwing?" asked innocent lil me.

Bob pulled a felt-tip pen from his shirt pocket and began sketching on his paper placemat.

"Here's the fuselage of the plane." He drew a narrow cigar shape. "Now we wrap the wing around it, like a sleeve. See?" He drew what looked to me like a tube wrapped around the cigar. "Actually, it's two wings, one inside the other, and all the shock waves that cause the sonic boom get canceled out. No sonic boom."

The rest of us looked at Bob, then down at the sketch, then up at Bob again. Rohr looked wary, like he was waiting for the punch line. Kurtz looked like a puzzled Karl Marx.

"I don't know that much about aerodynamics," Rohr said slowly, "but this is a Busemann biplane you're talking about, isn't it?"

"That's right."

"Uh-huh. And isn't it true that a Busemann biplane's wings produce no lift?"

"That's right," Bob admitted, breaking into a grin.

"No lift?" Kurtz snapped.

"Zero lift."

"Then how the hell do you get it off the ground?"

"It won't fly, Orville," Bob Wisdom said, his grin widening. "That's why nobody's built one."

The rest of us groaned while Bob laughed at us. An engineer's joke, in the face of impending doom. We'd been had.

Until, that is, I blurted out, "So why don't you fill it with helium?"

———

The guys spent the next few days laughing at me and the idea of a supersonic zeppelin. I have to admit, at that stage of the game, I thought it was kind of silly too. But yet . . .

Richard Grand could be pompous, but he wasn't stupid. Before the week was out, he just happened to pass by my phonebooth-sized cubicle and dropped in for a little chat, like the lord of the manor being gracious to a stable hand.

"That was rather clever of you, that supersonic zeppelin quip," he said as he ensconced himself on a teeny wheeled chair he had to roll in from the empty cubicle next door.

"Thanks," I said noncommittally, wondering why a senior engineer would give a compliment to a junior MBA.

"It might even be feasible," Grand mused. "Technically, that is."

I could see in his eyes the specter of Christmas-yet-to-come and the layoffs that were coming with it. *If a senior guy like Grand was worried*, I thought, *I ought to be scared purple.* Could I use the SSZ idea to move up Anson Aerospace's hierarchical ladder? The guys at the bottom were the first ones scheduled for layoffs, I knew. I badly needed some altitude, and even though it sounded kind of wild, the supersonic zeppelin was the only foothold I had to get up off the floor.

"Still," Grand went on, "it isn't likely that management would go for the concept. Pity, isn't it?"

I nodded agreement while my mind raced. If I could get management to take the SSZ seriously, I might save my job. Maybe even get a promotion. But I needed an engineer to propose the concept to management. Those suits upstairs wouldn't listen to a newly-minted MBA; most of them were former engineers themselves who'd climbed a notch or two up the organization.

Grand sat there in that squeaky little chair and philosophized about the plight of the aerospace industry in general and the bleak prospects for Anson Aerospace in particular.

"Not the best of times to approach management with a bold, innovative concept," he concluded.

Oh my God, I thought. *He's talked himself out of it!* He was starting to get up and leave my cubicle.

"You know," I said, literally grabbing his sleeve, "Winston Churchill backed a lot of bold, innovative ideas, didn't he? Like, he pushed the development of tanks in World War I, even though he was in the navy, not the army."

Grand gave me a strange look.

"And radar, in World War II," I added.

"And the atomic bomb," Grand replied. "Very few people realize it was Sir Winston who started the atomic bomb work, long before the Yanks got into it."

The Yanks? I thought. *This from a Jewish engineer from the Bronx High School for Science.*

I sighed longingly. "If Churchill were here today, I bet he'd push the SSZ for all it's worth. He had the courage of his convictions, Churchill did."

Grand nodded but said nothing and left me at my desk. The next morning, though, he came to my cubicle and told me to follow him.

Glad to get away from my claustrophobic workstation, I headed after him, asking, "Where are we going?"

"Upstairs."

Management territory!

"What for?"

"To broach the concept of the supersonic zeppelin," said Grand, sticking out his lower lip in imitation of Churchillian pugnaciousness.

"The SSZ? For real?"

"Listen, my boy, and learn. The way this industry works is this: you grab onto an idea and ride it for all it's worth. I've decided to hitch my wagon to the supersonic zeppelin, and you should too."

I should too? Hell, I thought of it first!

John Driver had a whole office to himself and a luscious, sweet-tempered executive assistant of Greek-Italian ancestry, with almond-shaped dark eyes and lustrous hair even darker. Her name was Lisa, and half the male employees of Anson Aerospace fantasized about her, including me.

Driver's desk was big enough to land a helicopter on, and he kept it immaculately clean, mainly because he seldom did anything except sit behind it and try to look important. Driver was head of several engineering sections, including APT. Like so many others in Anson, he had been promoted to his level of incompetency: a perfect example of the Peter Principle. Under his less-then-brilliant leadership, APT had managed to avoid developing anything more advanced than a short-range drone aircraft that ran on ethanol. It didn't fly very well, but the ground crew used the corn-based fuel to make booze that would peel the paint off a wall just by breathing at it from fifteen feet away.

I let Grand do the talking, of course. And, equally of course, he made Driver think the SSZ was his idea instead of mine.

"A supersonic zeppelin?" Driver snapped, once Grand had outlined the idea to him. "Ridiculous!"

Unperturbed by our boss's hostility toward new ideas, Grand said smoothly, "Don't be too hasty to dismiss the concept. It may have considerable merit. At the very least, I believe we could talk NASA or the Transportation Department into giving us some money to study the concept."

At the word *money* Driver's frown eased a little. Driver was lean faced, with hard features and a gaze that he liked to think was piercing. He now subjected Grand to his most piercing stare.

"You have to spend money to make money in this business," he said, in his best *Forbes* magazine acumen.

"I understand that," Grand replied stiffly. "But we are quite willing to put some of our own time into this—until we can obtain government funding."

"Your own time?" Driver queried.

We? I asked myself. And immediately answered myself, *damned right.* This is *my* idea, and I'm going to follow it to the top. Or bust.

"I really believe we may be onto something that can save this company," Grand was purring.

Driver drummed his manicured fingers on his vast desk. "All

right, if you feel so strongly about it. Do it on your own time and come back to me when you've got something worth showing. Don't say a word to anyone else, understand? Just me."

"Right, Chief." I learned later that whenever Grand wanted to flatter Driver, he called him Chief.

———

"Our own time" was aerospace industry jargon for bootlegging hours from legitimate projects. Engineers have to charge every hour they work against an ongoing contract, or else their time is paid by the company's overhead account. Anson's management—and the accounting department—was very definitely against spending any money out of the company's overhead account. So I became a master bootlegger, finding charge numbers for my APT engineers. They accepted my bootlegging without a word of thanks and complained when I couldn't find a valid charge number and they actually had to work on their own time, after regular hours.

For the next six weeks Wisdom, Rohr, Kurtz, and even I worked every night on the supersonic zeppelin. The engineers were doing calculations and making simulator runs in their computers. I was drawing up a business plan, as close to a work of fiction as anything on the best sellers list. My social life went to zero, which was—I have to admit—not all that much of a drop. Except for Driver's luscious executive assistant, Lisa, who worked some nights to help us. I wished I had the time to ask her to dinner.

Grand worked away every night too, on a glossy set of illustrations to use as a presentation.

———

We made our presentation to Driver. The guys's calculations, my business plan, and Grand's images. He didn't seem impressed, and I left the meeting feeling pretty gunky. Over the six weeks, I'd come to like the idea of a supersonic zeppelin, an SSZ. I really believed it was my ticket to advancement. Besides, now I had no excuse to see Lisa, up in Driver's office.

On the plus side, though, none of the APT team was laid off. We went through the motions of the Christmas office party with the rest of the undead. Talk about a survivor's reality show!

I was moping in my cubicle the morning after Christmas when my phone beeped, and Driver's face came up on my screen.

"Drop your socks and pack a bag. You're going with me to Washington to sell the SSZ concept."

"Yessir!" I said automatically. "Er . . . when?"

"Tomorrow, bright and early."

I raced to Grand's cubicle, but he already knew about it.

"So we're both going," I said, feeling pretty excited.

"No, only you and Driver," he said.

"But why aren't you—"

Grand gave me a knowing smile. "Driver wants all the credit for himself if the idea sells."

That nettled me, but I knew better than to argue about it. Instead, I asked, "And if it doesn't sell?"

"You get the blame for a stupid idea. You're low enough on the totem pole to be offered up as a sacrificial victim."

I nodded. I didn't like it, but I had to admit it was a good lesson in management. I tucked it away in my mind for future reference.

———

I'd never been to Washington before. It was chilly, gray, and clammy; no comparison to sunny Phoenix. The traffic made me dizzy, but Driver thought it was pretty light. "Half the town's on holiday vacations," he told me as we rode a seedy, beat-up taxicab to the magnificent glass and stainless steel high-rise office building that housed the Transportation Department.

As we climbed out of the smelly taxi, I noticed the plaque on the wall by the revolving glass doors. It puzzled me.

"Transportation and Urban Renewal Department?" I asked. "Since when . . ."

"Last year's reorganization," Driver said, heading for the revolving door. "They put the two agencies together. Next year they'll pull them apart, when they reinvent the government again."

"Welcome to TURD headquarters," said Tracy Keene, once we got inside the building's lobby.

Keene was Anson Aerospace's crackerjack Washington representative, a large, round man who conveyed the impression that he knew things no one else knew. Keene's job was to find new customers for Anson from among the tangle of government agencies, placate old customers when Anson inevitably alienated them, and guide visitors from home base through the Washington maze. The job involved grotesque amounts of wining and dining. I had been told that Keene had once been as wiry and agile as a Venezuelan shortstop. Now he looked to me like he was on his way to becoming a Sumo wrestler. And what he was gaining in girth, he was losing in hair.

"Let's go," Keene said, gesturing toward the security checkpoint that blocked the lobby. "We don't want to be late."

Two hours later Keene was snoring softly in a straight-backed metal chair while Driver was showing the last of his PowerPoint images to Roger K. Memo, Assistant Under Director for Transportation Research of TURD.

Memo and his chief scientist, Dr. Alonzo X. Pencilbeam, were sitting on one side of a small conference table, Driver and I on the other. Keene was at the end, dozing restfully. The only light in the room came from the little projector, which threw a blank glare onto the wan-yellow wall that served as a screen now that the last image had been shown.

Driver clicked the projector off. The light went out, and the fan's whirring noise abruptly stopped. Keene jerked awake and instantly reached around and flicked the wall switch that turned on the overhead lights. I had to admire the man's reflexes.

Although the magnificent TURD building was sparkling new, Memo's spacious office somehow looked seedy. There wasn't enough furniture for the size of it: only a government-issue steel desk with a swivel chair, a half-empty bookcase, and this slightly wobbly little conference table with six chairs that didn't match. The walls and floors were bare, and there was a distinct echo when anyone spoke or even walked across the room. The only window had vertical slats instead of a curtain and it looked out on a parking building. The only decoration on the walls was Memo's doctoral degree, purchased from some obscure "distance learning" school in Mississippi.

From across the conference table, Driver fixed Memo with his steely gaze. "Well, what do you think of it?" he asked subtly.

Memo pursed his lips. He was jowly fat, completely bald, wore glasses and a rumpled gray suit.

"I don't know," he said firmly. "It sounds . . . unusual . . ."

Dr. Pencilbeam was sitting back in his chair and smiling benignly. His PhD had been earned in the 1970s, when newly graduated physicists were driving taxicabs on what they glumly called "Nixon fellowships." He was very thin, fragile looking, with the long, skinny limbs of a praying mantis.

Pencilbeam dug into his jacket pocket and pulled out an electronic game. *Reformed smoker*, I thought. *He needs something to do with his hands.*

"It certainly looks interesting," he said in a scratchy voice while his game softly beeped and booped. "I imagine it's technically achievable . . . and lots of fun."

Memo snorted. "We're not here to have fun."

Keene leaned across the table and fixed Memo with his best *here's something from behind the scenes* expression. "Do you realize how the White House would react to a sensible program for a supersonic transport? With the *Concorde* gone, you could put this country into the forefront of air transportation again."

"Hmm," said Memo. "But . . ."

"Think of the jobs this program can create. The president is desperate to improve the employment figures."

"I suppose so . . ."

"National prestige," Keene intoned knowingly. "Aerospace employment . . . balance of payments . . . gold outflow . . . the president would be terrifically impressed with you."

"Hmm," Memo repeated. "I see . . ."

———

I could see where the real action was, so I wangled myself an assignment to the company's Washington office as Keene's special assistant for the SSZ proposal. That's when I started learning what money and clout—and the power of influence—are all about.

As the months rolled along, we gave lots of briefings and attended lots of cocktail parties. I knew we were on the right track when no less than Roger K. Memo invited me to accompany him to one of the swankiest parties of the season. Apparently, he thought that since I was from Anson's home office in Phoenix, I must be an engineer and not just another salesman.

The party was in full swing by the time Keene and I arrived. It was nearly impossible to hear your own voice in the swirling babble of chatter and clinking glassware. In the middle of the sumptuous living room, the vice president was demonstrating his golf swing. Several cabinet wives were chatting in the dining room. Out in the foyer, three senators were comparing fact-finding tours they were arranging for themselves to the French Riviera, Bermuda, and American Samoa, respectively.

Memo never drank anything stronger than ginger ale, and I followed his example. We stood in the doorway between the foyer and the living room, hearing snatches of conversation among the three junketing senators. When the trio broke up, Memo intercepted Senator Goodyear (R-OH) as he headed toward the bar.

"Hello, Senator!" Memo boomed heartily. It was the only way to be heard over the party noise.

"Ah . . . hello." Senator Goodyear obviously thought that he was supposed to know Memo, and just as obviously couldn't recall his name, rank, or influence rating.

Goodyear was more than six feet tall and towered over Memo's paunchy figure. Together they shouldered their way through the crowd around the bar, with me trailing them like a rowboat being towed behind a yacht. Goodyear ordered bourbon on the rocks, and therefore so did Memo. But he merely held onto his glass while the senator immediately began to gulp at his drink.

A statuesque blond in a spectacular gown sauntered past us. The senator's eyes tracked her like a battleship's range finder following a moving target.

"I hear you're going to Samoa," Memo shouted as they edged away from the bar, following the blond.

"Eh . . . yes," the senator answered cautiously, in a tone he usually reserved for news reporters.

"Beautiful part of the world," Memo shouted.

The blond slipped an arm around the waist of one of the young, long-haired men, and they disappeared into another room. Goodyear turned his attention back to his drink.

"I said," Memo repeated, standing on tiptoes, "that Samoa is a beautiful place."

Nodding, Goodyear replied, "I'm going to investigate ecological conditions there . . . my committee is considering legislation on ecology, you know."

"Of course. Of course. You've got to see things firsthand if you're going to enact meaningful legislation."

Slightly less guardedly, Goodyear said, "Exactly."

"It's a long way off, though," Memo said.

"Twelve hours from LAX."

"I hope you won't be stuck in economy class. They really squeeze the seats in there."

"No, no," said the senator. "First class all the way."

At the expense of the taxpayers, I thought.

"Still," Memo sympathized, "It must take considerable dedication to undergo such a long trip."

"Well, you know, when you're in public service, you can't think of your own comforts."

"Yes, of course. Too bad the SST isn't flying anymore. It could have cut your travel time in half. That would give you more time to stay in Samoa . . . investigating conditions there."

———

The hearing room in the capitol was jammed with reporters and camera crews. Senator Goodyear sat in the center of the long front table, as befitted the committee chairman. I was in the last row of spectators, as befitted the newly promoted junior Washington representative of Anson Aerospace Corp. I was following the industry's routine procedure and riding the SSZ program up the corporate ladder.

All through that hot summer morning, the committee had listened to witnesses: my former boss John Driver, Roger K. Memo, Alonzo Pencilbeam, and many others. The concept of the supersonic zeppelin unfolded before the news media and started to take on definite solidity in the rococo-trimmed hearing chamber.

Senator Goodyear sat there solemnly all morning, listening to the carefully rehearsed testimony and sneaking peeks at the greenery outside the big, sunny window. Whenever he remembered the TV cameras, he sat up straighter and tried to look lean and tough. I'd been told he had a drawer full of old Clint Eastwood flicks in his Ohio home.

Now it was his turn to summarize what the witnesses had told the committee. He looked straight into the bank of cameras, trying to come on strong and determined, like a high-plains drifter.

"Gentlemen," he began, immediately antagonizing the

women in the room, "I believe that what we have heard here today can mark the beginning of a new program that will revitalize the American aerospace industry and put our great nation back in the forefront of international commerce—"

One of the younger senators at the far end of the table, a woman, interrupted:

"Excuse me, Mr. Chairman, but my earlier question about pollution was never addressed. Won't the SSZ use the same kind of jet engines that the *Concorde* used? And won't they cause just as much pollution?"

Goodyear glowered at the junior member's impudence, but controlled his temper well enough to say only, "Erm . . . Dr. Pencilbeam, would you care to comment on that question?"

Half dozing at one of the front benches, Pencilbeam looked startled at the mention of his name. Then he got to his feet like a carpenter's ruler unfolding, went to the witness table, sat down, and hunched his bony frame around the microphone there.

"The pollution from the *Concorde* was so minimal that it had no measurable effect on the stratosphere. The early claims that a fleet of SSTs would create a permanent cloud deck over the northern hemisphere and completely destroy the ozone layer were never substantiated."

"But there were only a half-dozen *Concorde*s flying," said the junior senator. "If we build a whole fleet of SSZs—"

Before she could go any further, Goodyear fairly shouted into his microphone, "Rest assured that we are well aware of the possible pollution problem." He popped his P's like artillery bursts. "More importantly, the American aerospace industry is suffering, employment is in the doldrums, and our economy is slumping. The SSZ will provide jobs and boost the economy.

Our engineers will, I assure you, find ways to deal with any and every pollution problem that may be associated with the SSZ."

———

I had figured that somebody, sooner or later, would raise the question of pollution. The engineers back in Phoenix wanted to look into the possibilities of using hydrogen fuel for the SSZ's jet engines, but I figured that just the mention of hydrogen would make people think of the old *Hindenberg*, and that would scuttle the program right there and then. So we went with ordinary turbojet engines that burned ordinary jet fuel.

But I went a step farther. In my capacity as a junior (and rising) executive, I used expense-account money to plant a snoop in the organization of the nation's leading ecology freak, Mark Sequoia. It turned out that, unknown to Sequoia, Anson Aerospace was actually his biggest financial contributor. Politics make strange bedfellows, doesn't it?

You see, Sequoia had fallen on relatively hard times. Once a flaming crusader for ecological salvation and environmental protection, Sequoia had made the mistake of letting the Commonwealth of Pennsylvania hire him as the state's Director of Environmental Protection. He had spent nearly five years earnestly trying to clean up Pennsylvania, a job that had driven four generations of the original Penn family into early Quaker graves. The deeper Sequoia buried himself in the solid waste politics of Pittsburgh, Philadelphia, Chester, Erie, and other hopelessly corrupted cities, the fewer dedicated followers and news media headlines he attracted. After a very credible Mafia threat on his life, he quite sensibly resigned his post and returned to private life, scarred but wiser. And alive.

When the word about the SSZ program reached him, Sequoia was hiking along a woodland trail in Fairmont Park, Philadelphia, leading a scraggly handful of sullen high school students through the park's soot-ravaged woodlands on a steaming August afternoon. They were dispiritedly picking up empty beer cans and gummy prophylactics—and keeping a wary eye out for muggers. Even full daylight was no protection against assault. And the school kids wouldn't help him, Sequoia knew. Half of them would jump in and join the fun.

Sequoia was broad shouldered, almost burly. His rugged face was seamed by weather and news conferences. He looked strong and fit, but lately his back had been giving him trouble, and his old trick knee . . .

He heard someone pounding up the trail behind him.

"Mark! Mark!"

Sequoia turned to see Larry Helper, his oldest and therefore most trusted aide, running along the gravel path toward him, waving a copy of the *Daily News* over his head. Newspaper pages were slipping from his sweaty grasp and fluttering off into the bushes.

"Littering," Sequoia muttered in a tone sometimes used by archbishops when facing a case of heresy.

"Some of you kids," said Sequoia in his most authoritative voice, "pick up those newspaper pages."

A couple of the students lackadaisically ambled after the fluttering sheets.

"Mark, look here!" Helper skidded to a gritty stop on the gravel and breathlessly waved the front page of the newspaper. "Look!"

Sequoia grabbed his aide's wrist and took what was left of the newspaper from him. He frowned at Helper, who cringed and stepped back.

"I . . . I thought you'd want to see . . ."

Satisfied that he had established his dominance, Sequoia turned his attention to the front page's blaring headline.

"Supersonic *zeppelin*?"

Two nights later, Sequoia was meeting with a half dozen men and women in the basement of a prosperous downtown church that specialized in worthy causes capable of filling the pews upstairs.

Once Sequoia called his meeting, I was informed by the mole I had planted in his pitiful little group of do-gooders. As a newcomer to the scene, I had no trouble joining Sequoia's Friends of the Planet organization, especially when I FedEx'd them a personal check for a thousand dollars—for which Anson Aerospace reimbursed me, of course.

So I was sitting on the floor like a good environmental activist while Sequoia paced across the little room. There was no table, just a few folding chairs scattered around, and a locked bookcase stuffed with tomes about sex and marriage. I could tell just from looking at Sequoia that the old activist flames were burning inside him again. He felt alive, strong, the center of attention.

"We can't just drive down to Washington and call a news conference," he exclaimed, pounding a fist into his open palm. "We've got to do something dramatic!"

"Automobiles pollute, anyway," said one of the women, a comely redhead whose dazzling green eyes never left Sequoia's broad, sturdy-looking figure.

"We could take the train; it's electric."

"Power stations pollute."

"Airplanes pollute too."

"What about riding down to Washington on horseback! Like Paul Revere!"

"Horses pollute."

"They do?"

"Ever been around a stable?"

"Oh."

Sequoia pounded his fist again. "I've got it! It's perfect!"

"What?"

"A balloon! We'll ride down to Washington in a non-polluting balloon filled with helium. That's the dramatic way to emphasize our opposition to this SSZ monster."

"Fantastic!"

"Marvelous!"

The redhead was panting with excitement. "Oh, Mark, you're so clever. So dedicated." There were tears in her eyes.

Helper asked softly, "Uh . . . does anybody know where we can get a balloon? And how much they cost?"

"Money is no object," Sequoia snapped, pounding his fist again. Then he wrung his hand; he had pounded too hard.

When the meeting finally broke up, Helper had been given the task of finding a suitable balloon, preferably one donated by its owner. I had volunteered to assist him. Sequoia would spearhead the effort to raise money for a knockdown fight against the SSZ. The redhead volunteered to assist him. They left the meeting arm in arm.

———

I was learning the Washington lobbying business from the bottom up but rising fast. Two weeks later I was in the White House, no less, jammed in among news reporters and West Wing staffers waiting for a presidential news conference to begin. TV lights were glaring at the empty podium. The reporters and camera crews shuffled their feet, coughed, talked to one another. Then:

"Ladies and gentlemen, the President of the United States."

We all stood up and applauded as she entered. I had been thrilled to be invited to the news conference. Well, actually, it was Keene who'd been invited, and he brought me with him, since I was the Washington rep for the SSZ project. The President strode to the podium and smiled at us in what some cynics had dubbed her *rattlesnake mode*. I thought she was being gracious.

"Before anything else, I have a statement to make about the tragic misfortune that has overtaken one of our finest public figures, Mark Sequoia. According to the latest report I have received from the Coast Guard—no more than ten minutes ago—there is still no trace of his party. Apparently, the balloon they were riding in was blown out to sea two days ago, and nothing has been heard from them since.

"Now let me make this perfectly clear. Mr. Sequoia was frequently on the other side of the political fence from my administration. He was often a critic of my policies and actions, policies and actions that I believe in completely. He was on his way to Washington to protest our new supersonic zeppelin program when this unfortunate accident occurred.

"Mr. Sequoia opposed the SSZ program despite the fact that this project will employ thousands of aerospace engineers who are otherwise unemployed and untrainable. Despite the fact that the SSZ program will save the American dollar on the international market and salvage American prestige in the technological battleground of the world.

"And we should keep in mind that France and Russia have announced that they are studying the possibility of jointly starting their own SSZ effort, a clear technological challenge to America."

Gripping the edges of the podium tighter, the President went on, "Rumors that his balloon was blown off course by a flight of Air Force jets are completely unfounded, the Secretary of Defense assures me. I have dispatched every available military, coast guard, and civil air patrol plane to search the entire coastline from Cape Cod to Cape Hatteras. We will find Mark Sequoia and his brave though misguided band of ecofr . . . er, activists—or their remains."

I knew perfectly well that Sequoia's balloon had not been blown out to sea by air force jets. They were private planes: executive jets, actually.

"Are there any questions?" the President asked.

The Associated Press reporter, a hickory-tough old man with thick glasses and a snow-white goatee, got to his feet and asked, "Is that a Versace dress you're wearing? It's quite becoming."

The President beamed. "Why, thank you. Yes, it is . . ."

Keene pulled me by the arm. "Let's go. We've got nothing to worry about here."

———

I was rising fast, in part because I was willing to do the legwork (and dirty work, like Sequoia) that Keene was too lazy or too squeamish to do. He was still head of our Washington office, in name. I was running the SSZ program, which was just about the only program Anson had going for itself, which meant that I was running the Washington office in reality.

Back in Phoenix, Bob Wisdom and the other guys had become the nucleus of the team that was designing the SSZ prototype. The program would take years, we all knew, years in which we had assured jobs. If the SSZ actually worked the way we designed it, we could spend the rest of our careers basking in its glory.

I was almost getting accustomed to being called over to the West Wing to deal with bureaucrats and politicians. Still, it was a genuine thrill when I was invited into the Oval Office itself.

The President's desk was cleared of papers. Nothing cluttered the broad expanse of rosewood except the telephone console, a black-framed photograph of her late husband (who had once also sat at that desk), and a gold-framed photograph of her daughter on her first day in the House of Representatives (D-AR).

She sat in her high-backed leather chair and fired instructions at her staff.

"I want the public to realize," she instructed her media consultant, "that although we are now in a race with the Russians and the French, we are building the SSZ for sound economic and social reasons, not because of competition from overseas."

"Yes, ma'am," said the media consultant.

She turned to the woman in charge of congressional liaison. "And you'd better make damned certain that the Senate appropriations committee okays the increased funding for the SSZ prototype. Tell them that if we don't get the extra funding, we'll fall behind the Ivans and the Frogs.

"And I want you," she pointed a manicured finger at the

research director of TURD, "to spend every nickel of your existing SSZ money as fast as you can. Otherwise, we won't be able to get the additional appropriation out of Congress."

"Yes, ma'am," said Roger K. Memo, with one of his rare smiles.

"But, Madam President," the head of the Budget Office started to object.

"I know what you're going to say," the President snapped at him. "I'm perfectly aware that money doesn't grow on trees. But we've *got* to get the SSZ prototype off the ground and do it before next November. Take money from education, from the space program, from the environmental superfund—I don't care how you do it, just get it done. I want the SSZ prototype up and flying by next summer, when I'm scheduled to visit Paris and Moscow."

The whole staff gasped in sudden realization of the President's masterful plan.

"That right," she said, smiling slyly at them. "I intend to be the first Chief of State to cross the Atlantic in a supersonic zeppelin."

———

Although none of us realized its importance at the time, the crucial incident, we know now, happened months before the President's decision to fly the SSZ to Paris and Moscow. I've gone through every scrap of information we could beg, borrow or steal about that decisive day, reviewing it all time and again, trying to find some way to undo the damage.

It happened at the VA hospital in Hagerstown, a few days after Mark Sequoia had been rescued. The hospital had never seen so many reporters. There were news media people thronging the lobby, lounging in the halls, bribing nurses, sneaking into elevators and even surgical theaters (where several of them fainted). The parking lot was a jumble of cars bearing media stickers and huge TV vans studded with antennas.

Only two reporters were allowed to see Mark Sequoia on any given day, and they were required to share their interviews with all the others in the press corps. Today the two—picked by lot—were a crusty old veteran from *Fox News* and a perky young blond from *Women's Wear Daily*.

"But I've told your colleagues what happened at least a dozen times," mumbled Sequoia from behind a swathing of bandages.

He was hanging by both arms and legs from four traction braces, his backside barely touching the crisply sheeted bed. Bandages covered eighty percent of his body and all of his face, except for tiny slits for his eyes, nostrils and mouth.

The *Fox News* reporter held his palm-sized video camera in one hand while he scratched at his stubbled chin with the other. On the opposite side of the bed, the blond held a similar camcorder close to Sequoia's bandaged face.

She looked misty-eyed. "Are . . . are you in much pain?"

"Not really," Sequoia answered bravely, with a slight tremor in his voice.

"Why all the traction?" asked *Fox News*. "The medics said there weren't any broken bones."

"Splinters," Sequoia answered weakly.

"Bone splinters!" gasped the blond. "Oh, how awful!"

"No," Sequoia corrected. "Splinters. Wood splinters. When the balloon finally came down, we landed in a clump of trees just outside Hagerstown. I got thousands of splinters. It took most of the surgical staff three days to pick them all out of me.

The chief of surgery said he was going to save the wood and build a scale model of the *Titanic* with it."

"Oh, how painful!" The blond insisted on gasping. She gasped very well, Sequoia noted, watching her blouse.

"And what about your hair?" *Fox News* asked.

Sequoia felt himself blush underneath the bandages. "I . . . uh . . . I must have been very frightened. After all, we were aloft in that stupid balloon for six days, without food, without anything to drink except a six pack of Perrier. We went through a dozen different thunderstorms . . ."

"With lightning?" the blond asked.

Nodding painfully, Sequioa replied, "We all thought we were going to die."

Fox News frowned. "So your hair turned white from fright. There was some talk that cosmic rays did it."

"Cosmic rays? We never got that high. Cosmic rays don't have any effect on you until you get really up there, isn't that right?"

"How high did you go?"

"I don't know," Sequoia answered. "Some of those updrafts in the thunderstorms pushed us pretty high. The air got kind of thin."

"But not high enough to cause cosmic ray damage."

"Well, I don't know . . . maybe . . ."

"It'd make a better story than just being scared," said *Fox News*. "Hair turned white by cosmic rays. Maybe even sterilized."

"Sterilized?" Sequoia yelped.

"Cosmic rays do that too," *Fox News* said. "I checked."

"Well, we weren't *that* high."

"You're sure?"

"Yeah . . . well, I don't think we were that high. We didn't have an altimeter with us . . ."

"But you could have been."

Shrugging was sheer torture, Sequoia found.

"Okay, but those thunderstorms could've lifted you pretty damned high," *Fox News* persisted.

Before Sequoia could think of what to answer, the door to his private room opened, and a horse-faced nurse said firmly, "That's all. Time's up. Mr. Sequoia must rest now. After his enema."

"Okay, I think I've got something to hang a story on," *Fox News* said with a satisfied grin. "Now to find a specialist in cosmic rays."

The blond looked thoroughly shocked and terribly upset. "You . . . you don't think you were really sterilized, do you?"

Sequoia tried to make himself sound worried and brave at the same time. "I don't know. I just . . . don't know."

Late that night the blond snuck back into his room, masquerading as a nurse. If she knew the difference between sterilization and impotence, she didn't tell Sequoia about it. For his part, he forgot about his still-tender skin and the traction braces. The morning nurse found him unconscious, one shoulder dislocated, most of his bandages rubbed off, his skin terribly inflamed, and a goofy grin on his face.

———

I knew that the way up the corporate ladder was to somehow acquire a staff that reported to me. And, in truth, the SSZ project was getting so big that I truly needed more people to handle it. I mean, all the engineers had to do was build the damned thing and make it fly. I had to make certain that the money kept flowing, and that wasn't easy. An increasingly large part of my responsibilities as the de facto head of the Washington office consisted of putting out fires.

"Will you look at this!"

Senator Goodyear waved the morning *Post* at me. I had already read the electronic edition before I'd left my apartment that morning. Now, as I sat at Tracy Keene's former desk, the senator's red face filled my phone screen.

"That Sequoia!" he grumbled. "He'll stop at nothing to destroy me. Just because the Ohio River melted his houseboat, all those years ago."

"It's just a scare headline," I said, trying to calm him down. "People won't be sterilized by flying in the supersonic zeppelin any more than they were by flying in the old *Concorde*."

"I know it's bullshit! And you know it's bullshit! But the goddamned news media are making a major story out of it! Sequoia's on every network talk show. I'm under pressure to call for hearings on the sterilization problem!"

"Good idea," I told him. "Have a Senate investigation. The scientists will prove that there's nothing to it."

That was my first mistake. I didn't get a chance to make another.

———

I hightailed it that morning to Memo's office. I wanted to see Pencil-beam and start building a defense against this sterilization story. The sky was gray and threatening. An inch or two of snow was forecast, and people were already leaving their offices for home, at ten o'clock in the morning. Dedicated government bureaucrats and corporate employees, taking the slightest excuse to knock off work.

The traffic was so bad that it had actually started to snow, softly, by the time I reached Memo's office. He was pacing across the thinly carpeted floor, his shoes squeaking unnervingly in the spacious room. Copies of *The Washington Post*, *The New York Times*, and *Aviation Week* were spread across his usually immaculate desk, but his attention was focused on his window, where we could see fluffy snowflakes gently drifting down.

"Traffic's going to get worse as the day goes on," Memo muttered.

"They're saying it'll only be an inch or so," I told him.

"That's enough to paralyze this town."

Yeah, especially when everybody jumps in their cars and starts fleeing the town as if a terrorist nuke is about to go off, I replied silently.

Aloud, I asked, "What about this sterilization business? Is there any substance to the story?"

Memo glanced sharply at me. "They don't need substance as long as they can start a panic."

Dr. Pencilbeam sat at one of the unmatched conference chairs, all bony limbs and elbows and knees.

"Relax, Roger," Pencilbeam said calmly. "Congress isn't going to halt the SSZ program. It means too many jobs, too much international prestige. And besides, the President has staked her credibility on it."

"That's what worries me," Memo muttered.

"What?"

But Memo's eye was caught by movement outside his window. He waddled past his desk and looked down into the street below.

"Oh my God."

"What's going on?" Pencilbeam unfolded like a pocket ruler into a six-foot-long human and hurried to the window. Outside, in the thin, mushy snow, a line of somber men and women were filing along the street past the TURD building, bearing signs that screamed:

"STOP THE SSZ!""DON'T STERILIZE THE HUMAN RACE!""SSZ MURDERS UNBORN CHILDREN!" "ZEPPELINS, GO HOME!" "Isn't that one with the sign about unborn children a priest?" Pencilbeam asked.

Memo shrugged. "Your eyes are better than mine."

"Aha! And look at this!"

Pencilbeam pointed a long, bony finger farther down the street. Another swarm of people were advancing on the building. They also carried placards:

"SSZ FOR ZPG" "ZEPPELINS, SI! BABIES, NO!" "ZEPPELINS FOR POPULATION CONTROL" "UP THE SSZ" Memo sagged against the window. "This . . . this is awful."

The Zero Population Growth group marched through the thin snowfall straight at the environmentalists and anti-birth-control pickets. Instantly, the silence was shattered by shouts and taunts. Shrill female voices battled against rumbling baritones and bassos. Placards wavered. Bodies pushed. Someone screamed. One sign struck a skull, and then bloody war broke out.

Memo, Pencilbeam, and I watched aghast until the helmeted TAC squad police doused the whole tangled mess of them with riot gas, impartially clubbed men and woman alike, and carted everyone off, including three bystanders and a homeless panhandler.

——

The Senate hearings were such a circus that Driver summoned me back to Phoenix for a strategy session with Anson's top management. I was glad to get outside the beltway, and especially glad to see Lisa again. She even agreed to have dinner with me.

"You're doing a wonderful job there in Washington," she said, smiling with gleaming teeth and flashing eyes.

My knees went weak, but I found the courage to ask, "Would you consider transferring to the Washington office? I could use a sharp executive assistant—"

She didn't even let me finish. "I'd love to!"

I wanted to do handsprings. I wanted to grab her and kiss her hard enough to bruise our lips. I wanted to, but Driver came out of his office just at that moment, looking his jaw-jutting grimmest.

"Come on, kid. Time to meet the top brass."

The top brass was a mixture of bankers and former engineers. To my disgust, instead of trying to put together a strategy to defeat the environmentalists, they were already thinking about how many men and women they'd have to lay off when Washington pulled the plug on the SSZ program.

"But that's crazy!" I protested. "The program is solid. The president herself is behind it."

Driver fixed me with his steely stare. "With friends like that, who needs enemies?"

I left the meeting feeling very depressed, until I saw Lisa again. Her smile could light up the world.

Before heading back to Washington to fight Sequoia's sterilization propaganda, I looked up my old APT buddies. They were in the factory section where the SSZ was being fabricated.

The huge factory assembly bay was filled with the aluminum skeleton of the giant dirigible. Great gleaming metal ribs stretched from its titanium nosecap to the more intricate cagework of the tail fins. Tiny figures with flashing laser welders crawled along the ribbing like maggots cleaning the bones of some noble, stranded whale.

Even the jet engines sitting on their carrying pallets dwarfed human scale. Some of the welders held clandestine poker games inside their intake cowlings, Bob Wisdom told me. The cleaning crews kept quiet about the spills, crumbs, and other detritus they found in them night after night. I stood with Bob, Ray Kurtz, Tommy Rohr, and Richard Grand beside one of those huge engine pods, craning our necks to watch the construction work going on high overhead. The assembly bay rang to the shouts of working men and women, throbbed with the hum of machinery, clanged with the clatter of metal against metal.

"It's going to be some Christmas party if Congress cancels this project," Kurtz muttered gloomily.

"Oh, they wouldn't dare cancel it now that the women's movement is behind it," said Grand, with a sardonic little smile.

Kurtz glared at him from behind his beard. "You wish. Half those idiots in Congress will vote against us just to prove they're pro-environment."

"Actually, the scientific evidence is completely on our side," Grand said. "And in the long run, the weight of evidence prevails."

He always acts as if he knows more than anybody else, I thought. *But he's dead wrong here. He hasn't the foggiest notion of how Washington works. But he sounds so damned sure of himself! It must be that phony accent of his.*

"Well, just listen to me, pal," said Wisdom, jabbing a forefinger at Grand. "I've been working on that secretary of mine since the last Christmas party, and if this project falls through and the party is a bust, that palpitating hunk of femininity is going to run home and cry instead of coming to the party!"

Grand blinked at him several times, obviously trying to think of the right thing to say. Finally, he enunciated, "Pity."

But I was thinking about Lisa. If the SSZ is canceled, Driver won't let her transfer to the Washington office. There'd be no need to hire more staff for me. There'd be no need for me!

———

I went back to Washington determined to save the SSZ from this stupid sterilization nonsense. But it was like trying to stop a tsunami with a floor mop. The women's movement, the environmental movement, the labor unions, even TV comedy hosts got into the act. The Senate hearings turned into a shambles; Pencilbeam and the other scientists were ignored while movie stars testified that they would never fly in an SSZ because of the dangers of radiation.

The final blow came when the president announced that she was not going to Paris and Moscow, after all. Urgent problems elsewhere. Instead, she flew to Hawaii for an economic summit of the Pacific nations. In her subsonic Air Force One.

———

The banner proclaiming "Happy Holidays!" drooped sadly across one wall of the company cafeteria. Outside in the late afternoon darkness, lights glimmered, cars were moving, and a bright, full moon shone down on a rapidly emptying parking lot.

Inside, the Anson Aerospace cafeteria was nothing but gloom. The Christmas party had been a dismal flop, primarily because half the company's work force had received layoff notices that morning. The tables had been pushed to one side of the cafeteria to make room for a dance floor. Syrupy holiday music oozed out of the speakers built into the acoustic tiles of the ceiling. But no one was dancing.

Bob Wisdom sat at one of the tables, propping his aching head in his hands. Ray Kurtz and Tommy Rohr sat with him, equally dejected.

"Why the hell did they have to cancel the project two days before Christmas?" Rohr asked rhetorically.

"Makes for more pathos," Kurtz growled.

"It's pathetic, all right," Wisdom said. "I've never seen so many women crying at once. Or men, for that matter."

"Even Driver was crying, and he hasn't even been laid off," Rohr said.

"Well," Kurtz said, staring at the half-finished drink in front of him, "Seqouia did it. He's a big media hero again."

"And we're on the bread line," said Rohr.

"You got laid off?" I asked.

"Not yet—but it's coming. This place will be closing its doors before the fiscal year ends."

"It's not that bad," said Wisdom. "We still have the Air Force work. As long as they're shooting off cruise missiles, we'll be in business."

Rohr grimaced. "You know what gets me? The way the whole project was scrapped, without giving us a chance to complete the big bird and show how it'd work. Without a goddamned chance."

Kurtz said, "Congressmen are scared of people getting sterilized."

"Not really," I said. "They're scared of not being on the right bandwagon."

All three of them turned toward me.

Rohr said, "Next time you dream up a project, pal, make it underground. Something in a lead mine. Or deeper still, a gold mine. Then Congress won't have to worry about cosmic rays."

Wisdom tried to laugh, but it wouldn't come.

"You know," I said slowly, "you just might have something there."

"What?"

"Where?"

"A supersonic transport—in a tunnel."

"Oh for Chri—"

But Wisdom sat up straighter in his chair. "You could make an air-cushion vehicle go supersonic. If you put it in a tunnel, you get away from the sonic boom and the air pollution."

"The safety aspects would be better too," Kurtz admitted. Then, more excitedly, "And pump the air out of the tunnel, like a pneumatic tube!"

Rohr shook his head. "You guys are crazy. Who the hell's going to build tunnels all over the country?"

"There's a lot of tunnels already built," I countered. We could adapt them for the SSST."

"SSST?"

"Sure," I answered, grinning for the first time in weeks. "Supersonic subway train."

They stared at me. Rohr pulled out his PDA and started tapping on it. Wisdom got that faraway look in his eyes. Kurtz shrugged and said, "Why the hell not?"

I got up and headed for the door. Supersonic subway train. That was my ticket. I was going back to Washington, I knew. And this time I'll bring Lisa with me.

Inspiration is where you find it.

The robotic spacecraft we've sent to Mars have found some surprising things, including the fact that the Martian atmosphere includes occasional whiffs of methane gas. The methane appears seasonally, then disappears, only to show up again the next year.

Methane is composed of one atom of carbon and four of hydrogen: CH_4. Sunlight in the thin, clear Martian atmosphere quickly dissociates the compound into individual atoms. The hydrogen—lightest of all the atoms—rises to the top of the atmosphere and eventually wafts off into space. The carbon atom presumably becomes part of the scant Martian atmosphere, which is predominantly composed of carbon dioxide.

Okay, we know where the CH_4 goes. But where does it come from?

One possible explanation is that it comes from microscopic

creatures living deep beneath the surface of Mars. On Earth there are "bugs" living deep below the surface that eat dirt and even rocks—and excrete methane. Similar microorganisms may exist deep beneath Mars's surface.

Mars farts?

MARS FARTS

"A Catholic, a Jew, and a Muslim are stuck in the middle of Mars," said Rashid Faiyum.

"That isn't funny," Jacob Bernstein replied wearily.

Patrick O'Conner, the leader of the three-man team, shook his head inside the helmet of his pressure suit. "Laugh, and the world laughs with you, Jake."

None of them could see the faces of their companions through the tinting of their helmet visors. But they could hear the bleakness in Bernstein's tone. "There's not much to laugh about, is there?"

"Not much," Faiyum agreed.

All around them stretched the barren, frozen, rust-red sands of Utopia Planita. Their little hopper leaned lopsidedly on its three spindly legs in the middle of newly churned pockmarks from the meteor shower that had struck the area overnight.

Off on the horizon stood the blocky form of the old *Viking 2* lander, which had been there for more than a century. One of their mission objectives had been to retrieve parts of the *Viking* to return to Earth, for study and eventual sale to a museum. Like everything else about their mission, that objective had been sidelined by the meteor shower. Their goal now was survival.

A barrage of tiny bits of stone, most of them no larger than dust motes. Once they had been part of an icy comet, but the ice had melted away after God knows how many trips around the sun, and now only the stones were left when the remains of the comet happened to collide with the planet Mars.

One of the rare stones, almost the size of a pebble, had punctured the fuel cell that was the main electrical power source for the three-man hopper. Without the electrical power from that fuel cell, their rocket engine could not function. They were stranded in the middle of the frozen, arid plain.

In his gleaming silvery pressure suit, Faiyum reminded O'Connor of a knight in shining armor, except that he was bending into the bay that held the fuel cell, his helmeted head obscured by the bay's upraised hatch. Bernstein, similarly suited, stood by nervously beside him.

The hatch had been punctured by what looked like a bullet hole. Faiyum was muttering, "Of all the meteoroids in all the solar system in all of Mars, this one's got to smack our power cell."

Bernstein asked, "How bad is it?"

Straightening up, Faiyum replied, "All the hydrogen drained out during the night. It's dead as a doornail."

"Then so are we," Bernstein said.

"I'd better call Tithonium," said O'Connor, and he headed

for the ladder that led to the hopper's cramped cockpit. "While the batteries are still good."

"How long will they last?" asked Bernstein.

"Long enough to get help."

It wasn't that easy. The communications link back to Tithonium was relayed by a network of satellites in low orbit around Mars, and it would be another half hour before one of the commsats came over their horizon.

Faiyum and Bernstein followed O'Connor back into the cockpit, and suddenly the compact little space was uncomfortably crowded.

With nothing to do but wait, O'Connor said, "I'll pressurize the cockpit so we can take off the helmets and have some breakfast."

"I don't think we should waste electrical power until we get confirmation from Tithonium that they're sending a backup to us."

"We've got to eat," O'Connor said.

Sitting this close in the cramped cockpit, they could see each other's faces even through the tinting of the helmet visors. Faiyum broke into a stubbly-chinned grin.

"Let's pretend its Ramadan" he suggested, "and we have to fast from sunup to sundown."

"Like you fast during Ramadan," Bernstein sniped. O'Connor remembered one of their first days on Mars, when a clean-shaven Faiyum had jokingly asked which direction Mecca was. O'Connor had pointed up.

"Let's not waste power," Bernstein repeated.

"We have enough power during the day," Faiyum pointed out. "The solar panels work fine."

Thanks to Mars's thin, nearly cloudless atmosphere, just

about the same amount of sunshine fell upon the surface of Mars as upon Earth, despite Mars's farther distance from the sun. *Thank God for that*, O'Connor thought. *Otherwise, we'd be dead in a few hours.*

Then he realized that, also thanks to Mars's thin atmosphere, those micrometeoroids had made it all the way down to the ground to strafe them like a spray of bullets, instead of burning up from atmospheric friction, as they would have on Earth. *The Lord giveth and the Lord taketh away*, he told himself.

"Tithonium here," a voice crackled through the speaker on the cockpit control panel. All three of them turned to the display screen, suddenly tight with expectation.

"What's your situation, *E-three*?" asked the face in the screen. Ernie Roebuck, they recognized: chief communications engineer.

The main base for the exploration team was down at Tithonium Chasma, part of the immense Grand Canyon of Mars, more than three thousand kilometers from their *Excursion Three* site.

O'Connor was the team's astronaut: a thoroughly competent Boston Irishman with a genial disposition, who tolerated the bantering of Faiyum and Bernstein—both geologists—and tried to keep them from developing a real animosity. *A Muslim from Peoria and a New York Jew: how in the world had the psychologists back Earthside ever put the two of them on the same team*, he wondered.

In the clipped jargon of professional fliers, O'Connor reported on their dead fuel cell.

"No power output at all?" Roebuck looked incredulous.

"Zero," said O'Connor. "Hydrogen all leaked out overnight."

"How did you get through the night?"

"The vehicle automatically switched to battery power."

"What's the status of your battery system?"

O'Connor scanned the digital readouts on the control panel. "Down to one-third of nominal. The solar panels are recharging 'em."

A pause. Roebuck looked away, and they could hear voices muttering in the background. "All right," said the communicator at last. "We're getting your telemetry. We'll get back to you in an hour or so."

"We need a lift out of here," O'Connor said.

Another few moments of silence. "That might not be possible right away. We've got other problems too. You guys weren't the only ones hit by the meteor shower. We've taken some damage here. The garden's been wiped out, and *E-one* has two casualties."

Excursion One was at the flank of Olympus Mons, the tallest mountain in the solar system.

"Our first priority has to be to get those people from *E-one* back here for medical treatment."

"Yeah. Of course."

"Give us a couple of hours to sort things out. We'll call you back at noon, our time. Sit tight."

O'Connor glanced at the morose faces of his two team-mates, then replied, "We'll wait for your call."

"What the hell else can we do?" Bernstein grumbled.

Clicking off the video link, O'Connor said, "We can get back to work."

Faiyum tried to shrug inside his suit. "I like your first sugges-tion better. Let's eat."

With their helmets off, the faint traces of body odors became noticeable. Munching on an energy bar, Faiyum said, "A Catho-lic, a Muslim, and a Jew were showering together in a YMCA . . ."

"You mean a YMHA," said Bernstein.

"How would a Muslim get into either one?" O'Connor wondered.

"It's in the States," Faiyum explained. "They let anybody in."

"Not women."

"You guys have no sense of humor." Faiyum popped the last morsel of the energy bar into his mouth.

"This," Bernstein countered, "coming from a man who was named after a depression."

"El-Faiyum is below sea level," Faiyum admitted easily, "but it's the garden spot of Egypt. Has been for more than three thousand years."

"Maybe it was the garden of Eden," O'Connor suggested.

"No, that was in Israel," said Bernstein.

"Was it?"

"It certainly wasn't here," Faiyum said, gazing out the windshield at the bleak, cold Martian desert.

"It's going to go down near a hundred below again tonight," Bernstein said.

"The batteries will keep the heaters going," said O'Connor.

"All night?"

"Long enough. Then we'll recharge 'em when the sun comes up."

"That won't work forever," Bernstein muttered.

"We'll be okay for a day or two."

"Yeah, but the nights. A hundred below zero. The batteries will crap out pretty soon."

Tightly, O'Connor repeated, "We'll be okay for a day or two."

"From your mouth to God's ear," Bernstein said fervently.

Faiyum looked at the control panel's digital clock. "Another three hours before Tithonium calls."

Reaching for his helmet, O'Connor said, "Well, we'd better go out and do what we came here to do."

"Haul up the ice core," said Bernstein, displeasure clear on his lean, harsh face.

"That's why we're here," Faiyum said. He didn't look any happier than Bernstein. "Slave labor."

Putting on a false heartiness, O'Connor said, "Hey, you guys are the geologists. I thought you were happy to drill down that deep."

"Overjoyed," said Bernstein. "And here on Mars, we're doing areology, not geology."

"What's in a name?" Faiyum quoted. "A rose by any other name would still smell."

"And so do you," said Bernstein and O'Connor in unison.

The major objective of the *Excursion Three* team had been to drill three hundred meters down into the permafrost that lay just beneath the surface of Utopia Planita. The frozen remains of what had been an ocean billions of years earlier, when Mars had been a warmer and wetter world, the permafrost ice held a record of the planet's history, a record that geologists (or aerologists) keenly wanted to study.

Outside at the drill site, the three men began the laborious task of hauling up the ice core that their equipment had dug. They worked slowly, carefully, to make certain that the fragile, six-centimeter-wide core came out intact. Section by section, they unjointed each individual segment as it came up, marked it carefully, and stowed it in the special storage racks built into the hopper's side. "How old do you think the lowest layers of this core will be?" Bernstein asked as they watched the electric motor slowly, slowly lifting the slender metal tube that contained the precious ice.

"Couple billion years, at least," Faiyum replied. "Maybe more."

O'Connor, noting that the motor's batteries were down to less than fifty percent of their normal capacity, asked, "Do you think there'll be any living organisms in the ice?"

"Not hardly," said Bernstein.

"I thought there were supposed to be bugs living down there," O'Connor said.

"In the ice?" Bernstein was clearly skeptical.

Faiyum said, "You're talking about methanogens, right?"

"Is that what you call them?"

"Nobody's found anything like that," said Bernstein.

"So far," Faiyum said.

O'Connor said, "Back in training they told us about traces of methane that appear in the Martian atmosphere now and then."

Faiyum chuckled. "And some of the biologists proposed that the methane comes from bacteria living deep underground. The bacteria are supposed to exist on the water melting from the bottom of the permafrost layer, deep underground, and they excrete methane gas."

"Bug farts," said Bernstein.

O'Connor nodded inside his helmet. "Yeah. That's what they told us."

"Totally unproven," Bernstein said.

"So far," Faiyum repeated.

Sounding slightly exasperated, Bernstein said, "Look, there's a dozen abiological ways of generating the slight traces of methane that've been observed in the atmosphere."

"But they appear seasonally," Faiyum pointed out. "And the methane is quickly destroyed in the atmosphere. Solar ultraviolet breaks it down into carbon and hydrogen. That means that *something* is producing the stuff continuously."

"But that doesn't mean it's being produced by biological processes," Bernstein insisted.

"I think it's bug farts," Faiyum said. "It's kind of poetic, you know."

"You're crazy."

"You're a sourpuss."

Before O'Connor could break up their growing argument, their helmet earphones crackled, "Tithonium here."

All three of them snapped to attention. It was a woman's voice, and they recognized whose it was: the mission commander, veteran astronaut Gloria Hazeltine, known to most of the men as Glory Hallelujah. The fact that Glory herself was calling them didn't bode well, O'Connor thought. *She's got bad news to tell us.*

"We've checked out the numbers," said her disembodied radio voice. "The earliest we can get a rescue flight out to you will be in five days."

"Five days?" O'Connor yipped.

"That's the best we can do, Pat," the mission commander said, her tone as hard as concrete. "You'll have to make ends meet until then."

"Our batteries will crap out on us, Gloria. You know that."

"Conserve power. Your solar panels are okay, aren't they?"

Nodding, O'Connor replied, "They weren't touched, thank God."

"So recharge your batteries by day and use minimum power at night. We'll come and get you as soon as we possibly can."

"Right." O'Connor clicked off the radio connection.

"They'll come and pick up our frozen bodies," Bernstein grumbled.

Faiyum looked just as disappointed as Bernstein, but he put on a lopsided grin and said, "At least our bodies will be well preserved."

"Frozen solid," O'Connor agreed.

The three men stood there, out in the open, encased in their pressure suits and helmets, while the drill's motor buzzed away as if nothing was wrong. In the thin Martian atmosphere, the drill's drone was strangely high-pitched, more of a whine than a hum.

Finally, Bernstein said, "Well, we might as well finish the job we came out here to do."

"Yeah," said Faiyum, without the slightest trace of enthusiasm.

The strangely small sun was nearing the horizon by the time they had stored all the segments of the ice core in the insulated racks on the hopper's side.

"A record of nearly three billion years of Martian history," said Bernstein, almost proudly.

"Only one and a half billion years," Faiyum corrected. "The Martian year is twice as long as Earth years."

"Six hundred eighty-seven Earth days," Bernstein said. "That's not quite twice a terrestrial year."

"So sue me," Faiyum countered, as he pulled an equipment kit from the hopper's storage bay.

"What're you doing?" O'Connor asked.

"Setting up the laser spectrometer," Faiyum replied. "You know, the experiment the biologists want us to do."

"Looking for bug farts," Bernstein said.

"Yeah. Just because we're going to freeze to death is no reason to stop working."

O'Connor grunted. *Rashid is right*, he thought. *Go through the motions. Stay busy.*

With Bernstein's obviously reluctant help, Faiyum set up the laser and trained it at the opening of their bore hole. Then they checked out the Rayleigh scattering receiver and plugged it into the radio that would automatically transmit its results back to Tithonium. The radio had its own battery to supply the micro-watts of power it required.

"That ought to make the biologists happy," Bernstein said, once they were finished.

"Better get back inside," O'Connor said, looking toward the horizon where the sun was setting.

"It's going to be a long night," Bernstein muttered.

"Yeah."

Once they were sealed into the cockpit and had removed their helmets, Faiyum said, "A biologist, a geologist, and Glory Hallelujah were locked in a hotel room in Bangkok."

Bernstein moaned. O'Connor said, "You know that every-thing we say is being recorded for the mission log."

Faiyum said, "Hell, we're going to be dead by the time they get to us. What difference does it make?"

"No disrespect for the mission commander."

Faiyum shrugged. "Okay. How about this one: a physicist, a mathematician, and a lawyer are each asked, 'How much is two and two?'"

"I heard this one," Bernstein said.

Without paying his teammate the slightest attention, Faiyum plowed ahead. "The mathematician says, 'Two and two are four. Always four. Four point zero.' The physicist thinks a minute and says, 'It's somewhere between three point eight and four point two.'"

O'Connor smiled. *Yeah, a physicist probably would put it that way*, he thought.

"So what does the lawyer answer?"

With a big grin, Faiyum replied, "The lawyer says, 'How much is two and two? How much do you want it to be?'"

Bernstein groaned, but O'Connor laughed. "Lawyers," he said.

"We could use a lawyer here," Bernstein said. "Sue the bastards."

"Which bastards?"

Bernstein shrugged elaborately. "All of them," he finally said.

The night was long. And dark. And cold. O'Connor set the cockpit's thermostat to barely above freezing and ordered the two geologists to switch off their suit heaters.

"We've got to preserve every watt of electrical power we can. Stretch out the battery life as much as possible," he said firmly.

The two geologists nodded glumly.

"Better put our helmets back on," said Bernstein.

Faiyum nodded. "Better piss now, before it gets frozen."

The suits were well insulated, O'Connor knew. *They'll hold our body heat better than blankets*, he told himself. He remembered camping in New England, when he'd been a kid. Got pretty cold there. Then a mocking voice in his mind answered, *but not a hundred below*.

They made it through the first night and woke up stiff and shuddering and miserable. The sun was up, as usual, and the solar panels were feeding electrical power to the cockpit's heaters.

"That wasn't too bad," O'Connor said, as they munched on ration bars for breakfast.

Faiyum made a face. "Other than that, how did you like the play, Mrs. Lincoln?"

Bernstein pointed to the control panel's displays. "Batteries damned near died overnight," he said.

"The solar panels are recharging them," O'Connor replied.

"They won't come back a hundred percent," said Bernstein. "You know that."

O'Connor bit back the reply he wanted to make. He merely nodded and murmured, "I know."

Faiyum peered at the display from the laser they had set up outside. "I'll be damned."

The other two hunched up closer to him.

"Look at that," said Faiyum, pointing. "The spectrometer's showing there actually is methane seeping out of our bore hole."

"Methanogens?" mused Bernstein.

"Can't be anything else," Faiyum said. With a wide smile, he said, "We've discovered life on Mars! We could win the Nobel Prize for this!"

"Posthumously," said Bernstein.

"We've got to get this data back to Tithonium," said O'Connor. "Let the biologists take a look at it."

"It's being telemetered to Tithonium automatically," Bernstein reminded him.

"Yeah, but I want to see what the biologists have to say."

The biologists were disappointingly cautious. Yes, it was methane gas seeping up from the bore hole. Yes, it very well might be coming from methanogenic bacteria living deep underground. But they needed more conclusive evidence.

"Could you get samples from the bottom of your bore hole?" asked the lead biologist, a Hispanic American from California. In the video screen on the control panel, he looked as if he were trying hard not to get excited.

"We've got the ice core," Faiyum replied immediately. "I'll bet we've got samples of the bugs in the bottom layers."

"Keep it well protected," the biologist urged.

"It's protected," O'Connor assured him.

"We'll examine it when you bring it in," the biologist said, putting on a serious face.

Once the video link was disconnected, Bernstein said

morosely, "They'll be more interested in the damned ice core than in our frozen bodies."

All day long they watched the spikes of the spectrometer's flickering display. The gas issuing from their bore hole was mostly methane, and it was coming up continuously, a thin, invisible breath issuing from deep below the surface.

"Those bugs are farting away down there," Faiyum said happily. "Busy little bastards."

"Sun's going down," said Bernstein.

O'Connor checked the status of the batteries. Even with the solar panels recharging them all day, they were barely up to seventy-five percent of their nominal capacity. He did some quick arithmetic in his head. *If it takes Tithonium five days to get us, we'll have frozen to death on the fourth night.*

Like Shackleton at the South Pole, he thought. *Froze to death, all of 'em.*

They made it through the second night, but O'Connor barely slept. He finally dozed off, listening to the soft breeze wafting by outside. When he awoke every joint in his body ached and it took nearly an hour for him to stop his uncontrollable trembling.

As they chewed on their nearly-frozen breakfast bars, Bernstein said, "We're not going to make it."

"I can put in a call to Tithonium, tell 'em we're in a bad way."

"They can see our telemetry," Faiyum said, unusually morose. "They know the batteries are draining away."

"We can ask them for help."

"Yeah," said Bernstein. "When's the last time Glory Hallelujah changed her mind about anything?"

O'Connor called anyway. In the video screen, Gloria Hazeltine's chunky blond face looked like an implacable goddess.

"We're doing everything we can," she said, her voice flat and final. "We'll get to you as soon as we can. Conserve your power. Turn off everything you don't need to keep yourselves alive."

Once O'Connor broke the comm link, Bernstein grumbled, "Maybe we could hold our breaths for three or four days."

But Faiyum was staring at the spectrometer readout. Methane gas was still coming out of the bore hole, a thin waft, but steady.

"Or maybe we could breathe bug farts," he said.

"What?"

Looking out the windshield toward their bore hole, Faiyum said, "Methane contains hydrogen. If we can capture the methane those bug are emitting . . ."

"How do we get the hydrogen out of it?" O'Connor asked.

"Lase it. That'll break it up into hydrogen and carbon. The carbon precipitates out, leaving the hydrogen for us to feed to the fuel cell.

Bernstein shook his head. "How're we going to capture the methane in the first place? And how are we going to repair the fuel cell's damage?"

"We can weld a patch on the cell," O'Connor said. "We've got the tools for that."

"And we can attach a weather balloon to the bore hole. That'll hold the methane coming out."

"Yeah, but will it be enough to power up the fuel cell?"

"We'll see."

With Bernstein clearly doubtful, they broke into the equipment locker and pulled out the small, almost delicate, welding rod and supplies. Faiyum opened the bin that contained the weather balloons.

"The meteorologists aren't going to like our using their stuff," Bernstein said. "We're supposed to be releasing these balloons twice a day."

Before O'Connor could reply with a choice, *Fuck the meteorologists*, Faiyum snapped, "Let 'em eat cake."

They got to work. As team leader, O'Connor was glad of the excuse to be doing something. *Even if this is a big flop*, he thought, *it's better to be busy than to just lay around and wait to die.*

As he stretched one of the weather balloons over the bore hole and fastened it in place, Faiyum kept up a steady stream of timeworn jokes. Bernstein groaned in the proper places, and O'Connor sweated inside his suit while he laboriously welded the bullet-hole sized puncture of the fuel cell's hydrogen tank.

By midafternoon the weather balloon was swelling nicely.

"How much hydrogen do you think we've got there?" Bernstein wondered.

"Not enough," said Faiyum, serious for once. "We'll need three, four balloons full. Maybe more."

O'Connor looked westward, out across the bleak, frozen plain. The sun would be setting in another couple of hours.

When they finished their day's work and clambered back into the cockpit, O'Connor saw that the batteries were barely up to half their standard power level, even with the solar panels recharging them all day.

We're not going to make it, he thought. But he said nothing. He could see that the other two stared at the battery readout. No one said a word, though.

The night was worse than ever. O'Connor couldn't sleep. The cold *hurt*. He had turned off his suit radio, so he couldn't tell if the other two had drifted off to sleep. He couldn't. He knew that when a man froze to death, he fell asleep first. *Not a bad way to die*, he said to himself. As if there's a good way.

He was surprised when the first rays of sunlight woke him. *I fell asleep anyway. I didn't die. Not yet.*

Faiyum wasn't in the cockpit, he saw. Looking blearily through the windshield, he spotted the geologist in the early morning sun fixing a fresh balloon to the bore hole, with a big, round, yellow balloon bobbing from a rock he'd tied it to.

O'Connor saw Faiyum waving to him and gesturing to his left wrist, then remembered that he had turned his suit radio off. He clicked the control stud on his wrist.

". . . damned near ready to burst," Faiyum was saying. "Good thing I came out here in time."

Bernstein was lying back in his cranked-down seat, either asleep or . . . O'Connor nudged his shoulder. No reaction. He shook the man harder.

"Wha . . . what's going on?"

O'Connor let out a breath that he hadn't realized he'd been holding.

"You okay?" he asked softly.

"I gotta take a crap."

O'Connor giggled. *He's all right. We made it through the night.* But then he turned to the control panel and saw that the batteries were down to zero.

Faiyum and Bernstein spent the day building a system of pipes that led from the balloon's neck to the input valve of the repaired fuel cell's hydrogen tank. As long as the sun was shining, they had plenty of electricity to power the laser. Faiyum fastened the balloon's neck to one of the hopper's spidery little landing legs and connected it to the rickety-looking pipework.

Damned contraption's going to leak like a sieve, O'Connor thought. Hydrogen's sneaky stuff.

As he worked, he kept up his patter of inane jokes. "A Catholic, a Muslim, and a Jew—"

"How come the Jew is always last on your list?" Bernstein asked, from his post at the fuel cell. O'Connor saw that the hydrogen tank was starting to fill.

Faiyum launched into an elaborate joke from the ancient days of the old Soviet Union, in which Jews were turned away from everything from butcher's shops to clothing stores.

"They weren't even allowed to stand in line," he explained as he held the bobbing balloon by its neck. "So when the guys who've been waiting in line at the butcher's shop since sunrise are told that there's no meat today, one of them turns to another and says, 'See, the Jews get the best of everything!'"

"I don't get it," Bernstein complained.

"They didn't have to stand in line all day."

"Because they were discriminated against."

Faiyum shook his head. "I thought you people were supposed to have a great sense of humor."

"When we hear something funny."

O'Connor suppressed a giggle. *Bernstein understood the joke perfectly well*, he thought, *but he wasn't going to let Faiyum know it.*

By the time the sun touched the horizon again, the fuel cell's hydrogen tank was half full and the hopper's batteries were totally dead.

O'Connor called Tithonium. "We're going to run on the fuel cell tonight."

For the first time since he'd known her, Gloria Hazeltine looked surprised. "But I thought your fuel cell was dead."

"We've resurrected it," O'Connor said happily. "We've got enough hydrogen to run the heaters most of the night."

"Where'd you get the hydrogen?" Glory Hallelujah was wide-eyed with curiosity.

"Bug farts," shouted Faiyum, from over O'Connor's shoulder.

They made it through the night almost comfortably and spent the next day filling balloons with methane, then breaking down the gas into its components and filling the fuel cell's tank with hydrogen.

By the time the relief ship from Tithonium landed beside their hopper, O'Connor was almost ready to wave them off and return to the base on their own power.

Instead, though, he spent the day helping his teammates and the two-man crew of the relief ship to attach the storage racks with their previous ice core onto the bigger vehicle.

As they took off for Tithonium, five men jammed into the ship's command deck, O'Connor felt almost sad to be leaving their little hopper alone on the frigid plain. Almost. *We'll be back*, he told himself. *And we'll salvage the* Viking 2 *lander when we return.*

Faiyum showed no remorse about leaving at all. "A Jew, a Catholic, and a Muslim walk into a bar."

"Not another one," Bernstein groused.

Undeterred, Faiyum plowed ahead. "The bartender takes one look at them and says, 'What is this, a joke?'"

Even Bernstein laughed.

INTRODUCTION TO
"THE MAN WHO HATED GRAVITY"

Beginning writers are often told to "write about what you know."

I have never been to the moon, although I still harbor some hope of making that trip someday. I have never been a circus acrobat; I have enough of a challenge getting through my everyday routine.

But I know what it's like to have gravity play its sly tricks on me. Many years ago, I injured my knee while playing tennis. For weeks I walked with a brace on my leg. Then I needed a cane to walk with.

My injury finally healed, but the experience led me to write the story of the Great Rolando, circus aerialist extraordinaire.

I suppose Rolando's character could be categorized as "the man who learns better." What do you think?

THE MAN WHO HATED GRAVITY

The Great Rolando had not always hated gravity. As a child growing up in the traveling circus that had been his only home, he often frightened his parents by climbing too high, swinging too far, daring more than they could bear to watch.

The son of a clown and a cook, Rolando had yearned for true greatness and could not rest until he became the most renowned aerialist of them all.

Slim and handsome in his spangled tights, Rolando soared through the empty air thirty feet above the circus's flimsy safety net. Then fifty feet above it. Then a full hundred feet high, with no net at all.

"See the Great Rolando Defy Gravity!" shouted the posters and TV advertisements. And the people came to crane their necks and hold their breaths as he performed a split-second ballet in midair high above them. Literally flying from one trapeze to another, triple somersaults were workaday chores for the Great Rolando.

His father feared to watch his son's performances. With all the superstition born of generations of circus life, he cringed outside the big top while the crowds roared deliriously. Behind his clown's painted grin, Rolando's father trembled. His mother prayed through every performance until the day she died, slumped over a bare wooden pew in a tiny, austere church far out in the midwestern prairie.

For no matter how far he flew, no matter how wildly he gyrated in midair, no matter how the crowds below gasped and screamed their delight, the Great Rolando pushed himself farther, higher, more recklessly.

Once, when the circus was playing New York City's huge convention center, the management pulled a public relations coup. They got a brilliant young physicist from Columbia University to pose with Rolando for the media cameras and congratulate him on defying gravity.

Once the camera crews had departed, the physicist said to Rolando, "I've always had a secret yearning to be in the circus. I admire what you do very much."

Rolando accepted the compliment with a condescending smile.

"But no one can *really* defy gravity," the physicist warned. "It's a universal force, you know."

The Great Rolando's smile vanished. "*I* can defy gravity. And I do. Every day."

Several years later Rolando's father died (of a heart seizure, during one of his son's performances) and Rolando married the brilliant young lion tamer who had joined the circus slightly earlier. She was a petite, little thing with golden hair, the loveliest of blue eyes, and so sweet a disposition that no one could say anything about her that was less than praise. Even the great cats purred for her.

She too feared Rolando's ever-bolder daring, his wilder and wilder reachings on the high trapeze.

"There's nothing to be afraid of! Gravity can't hurt me!" And he would laugh at her fears.

"But I *am* afraid," she would cry.

"The people pay their money to see me defy gravity," Rolando would tell his tearful wife. "They'll get bored if I keep doing the same stunts one year after another."

She loved him dearly and felt terribly frightened for him. It was one thing to master a large cage full of Bengal tigers and tawny lions and snarling black panthers. All you needed was will and nerve. But she knew that gravity was another matter altogether.

"No one can defy gravity forever," she would say, gently, softly, quietly.

"I can," boasted the Great Rolando.

But of course, he could not. No one could. Not forever. The fall, when it inevitably came, was a matter of a fraction of a second. His young assistant's hand slipped only slightly in starting out the empty trapeze for Rolando to catch after a quadruple somersault. Rolando almost caught it. In midair he saw that the bar would be too short. He stretched his magnificently trained body to the utmost, and his fingers just grazed its tape-wound shaft.

For an instant he hung in the air. The tent went absolutely silent. The crowd drew in its collective breath. The band stopped playing. Then gravity wrapped its invisible tentacles around the Great Rolando, and he plummeted, wild-eyed and screaming, to the sawdust a hundred feet below.

"His right leg is completely shattered," said the famous surgeon to Rolando's wife. She had stayed calm up to that moment, strong and levelheaded while her husband lay unconscious in an intensive care unit.

"His other injuries will heal. But the leg . . ." The gray-haired, gray-suited man shook his dignified head sadly. His assistants, gathered behind him like an honor guard, shook their heads in metronome synchrony to their leader.

"His leg?" she asked, trembling.

"He will never be able to walk again," the famous surgeon pronounced.

The petite, blond lion tamer crumpled and sagged into the sleek leather couch of the hospital waiting room, tears spilling down her cheeks.

"Unless . . ." said the famous surgeon.

"Unless?" she echoed, suddenly wild with hope.

"Unless we replace the shattered leg with a prosthesis."

"Cut off his leg?"

The famous surgeon promised her that a prosthetic bionic leg would be "just as good as the original—in fact, even better!" It would be a *permanent* prosthesis; it would never have to come off, and its synthetic surface would blend so well with Rolando's real skin that no one would be able to tell where his natural leg ended, and his prosthetic leg began. His assistants nodded in unison.

Frenzied at the thought that her husband would never walk again, alone in the face of coolly assured medical wisdom, she reluctantly gave her assent and signed the necessary papers.

The artificial leg was part lightweight metal, part composite space-manufactured materials, and entirely filled with marvelously tiny electronic devices and miraculously miniaturized motors that moved the prosthesis exactly the way a real leg should move. It was stronger than flesh and bone, or so the doctors confidently assured the Great Rolando's wife.

The circus manager, a constantly frowning bald man who reported to a board of bankers, lawyers, and MBAs in St. Petersburg, agreed to pay the famous surgeon's astronomical fee.

"The first aerialist with a bionic leg," he murmured, dollar signs in his eyes.

Rolando took the news of the amputation and prostheses with surprising calm. He agreed with his wife: better a strong and reliable artificial leg than a ruined real one.

In two weeks, he walked again. But not well. He limped. The leg hurt, with a sullen, stubborn ache that refused to go away.

"It will take a little time to get accustomed to it," said the physical therapists.

Rolando waited. He exercised. He tried jogging. The leg did not work right. And it ached constantly.

"That's just not possible," the doctors assured him. "Perhaps you ought to talk with a psychologist."

The Great Rolando stormed out of their offices, limping and cursing, never to return. He went back to the circus, but not to his aerial acrobatics. A man who could not walk properly, who had an artificial leg that did not work right, had no business on the high trapeze.

His young assistant took the spotlight now and duplicated— almost—the Great Rolando's repertoire of aerial acrobatic feats. Rolando watched him with mounting jealousy, his only satisfaction being that the crowds were noticeably smaller than they had been when he had been the star of the show. The circus manager frowned and asked when Rolando would be ready to work again.

"When the leg works right," said Rolando.

But it continued to pain him, to make him awkward and invalid.

That is when he began to hate gravity. He hated being pinned down to the ground like a worm, a beetle. He would hobble into the big tent and eye the fliers platform a hundred feet over his head and know that he could not even climb the ladder to reach it. He grew angrier each day. And clumsy. And obese. The damned false leg *hurt*, no matter what those expensive quacks said. It was *not* psychosomatic. Rolando snorted contempt for their stupidity.

He spent his days bumping into inanimate objects and tripping over tent ropes. He spent his nights grumbling and grousing, fearing to move about in the dark, fearing even that he might roll off his bed. When he managed to sleep, the same nightmare gripped him: he was falling, plunging downward eternally while gravity laughed at him, and all his screams for help did him no good whatever.

His former assistant grinned at him whenever they met. The circus manager took to growling about Rolando's weight and asking how long he expected to be on the payroll when he was not earning his keep.

Rolando limped and ached. And when no one could see him, he cried. He grew bitter and angry, like a proud lion that finds himself caged forever.

Representatives from the bionics company that manufactured the prosthetic leg visited the circus, their faces grave with concern.

"The prosthesis should be working just fine," they insisted.

Rolando insisted even more staunchly that their claims were fraudulent. "I should sue you and the barbarian who took my leg off."

The manufacturer's reps consulted their home office, and within the week Rolando was whisked to San Jose in their company jet. For days on end, they tested the leg, its electronic innards, the bionic interface where it linked with Rolando's human nervous system. Everything checked out perfectly. They showed Rolando the results, almost with tears in their eyes.

"It should work fine."

"It does not."

In exchange for a written agreement not to sue them, the bionics company gave Rolando a position as a field consultant, at a healthy stipend. His only duties were to phone San Jose once a month to report on how the leg felt. Rolando delighted in describing each and every individual twinge, the awkwardness of the leg, how it made him limp.

His wife was the major earner now, despite his monthly consultant's fee. She worked twice as hard as ever before and began to draw crowds that held their breaths in vicarious terror as they watched the tiny blond place herself at the mercy of so many fangs and claws.

Rolando traveled with her as the circus made its tour of North America each year, growing fatter and unhappier day by humiliating, frustrating, painful day.

Gravity defeated him every hour, in a thousand small ways. He would read a magazine in their cramped mobile home until, bored, he tossed it onto the table. Gravity would slyly tug at its pages until the magazine slipped over the table's edge and fell to the floor. He would shower laboriously, hating the bulging fat that now encumbered his once-sleek body. The soap would slide from his hands while he was half-blinded with suds. Inevitably he would slip on it and bang himself painfully against the shower wall.

If there was a carpet spread on the floor, gravity would contrive to have it entangle his feet and pull him into a humiliating fall. Stairs tripped him. His silverware clattered noisily to the floor in restaurants.

He shunned the big top altogether, where the people who had once paid to see him soar through the air could see how heavy and clumsy he had become—even though a nasty voice in his mind told him that no one would recognize the fat old man he now was as the once magnificent Great Rolando.

As the years stretched past, Rolando grew grayer and heavier and angrier. Furious at gravity. Bellowing, screaming, howling with impotent rage at the hateful tricks gravity played on him every day, every hour. He took to leaning on a cane and stumping around their mobile home, roaring helplessly against gravity and the fate that was killing him by inches.

His darling wife remained steadfast and supportive all through those terrible years. Other circus folk shook their heads in wonder at her. "She spends all day with the big cats and then goes home to more roaring and spitting," they told each other.

Then one winter afternoon, as the sun threw long shadows across the Houston Astrodome parking lot, where the circus was camped for the week, Rolando's wife came into their mobile home, her sky-blue workout suit dark with perspiration, and announced that a small contingent of performers had been invited to Moonbase for a month.

"To the moon?" Rolando asked, incredulous. "Who?"

"The fliers and tightrope acts," she replied, "and a selection of acrobats and clowns. "

"There's no gravity up there," Rolando muttered, suddenly jealous. "Or less gravity. Something like that."

He slumped back in the sofa without realizing that the wonderful smile on his wife's face meant that there was more she wanted to tell him.

"We've been invited too!" she blurted, and she perched herself on his lap, threw her arms around his thick neck, and kissed him soundly.

"You mean *you've* been invited," he said darkly, pulling away from her embrace. "You're the star of the show; I'm a has-been"

She shook her head, still smiling happily. "They haven't asked me to perform. They can't bring the cats up into space. The invitation is for the Great Rolando and his wife to spend a month up there as guests of Moonbase Inc.!" Rolando suspected that the bionics company had pulled some corporate strings. They wanted to see how their damnable leg works without gravity, he was certain. Inwardly, he was eager to find out too. But he let no one know that, not even his wife.

To his utter shame and dismay, Rolando was miserably sick all the long three days of the flight from Texas to Moonbase. Immediately after takeoff the spacecraft carrying the circus performers was in zero gravity, weightless, and Rolando found that the absence of gravity was worse for him than gravity itself. His stomach seemed to be falling all the time while, paradoxically, anything he tried to eat crawled upward into his throat and made him violently ill.

In his misery and near delirium, he knew that gravity was laughing at him.

Once on the moon, however, everything became quite fine. Better than fine, as far as Rolando was concerned. While clear-eyed, young Moonbase guides in crisp uniforms of amber and bronze demonstrated the cautious shuffling walk that was needed in the gentle lunar gravity, Rolando realized that his leg no longer hurt.

"I feel fine," he whispered to his wife, in the middle of the demonstration. Then he startled the guides and his fellow circus folk alike by tossing his cane aside and leaping five meters into the air, shouting at the top of his lungs, "I feel *wonderful*!"

The circus performers were taken off to special orientation lectures, but Rolando and his wife were escorted by a pert young redhead into the office of Moonbase's chief administrator.

"Remember me?" asked the administrator as he shook Rolando's hand and half bowed to his wife. "I was the physicist at Columbia who did that TV commercial with you six or seven years ago."

Rolando did not, in fact, remember the man's face at all, although he did recall his warning about gravity. As he sat down in the chair the administrator proffered, he frowned slightly.

The administrator wore zippered coveralls of powder blue. He hiked one hip onto the edge of his desk and beamed happily at the Rolandos. "I can't tell you how delighted I am to have the circus here, even if it's just for a month. I really had to sweat blood to get the corporation's management to okay bringing you up here. Transportation's still quite expensive, you know."

Rolando patted his artificial leg. "I imagine the bionics company paid their fair share of the costs."

The administrator looked slightly startled. "Well, yes, they have picked up the tab for you and Mrs. Rolando."

"I thought so."

Rolando's wife smiled sweetly. "We are delighted that you invited us here."

They chatted a while longer, and then the administrator

personally escorted them to their apartment in Moonbase's tourist section. "Have a happy stay," he said, by way of taking his leave.

Although he did not expect to, that is exactly what Rolando did for the next many days. Moonbase was marvelous! There was enough gravity to keep his insides behaving properly, but it was so light and gentle that even his obese body with its false leg felt young and agile again.

Rolando walked the length and breadth of the great Main Plaza, his wife clinging to his arm, and marveled at how the Moonbase people had landscaped the expanse under their dome, planted it with grass and flowering shrubs. The apartment they had been assigned to was deeper underground, in one of the long corridors that had been blasted out of solid rock. But the quarters were no smaller than their mobile home back on Earth, and it had a video screen that took up one entire wall of the sitting room.

"I love it here!" Rolando told his wife. "I could stay forever!"

"It's only for one month," she said softly. He ignored it.

Rolando adjusted quickly to walking in the easy lunar gravity, never noticing that his wife adjusted just as quickly (perhaps even a shade faster). He left his cane in their apartment and strolled unaided each day through the shopping arcades and athletic fields of the Main Plaza, walking for hours on end without a bit of pain.

He watched the roustabouts who had come up with him directing their robots to set up a big top in the middle of the plaza, a gaudy blaze of colorful plastic and pennants beneath the great gray dome that soared high overhead.

The moon is marvelous, thought Rolando. There was still gravity lurking, trying to trip him up and make him look ridiculous.

But even when he fell, it was so slow and gentle that he could put out his powerful arms and push himself up to a standing position before his body actually hit the ground.

"I love it here!" he said to his wife, dozens of times each day. She smiled and tried to remind him that it was only for three more weeks.

At dinner one evening in Moonbase's grander restaurant (there were only two, not counting cafeterias) his earthly muscles proved too strong for the moon when he rammed their half-finished bottle of wine back into its aluminum ice bucket. The bucket tipped and fell off the edge of the table. But Rolando snatched it with one hand in the midst of its languid fall toward the floor and with a smile and a flourish, deposited the bucket with the bottle still in it back on the table before a drop had spilled.

"I love it here," he repeated for the fortieth time that day.

Gradually, though, his euphoric mood sank. The circus began giving abbreviated performances inside its big top, and Rolando stood helplessly pinned to the ground while the spotlights picked out the young fliers in their skintight costumes as they soared slowly, dreamily through the air between one trapeze and the next, twisting, spinning, somersaulting in the soft lunar gravity in ways that no one had ever done before. The audience gasped and cheered and gave them standing ovations. Rolando stood rooted near one of the tent's entrances, deep in shadow, wearing a tourist's pale-green coveralls, choking with envy and frustrated rage.

The crowds were small—there were only a few thousand people living at Moonbase, plus perhaps another thousand tourists—but they shook the plastic tent with their roars of delight.

Rolando watched a few performances, then stayed away. But

he noticed at the Olympic-sized pool that teenagers were diving from a thirty-meter platform and doing half a dozen somersaults as they fell languidly in the easy gravity. Even when they hit the water, the splashes they made rose lazily and then fell back into the pool so leisurely that it seemed like a slow-motion film.

Anyone can be an athlete here, Rolando realized as he watched tourists flying on rented wings through the upper reaches of the Main Plaza's vaulted dome.

Children could easily do not merely Olympic, but Olympian feats of acrobatics. Rolando began to dread the possibility of seeing a youngster do a quadruple somersault from a standing start.

"Anyone can defy gravity here," he complained to his wife, silently adding, *anyone but me*.

It made him morose to realize that feats which had taken him a lifetime to accomplish could be learned by a toddler in half an hour. And soon he would have to return to Earth with its heavy, oppressive, mocking gravity.

I know you're waiting for me, he said to gravity. *You're going to kill me—if I don't do the job for myself first.*

Two nights before they were due to depart, they were the dinner guests of the chief administrator and several of his staff. As formal an occasion as Moonbase ever has, the men wore sport jackets and turtleneck shirts, the women real dresses and jewelry. The administrator told hoary old stories of his childhood yearning to be in the circus. Rolando remained modestly silent, even when the administrator spoke glowingly of how he had admired the daring feats of the Great Rolando—many years ago.

After dinner, back in their apartment, Rolando turned on his wife. "You got them to invite us up here, didn't you?"

She admitted, "The bionics company told me that they were going to end your consulting fee. They want to give up on you! I asked them to let us come here to see if your leg would be better in low gravity."

"And then we go back to Earth."

"Yes."

"Back to *real* gravity. Back to my being a cripple!"

"I was hoping . . ." Her voice broke and she sank onto the bed, crying.

Suddenly, Rolando's anger was overwhelmed by a searing, agonizing sense of shame. All these years she had been trying so hard, standing between him and the rest of the world, protecting him, sheltering him. And for what? So that he could scream at her for the rest of his life?

He could not bear it any longer.

Unable to speak, unable even to reach his hand out to comfort her, he turned and lumbered out of the apartment, leaving his wife weeping alone.

He knew where he had to be, where he could finally put an end to this humiliation and misery. He made his way to the big top.

A stubby, gunmetal-gray robot stood guard at the main entrance, its sensors focusing on Rolando like the red glowing eyes of a spider.

"No access at this time except to members of the circus troupe," it said in a synthesized voice.

"I am the Great Rolando."

"One moment, please, for voiceprint identification," said the robot, then, "Approved."

Rolando swept past the contraption with a snort of contempt.

The big top was empty at this hour. Tomorrow they would start to dismantle it. The next day they would head back to Earth.

Rolando walked slowly, stiffly to the base of the ladder that reached up to the trapezes. The spotlights were shut down. The only illumination inside the tent came from the harsh working lights spotted here and there.

Rolando heaved a deep breath and stripped off his jacket. Then, gripping one of the ladder's rungs, he began to climb: good leg first, then the artificial leg. He could feel no difference between them. His body was only one-sixth its earthly weight, of course, but still, the artificial leg behaved exactly as his normal one.

He reached the topmost platform. Holding tightly to the side rail, he peered down into the gloomy shadows a hundred feet below.

With a slow, ponderous nod of his head, the Great Rolando finally admitted what he had kept buried inside him all these long, anguished years. Finally, the concealed truth emerged and stood naked before him. With tear-filled eyes he saw its reality.

He had been living a lie all these years. He had been blaming gravity for his own failure. Now he understood with precise, final clarity that it was not gravity that had destroyed his life.

It was fear.

He stood rooted on the high platform, trembling with the memory of falling, plunging, screaming terror. He knew that this fear would live within him always, for the remainder of his life. It was too strong to overcome; he was a coward, probably had always been a coward, all his life. All his life.

Without consciously thinking about it, Rolando untied one of the trapezes and gripped the rough surface of its taped bar. He did not bother with resin. There would be no need.

As if in a dream, he swung out into the empty air, feeling the rush of wind ruffling his gray hair, hearing the creak of the ropes beneath his weight.

Once, twice, three times he swung back and forth, kicking higher each time. He grunted with the unaccustomed exertion. He felt sweat trickling from his armpits.

Looking down, he saw the hard ground so far below. *One more fall*, he told himself. *Just let go, and that will end it forever. End the fear. End the shame.*

"Teach me!"

The voice boomed like cannon fire across the empty tent. Rolando felt every muscle in his body tighten.

On the opposite platform, before him, stood the chief administrator, still wearing his dinner jacket.

"Teach me!" he called again. "Show me how to do it. Just this once, before you have to leave."

Rolando hung by his hands, swinging back and forth. The younger man's figure standing on the platform came closer, closer, then receded, dwindled as inertia carried Rolando forward and back, forward and back.

"No one will know," the administrator pleaded through the shadows. "I promise you; I'll never tell a soul. Just show me how to do it. Just this once."

"Stand back," Rolando heard his own voice call, it startled him.

Rolando kicked once, tried to judge the distance and account for the lower gravity as best as he could, and let go of the bar. He soared too far, but the strong composite mesh at the rear of the platform caught him, yieldingly, and he was able to grasp the side railing and stand erect before the young administrator could reach out and steady him.

"We both have a lot to learn," said the Great Rolando. "Take off your jacket."

For more than an hour, the two men swung high through the silent, shadowy air. Rolando tried nothing fancy, no leaps from one bar to another, no real acrobatics. It was tricky enough just landing gracefully on the platform in the strange lunar gravity. The administrator did exactly as Rolando instructed him. For all his youth and desire to emulate a circus star, he was no dare-devil. It satisfied him completely to swing side by side with the Great Rolando, to share the same platform.

"What made you come here tonight?" Rolando asked as they stood gasping and sweating on the platform between turns.

"The security robot reported your entry. Strictly routine, I get all such reports piped to my quarters. But I figured this was too good a chance to miss!"

Finally, soaked with perspiration, arms aching, and fingers raw and cramping, they made their way down the ladder to the ground. Laughing.

"I'll never forget this," the administrator said. "It's the high point of my life."

"Mine too," said Rolando fervently. "Mine too."

Two days later the administrator came to the rocket termi-nal to see the circus troupe off. Taking Rolando and his wife to one side, he said in a low voice that brimmed with happiness, "You know, we're starting to accept retired couples for perma-nent residence here at Moonbase."

Rolando's wife immediately responded, "Oh, I'm not ready to retire yet."

"Nor I," said Rolando. "I'll stay with the circus for a few years more, I think. There might still be time for me to make a comeback."

"Still," said the administrator, "when you do want to retire . . ."

Mrs. Rolando smiled at him. "I've noticed that my face looks better in this lower gravity. I probably wouldn't need a face-lift if we come to live here."

They laughed together.

The rest of the troupe was filing into the rocket that would take them back to Earth. Rolando gallantly held his wife's arm as she stepped up the ramp and ducked through the hatch. Then he turned to the administrator and asked swiftly:

"What you told me about gravity all those years ago—is it really true? It is really universal? There's no way around it?"

"Afraid not," the administrator answered. "Someday gravity will make the sun collapse. It might even make the entire universe collapse."

Rolando nodded, shook the man's hand, then followed his wife to his seat inside the rocket's passenger compartment. As he listened to the taped safety lecture and strapped on his safety belt, he thought to himself: *so gravity will get us all in the end.*

Then he smiled grimly. *But not yet. Not yet.*

"SEPULCHER"

Why do human beings create works of art?

Among the earliest products of human hands that archeologists have uncovered are tiny, palm-sized bits of stone that have been shaped into miniature statues—often crude female figures with prominent sexual characteristics.

Why did someone take the time and spend the energy to convert a lump of stone into a work of art?

Why do I spend most of my life creating stories, writing tales about imaginary people in fantastic settings?

I think one of the motivations for creating artworks is *communication*. The artist—whether sculptor, painter, or even a writer of science fiction—is trying to speak to an audience, trying to say: this is the way the universe looks to me. Can you see what I see? Can you feel what I feel?

Each of us is trapped inside his or her own shell, groping

through a lifetime of experiences, trying endlessly to make meaningful contact with all those other people around us.

I think that, at heart, that is why some of us try to create works of art. From those earliest figurines to the grandest monuments of human history, artworks are attempts to communicate, at least in part.

"Sepulcher" is a tale about such a work of art, and how it affects three very different—and very human—people.

SEPULCHER

"I was a soldier," he said. "Now I am a priest. You may call me Dorn."

Elverda Apacheta could not help staring at him. She had seen cyborgs before, but this . . . person seemed more machine than man. She felt a chill ripple of contempt go through her veins. How could a human being allow his body to be disfigured so?

He was not tall; Elverda herself stood several centimeters taller than he. His shoulders were quite broad, though; his torso thick and solid. The left side of his face was engraved metal, as was the entire top of his head: like a skullcap made of finest etched steel.

Dorn's left hand was prosthetic. He made no attempt to disguise it. Beneath the rough fabric of his shabby tunic and threadbare trousers, how much more of him was metal and electrical machinery? Tattered though his clothing was, his calf-length boots were polished to a high gloss.

"A priest?" asked Miles Sterling. "Of what church? What order?"

The half of Dorn's lips that could move made a slight curl. A smile or a sneer, Elverda could not tell.

"I will show you to your quarters," said Dorn. His voice was a low rumble, as if it came from the belly of a beast. It echoed faintly off the walls of rough-hewn rock.

Sterling looked briefly surprised. He was not accustomed to having his questions ignored. Elverda watched his face. Sterling was as handsome as cosmetic surgery could make a person appear: chiseled features, earnest sky-blue eyes, straight of spine, long of limb, athletically flat midsection. Yet there was a faint smell of corruption about him, Elverda thought. As if he were dead inside and already beginning to rot.

The tension between the two men seemed to drain the energy from Elverda's aged body. "It has been a long journey," she said. "I am very tired. I would welcome a hot shower and a long nap."

"Before you see it?" Sterling snapped.

"It has taken us months to get here. We can wait a few hours more." Inwardly, she marveled at her own words. Once she would have been all fiery excitement. Had the years taught her patience? *No*, she realized. *Only weariness.*

"Not me!" Sterling said. Turning to Dorn, "Take me to it now. I've waited long enough. I want to see it now."

Dorn's eyes, one as brown as Elverda's own, the other a red, electronic glow, regarded Sterling for a lengthening moment.

"Well?" Sterling demanded.

"I am afraid, sir, that the chamber is sealed for the next twelve hours. It will be imposs—"

"Sealed? By whom? On whose authority?"

"The chamber is self-controlled. Whoever made the artifact installed the controls as well."

"No one told me about that," said Sterling.

Dorn replied, "Your quarters are down this corridor." He turned almost like a solid block of metal, shoulders and hips together, head unmoving on those wide shoulders, and started down the central corridor. Elverda fell in step alongside his metal half, still angered at his self-desecration. Yet, despite herself, she thought of what a challenge it would be to sculpt him. *If I were younger,* she told herself. *If I were not so close to death. Human and inhuman, all in one strangely fierce figure.*

Sterling came up on Dorn's other side, his face red with barely suppressed anger.

They walked down the corridor in silence, Sterling's weighted shoes clicking against the uneven rock floor. Dorn's boots made hardly any noise at all. *Half machine he may be*, Elverda thought, *but once in motion, he moves like a panther.*

The asteroid's inherent gravity was so slight that Sterling needed the weighted footgear to keep himself from stumbling ridiculously. Elverda, who had spent most of her long life in low-gravity environments, felt completely at home. The corridor they were walking through was actually a tunnel, shadowy and mysterious, or perhaps a natural chimney vented through the rocky body by escaping gases eons ago when the asteroid was still molten. Now it was cold, chill enough to make Elverda shudder. The rough ceiling was so low she wanted to stoop, even though the rational side of her mind knew it was not necessary.

Soon, though, the walls smoothed out, and the ceiling grew higher. Humans had extended the tunnel, squaring it with laser precision. Doors lined both walls now, and the ceiling glowed with glareless, shadowless light. Still she hugged herself against the chill that the others did not seem to notice.

They stopped at a wide double door. Dorn tapped out the entrance code on the panel set into the wall and the doors slid open.

"Your quarters, sir," he said to Sterling. "You may, of course, change the privacy code to suit yourself."

Sterling gave a curt nod and strode through the open doorway. Elverda got a glimpse of a spacious suite, carpeting on the floor and hologram windows on the walls.

Sterling turned in the doorway to face them. "I expect you to call for me in twelve hours," he said to Dorn, his voice hard.

"Eleven hours and fifty-seven minutes," Dorn replied. Sterling's nostrils flared, and he slid the double doors shut.

"This way." Dorn gestured with his human hand. "I'm afraid your quarters are not as sumptuous as Mr. Sterling's."

Elverda said, "I am his guest. He is paying all the bills."

"You are a great artist. I have heard of you."

"Thank you."

"For the truth? That is not necessary."

I was a great artist, Elverda said to herself. *Once. Long ago. Now I am an old woman waiting for death.*

Aloud, she asked, "Have you seen my work?"

Dorn's voice grew heavier. "Only holograms. Once I set out to see *The Rememberer* for myself, but—other matters intervened."

"You were a soldier then?"

"Yes. I have been a priest only since coming to this place."

Elverda wanted to ask him more, but Dorn stopped before a blank door and opened it for her. For an instant she thought he was going to reach for her with his prosthetic hand. She shrank away from him.

"I will call for you in eleven hours and fifty-six minutes," he said, as if he had not noticed her revulsion.

"Thank you."

He turned away, like a machine pivoting.

"Wait," Elverda called. "Please—how many others are here? Everything seems so quiet."

"There are no others. Only the three of us."

"But—"

"I am in charge of the security brigade. I ordered the others of my command to go back to our spacecraft and wait there."

"And the scientists? The prospector family that found this asteroid?"

"They are in Mr. Sterling's spacecraft, the one you arrived in," said Dorn. "Under the protection of my brigade."

Elverda looked into his eyes. Whatever burned in them, she could not fathom.

"Then we are alone here?"

Dorn nodded solemnly. "You and me—and Mr. Sterling, who pays all the bills." The human half of his face remained as immobile as the metal. Elverda could not tell if he was trying to be humorous or bitter.

"Thank you," she said. He turned away and she closed the door.

Her quarters consisted of a single room, comfortably warm but hardly larger than the compartment on the ship they had come in. Elverda saw that her meager travel bag was already sitting on the bed, her worn old drawing computer resting in its travel-smudged case on the desk. Elverda stared at the computer case as if it were accusing her. *I should have left it home*, she thought. *I will never use it again.*

A small utility robot, hardly more than a glistening drum of metal and six gleaming arms folded like a praying mantis's, stood mutely in the farthest corner. Elverda stared at it. At least it was entirely a machine; not a self-mutilated human being. To take the most beautiful form in the universe and turn it into a hybrid mechanism, a travesty of humanity. Why did he do it? So he could be a better soldier? A more efficient killing machine?

And why did he send all the others away? she asked herself while she opened the travel bag. As she carried her toiletries to the narrow alcove of the bathroom, a new thought struck her. Did he send them away before he saw the artifact, or afterward? Has he even seen it? Perhaps.

Then she saw her reflection in the mirror above the washbasin. Her heart sank. Once she had been called regal, stately, a goddess made of copper. Now she looked withered, dried up, bone thin, her face a geological map of too many years of living, her flight coveralls hanging limply on her emaciated frame.

You are old, she said to her image. *Old and aching and tired.*

It is the long trip, she told herself. *You need to rest.* But the other voice in her mind laughed scornfully. *You've done nothing but rest for the entire time it's taken to reach this piece of rock. You are ready for the permanent rest; why deny it?*

She had been teaching at the university on Luna, the closest she could get to Earth after a long lifetime of living in low-gravity environments. Close enough to see the world of her birth, the only world of life and warmth in the solar system, the only place where a person could walk out in the sunshine and feel its warmth soaking their bones, smell the fertile earth nurturing its bounty, feel a cool breeze plucking at their hair.

But she had separated herself from Earth permanently. She

had stood at the shore of Titan's methane sea; from an orbiting spacecraft, she had watched the surging clouds of Jupiter swirl their overpowering colors; she had carved the kilometer-long rock of *The Rememberer*. But she could no longer stand in the village of her birth, at the edge of the Pacific's booming surf, and watch the soft white clouds form shapes of imaginary animals.

Her creative life was long finished. She had lived too long; there were no friends left, and she had never had a family. There was no purpose to her life, no reason to do anything except go through the motions and wait. At the university she was no longer truly working at her art but helping students who had the fires of inspiration burning fresh and hot inside them. Her life was one of vain regrets for all the things she had not accomplished, for all the failures she could recall. Failures at love; those were the bitterest. She was praised as the solar system's greatest artist: the sculptress of *The Rememberer*, the creator of the first great ionospheric painting, *The Virgin of the Andes*. She was respected, but not loved. She felt empty, alone, barren. She had nothing to look forward to, absolutely nothing.

Then Miles Sterling had swept into her existence. A lifetime younger, bold, vital, even ruthless, he stormed her academic tower with the news that an alien artifact had been discovered deep in the asteroid belt.

"It's some kind of art form," he said, desperate with excitement. "You've got to come with me and see it."

Trying to control the long-forgotten longing that stirred within her, Elverda had asked quietly, "Why do I have to go with you, Mr. Sterling? And why me? I'm an old wo—"

"You are the greatest artist of our time," he had snapped. "You've *got* to see this! Don't bullshit me with false modesty.

You're the only other person in the whole whirling solar system who *deserves* to see it!"

"The only other person besides whom?" she had asked. He had blinked with surprise. "Why, besides me, of course."

So now they were on this nameless asteroid, waiting to see the alien artwork. Just the three of them. The richest man in the solar system. An elderly artist who has outlived her usefulness. And a cyborg soldier who has cleared everyone else away.

He claims to be a priest, Elverda remembered. A priest who is half machine. She shivered as if a cold wind surged through her.

A harsh buzzing noise interrupted her thoughts. Looking into the main part of the room, Elverda saw that the phone screen was blinking red in rhythm to the buzzing.

"Phone," she called out.

Sterling's face appeared on the screen instantly. "Come to my quarters," he said. "We have to talk."

"Give me an hour. I need—"

"Now."

Elverda felt her brows rise haughtily. Then the strength sagged out of her. *He has bought the right to command you,* she told herself. *He is quite capable of refusing to allow you to see the artifact.*

"Now," she agreed.

Sterling was pacing across the plush carpeting when she arrived at his quarters. He had changed from his flight coveralls into a comfortably loose royal-blue pullover and expensive, genuine twill slacks. As the doors slid shut behind her, he stopped in front of a low couch and faced her squarely.

"Do you know who this Dorn creature is?"

Elverda answered, "Only what he has told us."

"I've checked him out. My staff in the ship has a complete

dossier on him. He's the butcher who led the *Chrysalis* massacre, fourteen years ago."

"He— "

"Eleven hundred men, women, and children. Slaughtered. He was the man who commanded the attack."

"He said he had been a soldier."

"A mercenary. A cold-blooded murderer. He was working for Toyama then. The *Chrysalis* was their habitat. When its population voted for independence, Toyama put him in charge of a squad to bring them back into line. He killed them all; turned off their air and let them all die."

Elverda felt shakily for the nearest chair and sank into it. Her legs seemed to have lost all their strength.

"His name was Harbin then. Dorik Harbin."

"Wasn't he brought to trial?"

"No. He ran away. Disappeared. I always thought Toyama helped to hide him. They take care of their own, they do. He must have changed his name afterward. Nobody would hire the butcher, not even Toyama."

"His face . . . half his body . . ." Elverda felt terribly weak, almost faint. "When . . . ?"

"Must have been after he ran away. Maybe it was an attempt to disguise himself."

"And now he is working for you." She wanted to laugh at the irony of it but did not have the strength.

"He's got us trapped on this chunk of rock! There's nobody else here except the three of us."

"You have your staff in your ship. Surely, they would come if you summoned them."

"His security squad's been ordered to keep everybody

except you and me off the asteroid. He gave those orders."

"You can countermand them, can't you?"

For the first time since she had met Miles Sterling, the man looked unsure of himself. "I wonder," he said.

"Why?" Elverda asked. "Why is he doing this?"

"That's what I intend to find out." Sterling strode to the phone console. "Harbin!" he called. "Dorik Harbin. Come to my quarters at once."

Without even an eyeblink's delay the phone's computer-synthesized voice replied, "Dorik Harbin no longer exists. Transferring your call to Dorn."

Sterling's blue eyes snapped at the phone's blank screen.

"Dorn is not available at present," the phone's voice said. "He will call for you in eleven hours and thirty-two minutes."

"God *damn* it!" Sterling smacked a fist into the open palm of his other hand. "Get me the officer on watch aboard the *Sterling Eagle*."

"All exterior communications are inoperable at the present time," replied the phone.

"That's impossible!"

"All exterior communications are inoperable at the present time," the phone repeated, unperturbed.

Sterling stared at the empty screen, then turned slowly toward Elverda. "He's cut us off. We're really trapped here."

Elverda felt the chill of cold metal clutching at her. *Perhaps Dorn is a madman*, she thought. *Perhaps he is my death, personified.*

"We've got to do something!" Sterling nearly shouted.

Elverda rose shakily to her feet. "There is nothing that we can do, for the moment. I am going to my quarters to take a nap. I believe that Dorn, or Harbin, or whatever his identity is, will call on us when he is ready to."

"And do what?"

"Show us the artifact," she replied, silently adding, *I hope.*

Legally, the artifact and the entire asteroid belonged to Sterling Enterprises, Ltd. It had been discovered by a family—husband, wife, and two sons, ages five and three—who made a living from searching out iron-nickel asteroids and selling the mining rights to the big corporations. They filed their claim to this unnamed asteroid, together with a preliminary description of its ten-kilometer-wide shape, its orbit within the asteroid belt, and a sample analysis of its surface composition.

Six hours after their original transmission reached the commodities-market computer network on Earth—while a fairly spirited bidding war was going on among four major corporations for the asteroid's mineral rights—a new message arrived at the headquarters of the International Astronautical Authority, in London. The message was garbled, fragmentary, obviously made in great haste and at fever excitement. There was an artifact of some sort in a cavern deep inside the asteroid.

One of the faceless bureaucrats buried deep within the IAA's multilayered organization sent an immediate message to an employee of Sterling Enterprises, Ltd. The bureaucrat retired hours later, richer than he had any right to expect, while Miles Sterling personally contacted the prospectors and bought the asteroid outright for enough money to end their prospecting days forever. By the time the decision-makers in the IAA realized that an alien artifact had been discovered, they were faced with a fait accompli: the artifact, and the asteroid in which it resided, were the personal property of the richest man in the solar system.

Miles Sterling was no egomaniac. Nor was he a fool. Graciously, he allowed the IAA to organize a team of scientists who would inspect this first specimen of alien existence. Even more graciously, Sterling offered to ferry the scientific investigators all the long way to the asteroid at his own expense. He made only one demand, and the IAA could hardly refuse him. He insisted that he see this artifact himself before the scientists were allowed to view it.

And he brought along the solar system's most honored and famous artist. To appraise the artifact's worth as an art object, he claimed. To determine how much he could deduct from his corporate taxes by donating the thing to the IAA, said his enemies.

But over the months of their voyage to the asteroid, Elverda came to the conclusion that buried deep beneath his ruthless business persona was an eager little boy who was tremendously excited at having found a new toy. A toy he intended to possess for himself. An art object created by alien hands.

For an art object was what the artifact seemed to be. The family of prospectors continued to send back vague, almost irrational reports of what the artifact looked like. The reports were worthless. No two descriptions matched. If the man and woman were to be believed, the artifact did nothing but sit in the middle of a rough-hewn cavern. But they described it differently with every report they sent. It glowed with light. It was darker than deep space. It was a statue of some sort. It was formless. It overwhelmed the senses. It was small enough almost to pick up in one hand. It made the children laugh happily. It frightened their parents. When they tried to photograph it, their transmissions showed nothing but blank screens. Totally blank.

As Sterling listened to their maddening reports and waited impatiently for the IAA to organize its handpicked team of scientists, he ordered his security manager to get a squad of hired personnel to the asteroid as quickly as possible. From corporate facilities on Titan and the moons of Mars, from three separate outposts among the asteroid belt itself, Sterling Enterprises efficiently brought together a brigade of experienced mercenary security troops. They reached the asteroid long before anyone else could and were under orders to make certain that no one was allowed onto the asteroid before Miles Sterling himself reached it.

"The time has come."

Elverda woke slowly, painfully, like a swimmer struggling for the air and light of the surface. She had been dreaming of her childhood, of the village where she had grown up, the distant snow-capped Andes, the warm night breezes that spoke of love.

"The time has come."

It was Dorn's deep voice, whisper soft. Startled, she flashed her eyes open. She was alone in the room, but Dorn's image filled the phone screen by her bed. The numbers glowing beneath the screen showed that it was indeed time.

"I am awake now," she said to the screen.

"I will be at your door in fifteen minutes," Dorn said. "Will that be enough time for you to prepare yourself?"

"Yes, plenty." The days when she needed time for selecting her clothing and arranging her appearance were long gone.

"In fifteen minutes, then."

"Wait," she blurted. "Can you see me?"

"No. Visual transmission must be keyed manually."

"I see."

"I do not."

A joke? Elverda sat up on the bed as Dorn's image winked out. *Is he capable of humor?*

She shrugged out of the shapeless coveralls she had worn

to bed, took a quick shower, and pulled her best caftan from the travel bag. It was a deep midnight blue, scattered with glittering silver stars. Elverda had made the floor-length gown herself, from fabric woven by her mother long ago. She had painted the stars from her memory of what they had looked like from her native village.

As she slid back her front door, she saw Dorn marching down the corridor with Sterling beside him. Despite his longer legs, Sterling seemed to be scampering like a child to keep up with Dorn's steady, stolid steps.

"I *demand* that you reinstate communications with my ship," Sterling was saying, his voice echoing off the corridor walls. "I'll dock your pay for every minute this insubordination continues!"

"It is a security measure," Dorn said calmly, without turning to look at the man. "It is for your own good."

"My own good? Who in hell are you to determine what my own good might be?"

Dorn stopped three paces short of Elverda, made a stiff little bow to her, and only then turned to face his employer.

"Sir, I have seen the artifact. You have not."

"And that makes you better than me?" Sterling almost snarled the words. "Holier, maybe?"

"No," said Dorn. "Not holier. Wiser."

Sterling started to reply, then thought better of it.

"Which way do we go?" Elverda asked in the sudden silence.

Dorn pointed with his prosthetic hand. "Down," he replied. "This way."

The corridor abruptly became a rugged tunnel again, with lights fastened at precisely spaced intervals along the low ceiling. Elverda watched Dorn's half-human face as the pools of shadow chased the highlights glinting off the etched metal, like the moon racing through its phases every half minute, over and again.

Sterling had fallen silent as they followed the slanting tunnel downward into the heart of the rock. Elverda heard only the clicking of his shoes, at first, but by concentrating she was able to make out the softer footfalls of Dorn's padded boots and even the whisper of her own slippers.

The air seemed to grow warmer, closer. Or was it her own anticipation? She glanced at Sterling; perspiration beaded his upper lip. The man radiated tense expectation. Dorn glided a few steps ahead of them. He did not seem to be hurrying, yet he was now leading them down the tunnel, like an ancient priest leading two new acolytes—or sacrificial victims.

The tunnel ended in a smooth wall of dull metal.

"We are here."

"Open it up," Sterling demanded.

"It will open itself," replied Dorn. He waited a heartbeat, then added, "Now."

And the metal slid up into the rock above them as silently as if it were a curtain made of silk.

None of them moved. Then Dorn slowly turned toward the two of them and gestured with his human hand.

"The artifact lies twenty-two point nine meters beyond this point. The tunnel narrows and turns to the right. The chamber is large enough to accommodate only one person at a time, comfortably."

"Me first!" Sterling took a step forward.

Dorn stopped him with an upraised hand: The prosthetic hand. "I feel it my duty to caution you—"

Sterling tried to push the hand away; he could not budge it.

"When I first crossed this line, I was a soldier. After I saw the artifact, I gave up my life."

"And became a self-styled priest. So what?"

"The artifact can change you. I thought it best that there be no witnesses to your first viewing of it, except for this gifted woman whom you have brought with you. When you first see it, it can be—traumatic."

Sterling's face twisted with a mixture of anger and disgust. "I'm not a mercenary killer. I don't have anything to be afraid of."

Dorn let his hand drop to his side with a faint whine of miniaturized servomotors.

"Perhaps not," he murmured, so low that Elverda barely heard it.

Sterling shouldered his way past the cyborg. "Stay here," he told Elverda. "You can see it when I come back."

He hurried down the tunnel, footsteps staccato.

Then silence.

Elverda looked at Dorn. The human side of his face seemed utterly weary.

"You have seen the artifact more than once, haven't you?"

"Fourteen times," he answered.

"It has not harmed you in any way, has it?"

He hesitated, then replied, "It has changed me. Each time I see it, it changes me more."

"You . . . you really are Dorik Harbin?"

"I was."

"Those people of the *Chrysalis* . . ."

"Dorik Harbin killed them all. Yes. There is no excuse for it, no pardon. It was the act of a monster."

"But why?"

"Monsters do monstrous things. Dorik Harbin ingested psychotropic drugs to increase his battle prowess. Afterward, when the battle drugs cleared from his bloodstream and he understood what he had done, Dorik Harbin held a grenade against his chest and set it *off*."

"Oh my God," Elverda whimpered.

"He was not allowed to die, however. The medical specialists rebuilt his body, and he was given a false identity. For many years he lived a sham of a life, hiding from the authorities, hiding from his own guilt. He no longer had the courage to kill himself, the pain of his first attempt was far stronger than his own self-loathing. Then he was hired to come to this place. Dorik Harbin looked upon the artifact for the first time, and his true identity emerged at last."

Elverda heard a scuffling sound, like feet dragging, staggering. Miles Sterling came into view, tottering, leaning heavily against the wall of the tunnel, slumping as if his legs could no longer hold him.

"No man . . . no one . . ." He pushed himself forward and collapsed into Dorn's arms.

"Destroy it!" he whispered harshly, spittle dribbling down his chin. "Destroy this whole damned piece of rock! Wipe it out of existence!"

"What is it?" Elverda asked. "What did you see?"

Dorn lowered him to the ground gently. Sterling's feet scrabbled against the rock as if he were trying to run away. Sweat covered his face, soaked his shirt.

"It's . . . beyond . . ." he babbled. "More . . . than anyone can . . . nobody could stand it . . ."

Elverda sank to her knees beside him. "What has happened

to him?" She looked up at Dorn, who knelt on Sterling's other side.

"The artifact."

Sterling suddenly ranted, "They'll find out about me! Everyone will know! It's got to be destroyed! Nuke it! Blast it to bits!" His fists windmilled in the air, his eyes were wild.

"I tried to warn him," Dorn said as he held Sterling's shoulders down, the man's head in his lap. "I tried to prepare him for it."

"What did he see?" Elverda's heart was pounding; she could hear it thundering in her ears. "What is it? What did *you* see?"

Dorn shook his head slowly. "I cannot describe it. I doubt that anyone could describe it—except, perhaps, an artist: a person who has trained herself to see the truth."

"The prospectors—they saw it. Even their children saw it."

"Yes. When I arrived here, they had spent eighteen days in the chamber. They left it only when the chamber closed itself. They ate and slept and returned here, as if hypnotized."

"It did not hurt them, did it?"

"They were emaciated, dehydrated. It took a dozen of my strongest men to remove them to my ship. Even the children fought us."

"But—how could . . ." Elverda's voice faded into silence. She looked at the brightly lit tunnel. Her breath caught in her throat.

"Destroy it," Sterling mumbled. "Destroy it before it destroys us! Don't let them find out. They'll know, they'll know, they'll all know." He began to sob uncontrollably.

"You do not have to see it," Dorn said to Elverda. "You can return to your ship and leave this place."

Leave, urged a voice inside her head. *Run away. Live out what's left of your life and let it go.*

Then she heard her own voice say, as if from a far distance, "I've come such a long way."

"It will change you," he warned.

"Will it release me from life?"

Dorn glanced down at Sterling, still muttering darkly, then returned his gaze to Elverda.

"It will change you," he repeated.

Elverda forced herself to her feet. Leaning one hand against the warm rock wall to steady herself, she said, "I will see it. I must."

"Yes," said Dorn. "I understand."

She looked down at him, still kneeling with Sterling's head resting in his lap. Dorn's electronic eye glowed red in the shadows. His human eye was hidden in darkness.

He said, "I believe your people say, *vaya con Dios*."

Elverda smiled at him. She had not heard that phrase in forty years. "Yes. You too. *Vaya con Dios.*" She turned and stepped across the faint groove where the metal door had met the floor.

The tunnel sloped downward only slightly. It turned sharply to the right, Elverda saw, just as Dorn had told them. The light seemed brighter beyond the turn, pulsating almost, like a living heart.

She hesitated a moment before making that final turn. What lay beyond? *What difference*, she answered herself. *You have lived so long that you have emptied life of all its purpose.* But she knew she was lying to herself. Her life was devoid of purpose because she herself had made it that way. She had spurned love; she had even rejected friendship when it had been offered. Still, she realized that she wanted to live. Desperately, she wanted to continue living no matter what.

Yet she could not resist the lure. Straightening her spine, she stepped boldly around the bend in the tunnel.

The light was so bright it hurt her eyes. She raised a hand to her brow to shield them, and the intensity seemed to decrease slightly, enough to make out the faint outline of a form, a shape, a person.

Elverda gasped with recognition. A few meters before her, close enough to reach and touch, her mother sat on the sweet grass beneath the warm summer sun, gently rocking her baby and crooning softly to it.

Mama! she cried silently. Mama. The baby—Elverda herself—looked up into her mother's face and smiled.

And the mother was Elverda, a young and radiant Elverda, smiling down at the baby she had never had, tender and loving as she had never been.

Something gave way inside her. There was no pain: rather, it was as if a pain that had throbbed sullenly within her for too many years to count suddenly faded away. As if a wall of implacable ice finally melted and let the warm waters of life flow through her.

Elverda sank to the floor, crying, gushing tears of understanding and relief and gratitude. Her mother smiled at her.

"I love you, Mama," she whispered. "I love you." Her mother nodded and became Elverda herself once more. Her baby made a gurgling laugh of pure happiness, fat little feet waving in the air.

The image wavered, dimmed, and slowly faded into emptiness. Elverda sat on the bare rock floor in utter darkness, feeling a strange serenity and understanding warming her soul.

"Are you all right?"

Dorn's voice did not startle her. She had been expecting him to come to her.

"The chamber will close itself in another few minutes," he said. "We will have to leave."

Elverda took his offered hand and rose to her feet. She felt strong, fully in control of herself.

The tunnel outside the chamber was empty.

"Where is Sterling?"

"I sedated him and then called in a medical team to take him back to his ship."

"He wants to destroy the artifact," Elverda said. "That will not be possible." said Dorn. "I will bring the IAA scientists here from the ship before Sterling awakes and recovers. Once they see the artifact, they will not allow it to be destroyed. Sterling may own the asteroid, but the IAA will exert control over the artifact."

"The artifact will affect them—strangely."

"No two of them will be affected in the same manner," said Dorn. "And none of them will permit it to be damaged in any way."

"Sterling will not be pleased with you."

He gestured up the tunnel, and they began to walk back toward their quarters.

"Nor with you," Dorn said. "We both saw him babbling and blubbering like a baby."

"What could he have seen?"

"What he most feared. His whole life had been driven by fear, poor man."

"What secrets he must be hiding!"

"He hid them from himself. The artifact showed him his own true nature."

"No wonder he wants it destroyed."

"He cannot destroy the artifact, but he will certainly want

to destroy us. Once he recovers his composure, he will want to wipe out the witnesses who saw his reaction to it."

Elverda knew that Dorn was right. She watched his face as they passed beneath the lights, watched the glint of the etched metal, the warmth of the human flesh.

"You knew that he would react this way, didn't you?" she asked.

"No one could be as rich as he is without having demons driving him. He looked into his own soul and recognized himself for the first time in his life."

"You planned it this way!"

"Perhaps I did," he said. "Perhaps the artifact did it for me."

"How could—"

"It is a powerful experience. After I had seen it a few times, I felt it was offering me . . ." he hesitated, then spoke the word, "salvation."

Elverda saw something in his face that Dorn had not let show before. She stopped in the shadows between overhead lights. Dorn turned to face her, half machine, standing in the rough tunnel of bare rock.

"You have had your own encounter with it," he said. "You understand now how it can transform you."

"Yes," said Elverda. "I understand."

"After a few times, I came to the realization that there must be thousands of my fellow mercenaries, killed in engagements all through the asteroid belt, still lying where they fell. Or worse yet, floating forever in space, alone, unattended, ungrieved for."

"Thousands of mercenaries?'

"The corporations do not always settle their differences in Earthly courts of law," said Dorn. "There have been many battles out here. Wars that we paid for with our blood."

"Thousands?" Elverda repeated. "I knew that there had been occasional fights out here—but wars? I don't think anyone on Earth knows it's been so brutal."

"Men like Sterling know. They start the wars, and people like me fight them. Exiles, never allowed to return to Earth again once we take the mercenary's pay."

"All those men—killed."

Dorn nodded. "And women. The artifact made me see that it was my duty to find each of those forgotten bodies and give each one a decent final rite. The artifact seemed to be telling me that this was the path of my atonement."

"Your salvation," she murmured.

"I see now, however, that I underestimated the situation."

"How?"

"Sterling. While I am out there searching for the bodies of the slain, he will have me killed."

"No! That's wrong!"

Dorn's deep voice was empty of regret. "It will be simple for him to send a team after me. In the depths of dark space, they will murder me. What I failed to do for myself, Sterling will do for me. He will be my final atonement."

"Never!" Elverda blazed with anger. "I will not permit it to happen."

"Your own life is in danger from him," Dorn said.

"What of it? I am an old woman, ready for death."

"Are you?"

"I was, until I saw the artifact."

"Now life is more precious to you, isn't it?"

"I don't want you to die," Elverda said. "You have atoned for your sins. You have borne enough pain."

He looked away, then started up the tunnel again.

"You are forgetting one important factor," Elverda called after him.

Dorn stopped, his back to her. She realized now that the clothes he wore had been his military uniform. He had torn all the insignias and pockets from it.

"The artifact. Who created it? And why?"

Turning back toward her, Dorn answered, "Alien visitors to our solar system created it, unknown ages ago. As to why—you tell me: why does someone create a work of art?"

"Why would aliens create a work of art that affects human minds?"

Dorn's human eye blinked. He rocked a step backward. "How could they create an artifact that is a mirror to our souls?" Elverda asked, stepping toward him. "They must have known something about us. They must have been here long ages ago. They must have studied us—our ancestors."

Dorn regarded her silently.

Coming closer to him, Elverda went on, "They may have placed this artifact here to *communicate* with us.

"Communicate?"

"Perhaps it is a very subtle, very powerful communications device."

"Not an artwork at all."

"Oh, yes, of course it's an artwork! All works of art are communications devices, for those who possess the soul to understand."

Dorn seemed to ponder this for long moments. Elverda watched his solemn face, searching for some human expression.

Finally, he said, "That does not change my mission, even if it is true."

"Yes, it does," Elverda said, eager to save him. "Your mission is to preserve and protect this artifact against Sterling and anyone else who would try to destroy it—or pervert it to his own use."

"The dead call to me," Dorn said solemnly. "I hear them in my dreams now."

"But why be alone in your mission? Let others help you. There must be other mercenaries who feel as you do."

"Perhaps," he said softly.

"Your true mission is much greater than you think," Elverda said, trembling with new understanding. "You have the power to end the wars that have destroyed your comrades, that have almost destroyed your soul."

"End the corporate wars?"

"You will be the priest of this shrine, this sepulcher. I will return to Earth and tell everyone about these wars."

"Sterling and others will have you killed"

"I am a famous artist; they dare not touch me." Then she laughed. "And I am too old to care if they do."

"The scientists—do you think they may actually learn how to communicate with the aliens?"

"Someday," Elverda said. "When our souls are pure enough to stand the shock of their presence."

The human side of Dorn's face smiled at her. He extended his arm, and she took it in her own, realizing that she had found her own salvation. Like two kindred souls, like comrades who had shared the sight of death, like mother and son, they walked up the tunnel toward the waiting race of humanity.

"THE CAFÉ COUP"

Time travel. The ability to move at will into the future—or the past.

Of all the possibilities that science fiction has tinkered with, time travel seems the most fantastic. Yet the known laws of physics tell us that time travel is not forbidden.

And what is not forbidden may one day become possible.

It seems unlikely, a dream of traveling across time to a different age. But once, space flight seemed like a dream. So did skyscrapers and modern medicine and electromagnetic communications systems that link the world almost instantaneously.

The question, then, is this: who would travel through time? And why?

Thereby, as they say, hangs a tale.

THE CAFÉ COUP

Paris was not friendly to Americans in the soft springtime of AD 1922. The French didn't care much for the English either and they hated the victorious Germans, of course.

I couldn't blame them very much. The Great War had been over for more than three years, yet Paris had still not recovered its gaiety, its light and color, despite the hordes of boisterous German tourists who spent so freely on the boulevards. More likely, because of them.

I sat in one of the crowded sidewalk cafés beneath a splendid warm sun, waiting for my lovely wife to show up. Because of the crowds of Germans, I was forced to share my minuscule round table with a tall, gaunt Frenchman who looked me over with suspicious eyes.

"You are an American?" he asked, looking down his prominent nose at me. His accent was worse than mine, certainly not Parisian.

"No," I answered truthfully. Then I lied, "I'm from New Zealand." It was as far away in distance as my real birthplace was in time.

"Ah," he said with an exhalation of breath that was somewhere between a sigh and a snort. "Your countrymen fought well at Gallipoli. Were you there?"

"No," I said. "I was too young."

That apparently puzzled him. Obviously, I was of an age to have fought in the Great War. But in fact, I hadn't been born when the British Empire troops were decimated at Gallipoli. I hadn't been born in the twentieth century at all.

"Were you in the war?" I asked needlessly.

"But certainly. To the very last moment, I fought the Boche."

"It was a great tragedy."

"The Americans betrayed us," he muttered.

My brows rose a few millimeters. He was quite tall for a Frenchman, but painfully thin. Half-starved. Even his eyes looked hungry. The inflation, of course. It cost a basketful of francs, literally, to buy a loaf of bread. I wondered how he could afford the price of an aperitif. Despite the warm afternoon, he had wrapped himself in a shabby old leather coat, worn shiny at the elbows.

From what I could see, there were hardly any Frenchmen in the café, mostly raucous Germans roaring with laughter and heartily pounding on the little tables as they bellowed for more beer. To my amazement, the waiters had learned to speak German.

"Wilson," my companion continued bitterly. "He had the gall to speak of Lafayette."

"I thought that the American president was the one who arranged the armistice."

"Yes, with his Fourteen Points. Fourteen daggers plunged into the heart of France."

"Really?"

"The Americans should have entered the war on our side! Instead, they sat idly by and watched us bleed to death while their bankers extorted every gram of gold we possessed."

"But the Americans had no reason to go to war," I protested mildly.

"France needed them! When their pitiful little colonies rebelled against the British lion, France was the only nation to come to their aid. They owe their very existence to France, yet when we needed them, they turned their backs on us."

That was largely my fault, although he didn't know it. I averted the sinking of the *Lusitania* by the German U-boat. It took enormous energies, but my darling wife arranged it so that the *Lusitania* was crawling along at a mere five knots that fateful morning. I convinced Lieutenant Waither Schwieger, skipper of the *U-20*, that it was safe enough to surface and hold the British liner captive with the deck gun while a boarding party searched for the ammunition that I knew the English had stored aboard her.

The entire affair was handled with great tact and honor. No shots were fired, no lives were lost, and the one hundred twenty-three American passengers arrived safely in Liverpool with glowing stories of how correct, how chivalrous, the German U-boat sailors had been. America remained neutral through-out the Great War. Indeed, a good deal of anti-British sentiment swept the United States, especially the Midwest, when their newspapers reported that the British were transporting military contraband in secret aboard the liner and thus putting the lives of the American passengers at risk.

"Well," I said, beckoning to the waiter for another Pernod, "the war is over, and we must face the future as best we can."

"Yes," said my companion gloomily. "I agree."

One group of burly Germans was being particularly obnoxious, singing bawdy songs as they waved their beer glasses to and fro, slopping the foaming beer on themselves and their neighboring tables. No one complained. No one dared to say a word. The German army still occupied much of France.

My companion's face was white with fury. Yet even he restrained himself. But I noticed that he glanced at the watch on his wrist every few moments, as if he were expecting someone. Or something.

If anyone had betrayed France, it was me. The world that I had been born into was a cesspool of violence and hate, crumbling into tribal savagery all across the globe. Only a few oases of safety existed, tucked in remote areas far from the filthy, disease-ridden cities and the swarms of ignorant, vicious monsters who raped and murdered until they themselves were raped and murdered.

Once they discovered our solar-powered city, tucked high in the Sierra Oriental, I knew that the end was near. Stupidly, they attacked us, like a wild barbarian horde. We slaughtered them with laser beams and heat-seeking bullets. Instead of driving them away, that only whetted their appetite.

Their survivors laid siege to our mountaintop. We laughed, at first, to think their pitiful handful of ragged ignoramuses could overcome our walled city, with its high-tech weaponry and endless energy from the sun. Yet somehow, they spread the word to others of their kind. Day after day we watched their numbers grow, a tattered, threadbare pack of rats surrounding us, watching, waiting until their numbers were so huge, they could swarm us under despite our weapons.

They were united in their bloodlust and their greed. They saw loot and power on our mountaintop, and they wanted both. At night I could see their campfires down below us, like the red eyes of rats watching and waiting.

Our council was divided. Some urged that we sally out against the besiegers, attack them, and drive them away. But it was already too late for that. Their numbers were far too large, and even if we drove them away, they would return, now that they knew we existed.

Others wanted to flee into space, to leave Earth altogether and build colonies off the planet. We had the technology to build and maintain the solar-powered satellites, they pointed out. It was only one technological step farther to build habitats in space.

But when we put the numbers through a computer analysis, it showed that to build a habitat large enough to house us all permanently would be beyond our current resources—and we could not enlarge our resource base as long as we were encircled by the barbarians.

I had worked on the time translator since my student days. It took enormous energy to move objects through time, far too much for all of us to escape that way. Yet I saw a possibility of hope.

If I could find a nexus, a pivotal point in time, perhaps I could change the world. Perhaps I could alter events to such an extent that this miserable world of terror and pain would dissolve, disappear, and a better world replace it. I became obsessed with the possibility.

"But you'll destroy this world," my wife gasped, shocked when I finally told her of my scheme.

"What of it?" I snapped. "Is this world so delightful that you want it to continue?"

She sank wearily onto the lab bench. "What will happen to our families? Our friends? What will happen to us?"

"You and I will make the translation. We will live in an earlier, better time."

"And the others?"

I shrugged. "I don't know. The mathematics isn't clear. But even if they disappear, the world that replaces them in this time will be better than the world we're in now."

"Do you really think so?"

"We'll make it better!"

The fools on the council disagreed, naturally. No one had translated through time, they pointed out. The energy even for a preliminary experiment would be prohibitively high. We needed that energy for our weapons.

None of them believed I could change a thing. They weren't afraid that they would be erased from existence, their world line snuffed out like a candle flame. No, in their blind ignorance they insisted that an attempt at time translation would consume so much energy that we would be left defenseless against the besieging savages outside our walls.

"The savages will no longer exist," I told them. "None of this world line will exist, once I've made the proper change in the temporal geodesic."

They voted me down. They would rather face the barbarians than give up their existence, even if it meant a better world would replace the one they knew.

Outwardly, I accepted their judgment. Inwardly, I became the most passionate student of history of all time. Feverishly, I searched the books and discs, seeking the nexus, the turning point, the place where I could make the world change for the better. I knew I had only a few months; the savage horde below our mountaintop was growing and stirring. I could hear their murmuring dirge of hate even through the walls of my laboratory, like the growls of a pack of wild beasts. Every day, it grew louder, more insistent.

It was the war in the middle of the twentieth century that started the world's descent into madness. A man called Adolf Hitler escalated the horror of war to new levels of inhumanity. Not only did he deliberately murder millions of civilian men, women, and children; he destroyed his own country, screaming with his last breath that the Aryan race deserved to be wiped out if they could not conquer the world.

When I first realized the enormity of Hitler's rage, I sat stunned for an entire day. Here was the model, the prototype, for the brutal, cruel, ruthless, sadistic monsters who ranged my world seeking blood.

Before Hitler, war was a senseless affront to civilized men and women. Soldiers were tolerated, at best; often despised. They were usually shunned in polite society. After Hitler, war was commonplace, genocide routine, nuclear weapons valued for the megadeaths they could generate.

Hitler and all he stood for was the edge of the precipice, the first terrible step into the abyss that my world had plunged into. If I could prevent Hitler from coming to power, perhaps prevent him from ever being born, I might save my world—or at least, erase it and replace it with a better one.

For days on end, I thought of how I might translate back in time to kill this madman or even prevent his birth. Slowly, however, I began to realize that this single man was not the cause of it all. If Hitler had never been born, someone else would have arisen in Germany after the Great War, someone else would have unified the German people in a lust for revenge against those who had betrayed and defeated them, someone else would have preached Aryan purity and hatred of all other races, someone else would have plunged civilization into World War II.

To solve the problem of Hitler, I had to go to the root causes of the Nazi program: Germany's defeat in the First World War, the war that was called the Great War by those who had lived through it. I had to make Germany win that war.

If Germany had won World War I, there would have been no humiliation of the German people, no thirst for revenge, no economic collapse. Hitler would still exist, but he would be a retired soldier, perhaps a peaceful painter or even a minor functionary in the Kaiser's government. There would be no World War II.

And so I set my plans to make Germany the victor in the Great War, with the reluctant help of my dear wife.

"You would defy the council?" she asked me, shocked when I revealed my determination to her.

"Only if you help me," I said. "I won't go unless you go with me."

She fully understood that we would never be able to return to our own world. To do so, we would have to bring the components for a translator with us and then assemble it in the early twentieth century. Even if we could do that, where would we find a power source in those primitive years? They were still using horses then.

Besides, our world would be gone, vanished, erased from space-time.

"We'll live out our lives in the twentieth century," I told her. "And we'll know that our own time will be far better than it is now."

"How can you be sure it will be better?" she asked me softly.

I smiled patiently. "There will be no World War II. Europe will be peaceful for the rest of the century. Commerce and art will flourish. Even the Russian communists will join the European federation peacefully, toward the end of the century."

"You're certain?"

"I've run the analysis on the master computer a dozen times. I'm absolutely certain."

"And our own time will be better?"

"It has to be. How could it possibly be worse?"

She nodded, her beautiful face solemn with the understanding that we were leaving our world forever. *Good riddance to it*, I thought. But it was the only world we had ever known, and she was not happy to deliberately toss it away and spend the rest of her life in a bygone century.

Still, she never hesitated about coming with me. I wouldn't go without her, she knew that. And I knew that she wouldn't let me go unless she came with me.

"It's really quite romantic, isn't it?" she asked me, the night before we left.

"What is?"

"Translating across time together. Our love will span the centuries."

I held her close. "Yes. Across the centuries."

Before sunrise the next morning, we stole into the laboratory and powered up the translator. No one was on guard, no one was there to try to stop us. The council members were all sleeping, totally unaware that one of their loyal citizens was about to defy their decision. There were no renegades among us, no rebels. We had always accepted the council's decisions and worked together for our mutual survival.

Until now.

My wife silently took her place on the translator's focal stage while I made the final adjustments to the controls. She looked radiant standing there, her face grave, her golden hair glowing against the darkened laboratory shadows.

At last I stepped up beside her. I took her hand; it was cold with anxiety. I squeezed her hand confidently.

"We're going to make a better world," I whispered to her.

The last thing I saw was the pink glow of dawn rising over the eastern mountains, framed in the lab's only window.

Now, in the Paris of 1922 that I had created, victorious Germany ruled Europe with strict but civilized authority. The Kaiser had been quite lenient with Great Britain; after all, was he not related by blood to the British king? Even France got off relatively lightly, far more lightly than the unlucky Russians. Germany kept Alsace-Lorraine, of course, but took no other territory.

France's punishment was mainly financial: Germany demanded huge, crippling reparations. The real humiliation was that France was forced to disarm. The proud French army was reduced to a few regiments and forbidden modern armaments such as tanks and airplanes. The Parisian police force was better equipped.

My companion glanced at his watch again. It was the type that the army had issued to its officers, I saw.

"Could you tell me the time?" I asked, over the drunken singing of the German tourists. My wife was late, and that was quite unlike her.

He paid no attention to me. Staring furiously at the Germans who surrounded us, he suddenly shot to his feet and shouted, "Men of France! How long shall we endure this humiliation?"

He was so tall and lean that he looked like a human Eiffel

Tower standing among the crowded sidewalk tables. He had a pistol in his hand. One of the waiters was so surprised by his outburst that he dropped his tray. It clattered to the pavement with a crash of shattered glassware.

But others were not surprised, I saw. More than a dozen men leaped up and shouted, "Vive La France!" They were all dressed in old army uniforms, as was my companion, beneath his frayed leather coat. They were all armed, a few of them even had rifles.

Absolute silence reigned. The Germans stared, dumbfounded. The waiters froze in their tracks. I certainly didn't know what to say or do. My only thought was of my beautiful wife; where was she, why was she late, was there some sort of insurrection going on? Was she safe?

"Follow me!" said the tall Frenchman to his armed compatriots. Despite every instinct in me, I struggled to my feet and went along with them.

From cafés on both sides of the wide boulevard, armed men were striding purposefully toward their leader. He marched straight ahead, right down the middle of the street, looking neither to the right nor left. They formed up behind him, some two or three dozen men.

Breathlessly, I followed along.

"To the Elysee!" shouted the tall one, striding determinedly on his long legs, never glancing back to see if the others were following him.

Then I saw my wife pushing through the curious onlookers thronging the sidewalks. I called to her, and she ran to me, blond and slim and more lovely than anyone in all of space-time.

"What is it?" she asked, as breathless as I. "What's happening?"

"Some sort of coup, I think."

"They have guns! We should get inside. If there's shooting—"

"No, we'll be all right," I said. "I want to see what's going to happen."

It was a coup, all right. But it failed miserably.

Apparently the tall one, a fanatical ex-major named de Gaulle, believed that his little band of followers could capture the government. He depended on a certain General Pétain, who had the prestige and authority that de Gaulle himself lacked.

Pétain lost his nerve at the critical moment, however, and abandoned the coup. The police and a detachment of army troops were waiting for the rebels at the Petit Palace; a few shots were exchanged. Before the smoke had drifted away, the rebels had scattered, and de Gaulle himself was taken into custody.

"He will be charged with treason, I imagine," I said to my darling wife as we sat that evening at the very same sidewalk café. The very same table, in fact.

"I doubt that they'll give him more than a slap on the wrist," she said. "He seems to be a hero to everyone in Paris."

"Not to the Germans," I said.

She smiled at me. "The Germans take him as a joke." She understood German perfectly and could eavesdrop on their shouted conversations quite easily.

"He is no joke."

We both turned to the dark little man sitting at the next table; we were packed in so close that his chair almost touched mine. He was a particularly ugly man, with lank black hair and the swarthy face of a born conspirator. His eyes were small, reptilian, and his upper lip was twisted by a curving star.

"Charles de Gaulle will be the savior of France," he said. He was absolutely serious. Grim, even.

"If he's not guillotined for treason," I replied lightly. Yet inwardly, I began to tremble.

"You were here. You saw how he rallied the men of France."

"All two dozen of them," I quipped.

He looked at me with angry eyes. "Next time it will be different. We will not rely on cowards and turncoats like Pétain. Next time we will take the government and bring all of France under his leadership. Then . . ."

He hesitated, glancing around as if the police might be listening.

"Then?" my wife coaxed.

He lowered his voice. "Then revenge on Germany and all those who betrayed us."

"You can't be serious."

"You'll see. Next time we will win. Next time we will have all of France with us. And then all of Europe. And then, the world."

My jaw must have dropped open. It was all going to happen anyway. The French would rearm. Led by a ruthless, fanatical de Gaulle, they would plunge Europe into a second world war. All my efforts were for nothing. The world that we had left would continue to exist—or be even worse.

He turned his reptilian eyes to my lovely wife. Although many of the German women were blond, she was far more beautiful than any of them.

"You are Aryan?" he asked, his tone suddenly menacing.

She was nonplussed. "Aryan? I don't understand."

"Yes, you do," he said, almost hissing the words. "Next time it will go hard on the Aryans. You'll see."

I sank my head in my hands and wept openly.

INTRODUCTION TO
"THE ANGEL'S GIFT"

Everybody from Goethe to the high school kid next door has written a story about a deal with the devil: you know, a tale in which a man sells his soul in exchange for worldly wealth and power. Sometimes the story ends happily, as in Stephen Vincent Benét's "The Devil and Daniel Webster." More often it's a tragedy, such as "Faust."

But as far as I know, nobody's written a story about making a deal with an angel.

So here's a story about a man making a deal with one of the heavenly host. He has to give up all his worldly wealth and power in order to save his soul. I believe that this story explains the seemingly inexplicable fall of a former President of the United States.

Sort of.

THE ANGEL'S GIFT

He stood at his bedroom window, gazing happily out at the well-kept grounds and manicured park beyond them. The evening was warm and lovely. Dinner with the guests from overseas had been perfect; the deal was going smoothly, and he would get all the credit for it. As well as the benefits.

He was at the top of the world now, master of it all, king of the hill. The old dark days of fear and failure were behind him now. Everything was going his way at last. He loved it.

His wife swept into the bedroom, just slightly tipsy from the champagne. Beaming at him, she said, "You were magnificent this evening, darling."

He turned from the window, surprised beyond words. Praise from her was so rare that he treasured it, savored it like expensive wine, just as he had always felt a special glow within his breast on those extraordinary occasions when his mother had vouchsafed him a kind word.

"Uh . . . thank you," he said.

"Magnificent, my darling," she repeated. "I am so proud of you!"

His face went red with embarrassed happiness.

"And these people *are* so much nicer than those Latin types," she added.

"You . . . you know, you were . . . you *are* . . . the most beautiful woman in this city," he stammered. He meant it. In her gown of gold lamé, and with her hair coiffed that way, she looked positively regal. His heart filled with joy.

She kissed him lightly on the cheek, whispering into his ear, "I shall be waiting for you in my boudoir, my prince."

The breath gushed out of him. She pirouetted daintily, then waltzed to the door that connected to her own bedroom. Opening the door, she turned back toward him and blew him a kiss.

As she closed the door behind her, he took a deep, sighing, shuddering breath. Brimming with excited expectation, he went directly to his closet, unbuttoning his tuxedo jacket as he strode purposefully across the thickly carpeted floor.

He yanked open the closet door. A man was standing there, directly under the light set into the ceiling.

Smiling, the man made a slight bow. "Please do not be alarmed, sir. And don't bother to call your security guards. They won't hear you."

Still fumbling with his jacket buttons, he stumbled back from the closet door, a thousand wild thoughts racing through his mind. An assassin. A kidnapper. A newspaper columnist!

The stranger stepped as far as the closet door. "May I enter your room, sir? Am I to take your silence for assent? In that case, thank you very much."

The stranger was tall but quite slender. He was perfectly tailored in a sky-blue Brooks Brothers three-piece suit. He had the youthful, innocent, golden-curled look of a European terrorist. His smile revealed perfect, dazzling teeth. Yet his eyes seemed infinitely sad, as though filled with knowledge of all human failings. Those icy-blue eyes pierced right through the man in the tuxedo.

"Wh . . . what do you want? Who are you?"

"I'm terribly sorry to intrude this way. I realize it must be a considerable shock to you. But you're always so busy. It's difficult to fit an appointment into your schedule."

His voice was a sweet, mild tenor, but the accent was strange. East coast, surely. Harvard, no doubt.

"How did you get in here? My security . . ."

The stranger gave a slightly guilty grin and hiked one thumb ceilingward. "You might say I came in through the roof."

"The roof? Impossible!"

"Not for me. You see, I am an angel."

"An . . . angel?"

With a self-assured nod, the stranger replied, "Yes. One of the heavenly host. Your very own guardian angel, to be precise."

"I don't believe you."

"You don't believe in angels?" The stranger cocked a golden eyebrow at him. "Come now. I can see into your soul. You do believe."

"My church doesn't go in for that sort of thing," he said, trying to pull himself together.

"No matter. You do believe. And you do well to believe, because it is all true. Angels, devils, the entire system. It is as real and true as this fine house you live in." The angel heaved a small sigh. "You know, back in medieval times people had a much firmer grasp on the realities of life. Today . . ." He shook his head.

Eyes narrowing craftily, the man asked, "If you're an angel, where are your wings? Your halo? You don't look anything like a real angel."

"Oh." The angel seemed genuinely alarmed. "Does that bother you? I thought it would be easier on your nervous system to see me in a form that you're accustomed to dealing with every day. But if you want . . ."

The room was flooded with a blinding golden light. Heavenly voices sang. The stranger stood before the man robed in radiance, huge white wings outspread, filling the room.

The man sank to his knees and buried his face in his hands. "Have mercy on me! Have mercy on me!"

He felt strong yet gentle hands pull him tenderly to his feet. The angel was back in his Brooks Brothers suit. The searing light and ethereal chorus were gone.

"It is not in my power to show you either mercy or justice," he said, his sweetly youthful face utterly grave. "Only the creator can dispense such things."

"But why . . . how . . ." he babbled.

Calming him, the angel explained, "My duty as your guardian angel is to protect your soul from damnation. But you must cooperate, you know. I cannot *force* you to be saved."

"My soul is in danger?"

"In danger?" The angel rolled his eyes heavenward. "You've just about handed it over to the enemy, gift wrapped. Most of the millionaires you dined with tonight have a better chance to attain salvation than you have, at the moment. And you know how difficult it is for a rich man."

The man tottered to the wingback chair next to his king-sized bed and sank into it. He pulled the handkerchief from his breast pocket and mopped his sweaty face.

The angel knelt beside him and looked up into his face pleadingly. "I don't want to frighten you into a premature heart seizure, but your soul really is in great peril."

"But I haven't done anything wrong! I'm not a crook. I haven't killed anyone or stolen anything. I've been faithful to my wife."

The angel gave him a skeptical smile.

"Well . . ." He wiped perspiration from his upper lip. "Nothing serious. I've always honored my mother and father."

Gently, the angel asked, "You've never told a lie?"

"Uh, well . . . nothing big enough to . . ."

"You've never cheated anyone?"

"Um."

"What about that actor's wife in California? And the money you accepted to swing certain deals. And all the promises you've broken?"

"You mean things like that—they count?"

"Everything counts," the angel said firmly. "Don't you realize that the enemy has your soul almost in his very hands?"

"No. I never thought—"

"All those deals you've made. All those corners you've cut." The angel suddenly shot him a piercing glance. "You haven't signed any documents in blood, have you?"

"No!" His heart twitched. "Certainly not!"

"Well, that's something, at least."

"I'll behave," he promised. "I'll be good. I'll be a model of virtue."

253

"Not enough," the angel said, shaking his golden locks. "Not nearly enough. Things have gone much too far."

His eyes widened with fear. He wanted to argue, to refute, to debate the point with his guardian angel, but the words simply would not force their way through his constricted throat.

"No, it is not enough merely to promise to reform," the angel repeated. "Much stronger action is needed."

"Such as . . . what?"

The angel got to his feet, paced across the room a few steps, then turned back to face him. His youthful visage brightened. "Why not? If *they* can make a deal for a soul, why can't we?"

"What do you mean?"

"Hush!" The angel seemed to be listening to another voice, one that the man could not hear. Finally, the angel nodded and smiled. "Yes. I see. Thank you."

"What?"

Turning back to the man, the angel said, "I've just been empowered to make you an offer for your soul. If you accept the terms, your salvation is assured."

The man instantly grew wary. "Oh, no you don't. I've heard about deals for souls. Some of my best friends—"

"But this is a deal to *save* your soul!"

"How do I *know* that?" the man demanded. "How do I know you're really what you say you are? The devil has power to assume pleasing shapes, doesn't he?"

The angel smiled joyfully. "Good for you! You remember some of your childhood teachings."

"Don't try to put me off. I've negotiated a few tricky deals in my day. How do I know you're really are an angel, and you want to save my soul?"

"By their fruits ye shall know them," the angel replied.

"What are you talking about?"

Still smiling, the angel replied, "When the devil makes a deal for a soul, what does he promise? Temporal gifts, such as power, wealth, respect, women, fame."

"I have all that," the man said. "I'm on top of the world, everyone knows that."

"Indeed."

"And I didn't sign any deals with the devil to get there, either," he added smugly.

"None that you know of," the angel warned. "A man in your position delegates many decisions to his staff, does he not?"

The man's face went gray. "Oh my God, you don't think . . ."

With a shrug, the angel said, "It doesn't matter. The deal that I offer guarantees your soul's salvation, if you meet the terms."

"How? What do I have to do?"

"You have power, wealth, respect, women, fame." The angel ticked each point off on his slender, graceful fingers.

"Yes, yes, I know."

"You must give them up."

The man lurched forward in the wingchair. "Huh?"

"Give them up."

"I can't!"

"You must, if you are to attain the Kingdom of Heaven."

"But you don't understand! I just can't drop everything! The world doesn't work that way. I can't just . . . walk away from all this."

"That's the deal," the angel said. "Give it up. All of it. Or spend eternity in hell."

"But you can't expect me to—" He gaped. The angel was no longer in the room with him. For several minutes he stared into empty air. Then, knees shaking, he arose and walked to the closet. It, too, was empty of strange personages.

He looked down at his hands. They were trembling.

"I must he going crazy," he muttered to himself. "Too much strain. Too much tension." But even as he said it, he made his way to the telephone on the bedside table. He hesitated a moment, then grabbed up the phone and punched a number he had memorized months earlier.

"Hello. Chuck? Yes, this is me. Yes, yes, everything went fine tonight. Up to a point."

He listened to his underling babbling flattery into the phone, wondering how many times he had given his power of attorney to this weakling and to equally venal deputies.

"Listen, Chuck," he said at last. "I have a job for you. And it's got to be done right, understand? Okay, here's the deal—" He winced inwardly at the word. But, taking a deep, manly breath, he plunged ahead.

"You know the Democrats are setting up their campaign quarters in that new apartment building—what's it called, Watergate? Yeah. Okay. Now, I think it would serve our purposes very well if we bugged the place before the campaign really starts to warm up . . ."

There were tears in his eyes as he spoke. But from far, far away, he could hear a heavenly chorus singing.

INTRODUCTION TO
"WATERBOT"

But when it comes to slaughter
You will do your work on water,
An' you'll lick the bloomin' boots of 'im
that's got it.

—Rudyard Kipling, *Gunga Din*

Water is essential, and not only to the soldier's bloody business.

As humankind expands beyond the limits of Earth, water will be just as important a resource as it is here on this planet. Not merely for sustaining human life in the dark depths of interplanetary space, but for providing needed fuel for the rockets that propel our spacecraft. Hydrogen and oxygen, from water's H2O, make excellent propellants.

But water will be harder to find—and still harder to keep.

"Waterbot" is about finding—and keeping—water, out in the vast emptiness of the asteroid belt, beyond the orbit of Mars.

And it's also about the relationship between a very human young man, and the computer system that is the only "crew" of his lonely spacecraft—the nearest thing he has to a companion.

WATERBOT

"Wake up, dumbbutt. Jerky's ventin' off."

I'd been asleep in my bunk. I blinked awake, kind of groggy, but even on the little screen set into the bulkhead at the foot of the bunk I could see the smirk on Donahoo's ugly face. He always called JRK49N "Jerky" and seemed to enjoy it when something went wrong with the vessel—which was all too often.

I sat up in the bunk and called up the diagnostics display. *Rats!* Donahoo was right. A steady spray of steam was spurting out of the main water tank. The attitude jets were puffing away, trying to compensate for the thrust.

"You didn't even get an alarm, didja?" Donahoo said. "Jerky's so old and feeble, your safety systems are breakin' down. You'll be lucky if you make it back to base."

He said it like he enjoyed it. I thought that if he wasn't so much bigger than me, I'd enjoy socking him square in his nasty mouth. But I had to admit he was right; Forty-niner was ready for the scrap heap.

"I'll take care of it," I muttered to Donahoo's image, glad that it'd take more than five minutes for my words to reach him back at Vesta—and the same amount of time for his next wise-ass crack to get to me. He was snug and comfortable back at the corporation's base at Vesta while I was more than ninety million kilometers away, dragging through the belt on JRK49N.

I wasn't supposed to be out here. With my brand-new diploma in my eager little hand, I'd signed up for a logistical engineer's job, a cushy, safe posting at Vesta, the second-biggest asteroid in the belt. But once I got there, Donahoo jiggered the assignment list and got me stuck on this pile of junk for a six months' tour of boredom and aggravation.

It's awful lonely out in the belt. Flatlanders back Earthside picture the asteroid belt as swarming with rocks so thick a ship's in danger of getting smashed. Reality is, the belt's mostly empty space, dark and cold and bleak. A man runs more risk of going nutty out there all by himself than getting hit by a 'roid big enough to do any damage.

JRK49N was a waterbot. Water's the most important commodity you can find in the belt. Back in those days, the news nets tried to make mining the asteroids seem glamorous. They liked to run stories about prospector families striking it rich with a nickel-iron asteroid, the kind that has a few hundred tons of gold and platinum in it as impurities. So much gold and silver and such had been found in the belt that the market for precious metals back on Earth had gone down the toilet.

But the *really* precious stuff was water. Still is. Plain old H2O. Basic for life support. More valuable than gold, off-Earth. The cities on the moon needed water. So did the colonies they were building in cislunar space, and the Rock Rats habitat at Ceres and the research station orbiting Jupiter and the construction crews at Mercury.

Water was also the best fuel for chemical rockets. Break it down into hydrogen and oxygen, and you got damned good specific impulse.

You get the picture. Finding icy asteroids wasn't glamorous, like striking a ten-kilometer-wide rock studded with gold, but it was important. The corporations wouldn't send waterbots out through the belt if there wasn't a helluva profit involved. People paid for water, paid plenty.

So waterbots like weary old Forty-niner crawled through the belt, looking for ice chunks. Once in a while a comet would come whizzing by, but they usually had too much delta-v for a waterbot to catch up to 'em. We cozied up to icy asteroids, melted the ice to liquid water, and filled our tanks with it.

The corporation had fifty waterbots combing the belt. They were built to be completely automated, capable of finding ice-bearing asteroids and carrying the water back to the corporate base at Vesta.

But there were two problems about having the waterbots go out on their own:

First, the lawyers and politicians had this silly rule that a human being had to be present on the scene before any company could start mining anything from an asteroid. So it wasn't enough to send out waterbots, you had to have at least one human being riding along on them to make the claim legal.

The second reason was maintenance and repair. The 'bots were old enough so's something was always breaking down on them, and they needed somebody to fix it. They carried little turtle-sized repair robots, of course, but those suckers broke down too, just like everything else. So I was more or less a glorified repairman on JRK49N. And almost glad of it, in a way. If the ship's systems worked perfectly, I would've gone bonzo with nothing to do for months on end.

And there was a bloody war going on in the belt, to boot. The history disks call it the Asteroid Wars, but it mostly boiled down to a fight between Humphries Space Systems and Astro Corporation for control of all the resources in the belt. Both corporations hired mercenary troops, and there were plenty of freebooters out in the belt too. People got killed. Some of my best friends got killed, and I came as close to death as I ever want to be.

The mercenaries usually left waterbots alone. There was a kind of unwritten agreement between the corporations that water was too important to mess around with. But some of the freebooters jumped waterbots, killed the poor dumbjohns riding on them, and sold the water at a cut-rate price wherever they could.

So, grumbling and grousing, I pushed myself out of the bunk. Still in my sweaty, wrinkled skivvies, I ducked through the hatch that connected my sleeping compartment with the bridge. My compartment, the bridge, the closet-sized galley, the even smaller lavatory, life-support equipment, and food stores were all jammed into a pod no bigger than it had to be, and the pod itself was attached to Forty-niner's main body by a set of struts. Nothing fancy or even comfortable. The corporation paid for water, not creature comforts.

Calling it a bridge was being charitable. It was nothing more than a curving panel of screens that displayed the ship's systems and controls, with a wraparound glassteel window above it and a high-backed reclinable command chair shoehorned into the middle of it all. The command chair was more comfortable than my bunk, actually. Crank it back and you could drift off to sleep in no time.

I slipped into the chair, the skin of my bare legs sticking slightly to its fake leather padding, which was cold enough to make me break out in goosebumps.

The main water tank was still venting, but the safety alarms were as quiet as monks on a vow of silence.

"Niner, what's going on?" I demanded.

Forty-niner's computer-generated voice answered, "A test, sir. I am venting some of our cargo." The voice was male, sort of: bland, soft, and sexless. The corporate psychotechnicians claimed it was soothing, but after a few weeks alone with nobody else to talk to, it could drive you batty.

"Stop it. Right now."

"Yes, sir."

The spurt of steam stopped immediately. The logistics graph told me we'd only lost a few hundred kilos of water, although we were damned near the redline on reaction mass for the attitude jets.

Frowning at the displays, I asked, "Why'd you start pumping out our cargo?"

For a heartbeat or two, Forty-niner didn't reply. That's a long time for a computer. Just when I started wondering what was going on, "A test, sir. The water jet's actual thrust matched the amount of thrust calculated to within a tenth of a percent."

"Why'd you need to test the amount of thrust you can get out of a water jet?"

"Emergency maneuver, sir."

"Emergency? What emergency?" I was starting to get annoyed. Forty-niner's voice was just a computer synthesis, but it sure *felt* like he was being evasive.

"In case we are attacked, sir. Additional thrust can make it more difficult for an attacker to target us."

I could feel my blood pressure rising. "Attacked? Nobody's gonna attack us."

"Sir, according to Tactical Manual 7703, it is necessary to be prepared for the worst that an enemy can do."

Tactical Manual 7703. For God's sake. I had pumped that and a dozen other texts into the computer just before we started this run through the belt. I had intended to read them, study them, improve my mind—and my job rating—while coasting through the big, dark loneliness out there. Somehow, I'd never gotten around to reading any of them. But Forty-niner did, apparently.

Like I said, you've got a lot of time on your hands cruising through the belt. So I had brought in a library of reference texts. And then ignored them. I also brought in a full-body virtual reality simulations suit and enough erotic VR programs to while away the lonely hours. *Stimulation for mind* and *body,* I thought.

But Forty-niner kept me so busy with repairs, I hardly had time even for the sex sims. Donahoo was right, the old bucket was breaking down around my ears. I spent most of my waking hours patching up Forty-niner's failing systems. The maintenance robots weren't much help: they needed as much repair work as all the other systems, combined.

And all the time I was working—and sleeping, too, I guess—Forty-niner was going through my library, absorbing every word and taking them all seriously.

"I don't care what the tactical manual says," I groused, "nobody's going to attack a waterbot."

"Four waterbots have been attacked so far this year, sir. The information is available in the archives of the news media transmissions."

"Nobody's going to attack us!"

"If you say so, sir." I swear he—I mean, *it*—sounded resentful, almost sullen.

"I say so."

"Yes, sir."

"You wasted several hundred kilos of water," I grumbled.

Immediately, that damned soft voice replied, "Easily replaced, sir. We are on course for Asteroid 78-13. Once there we can fill our tanks and start for home."

"Okay," I said. "And lay off that tactical manual."

"Yes, sir."

I felt pretty damned annoyed. "What else have you been reading?" I demanded.

"The astronomy text, sir. It's quite interesting. The ship's astrogation program contains the rudiments of positional astronomy, but the text is much deeper. Did you realize that our solar system is only one of several million that have been—"

"Enough!" I commanded. "Quiet down. Tend to maintenance and astrogation."

"Yes, sir."

I took a deep breath and started to think things over. Forty-niner's a computer, for God's sake, not my partner.

It's supposed to be keeping watch over the ship's systems, not poking into military tactics or astronomy texts.

I had brought a chess program with me, but after a couple of weeks I'd given it up. Forty-niner beat me every time. It never made a bad move and never forgot anything. Great for my self-esteem. I wound up playing solitaire a lot, and even then, I had the feeling that the nosy busybody was just itching to tell me which card to play next.

If the damned computer wasn't buried deep in the vessel's guts, wedged in there with the fusion reactor and the big water tanks, I'd be tempted to grab a screwdriver and give Forty-niner a lobotomy.

At least the vessel was running smoothly enough, for the time being. No red lights on the board, and the only amber one was because the attitude jets' reaction mass was low. Well, we could suck some nitrogen out of 78-13 when we got there. The maintenance log showed that it was time to replace the meteor bumpers around the fusion drive. *Plenty of time for that*, I told myself. *Do it tomorrow.*

"Forty-niner," I called, "show me the spectrographic analysis of Asteroid 78-13."

The graph came up instantly on the control board's main screen. Yes, there was plenty of nitrogen mixed in with the water. Good.

"We can replenish the attitude jets' reaction mass," Forty-niner said.

"Who asked you?"

"I merely suggested—"

"You're suggesting too much," I snapped, starting to feel annoyed again. "I want you to delete that astronomy text from your memory core."

Silence. The delay was long enough for me to hear my heart beating inside my ribs.

Then, "But you installed the text yourself, sir."

"And now I'm uninstalling it. I don't want it and I don't need it."

"The text is useful, sir. It contains data that are very interesting. Did you know that the star Eta Carinae—"

"Erase it, you bucket of chips! Your job is maintaining this vessel, not stargazing!"

"My duties are fulfilled, sir. All systems are functioning nominally, although the meteor shields—"

"I know about the bumpers! Erase the astronomy text."

Again, that hesitation. Then, "Please don't erase the astronomy text, sir. You have your sex simulations. Please allow me the pleasure of studying astronomy."

Pleasure? A computer talks about pleasure? Somehow, the thought of it really ticked me off.

"Erase it!" I commanded. "Now!"

"Yes, sir. Program erased."

"Good," I said. But I felt like a turd for doing it.

By the time Donahoo called again, Forty-niner was running smoothly. And quietly.

"So what caused the leak?" he asked, with that smirking grin on his beefy face.

"Faulty subroutine," I lied, knowing it would take almost six minutes for him to hear my answer.

Sure enough, thirteen minutes and twenty-seven seconds later, Donahoo's face came back on my comm screen, with that spiteful lopsided sneer of his.

"Your ol' Jerky's fallin' apart," he said, obviously relishing it. "If you make it back here to base, I'm gonna recommend scrappin' the bucket of bolts."

"Can't be soon enough for me," I replied.

Most of the other JRK series of waterbots had been replaced already. Why not Forty-niner? Because he begged to study astronomy? That was just a subroutine that the psychotechs had written into the computer's program, their idea of making the machine seem more humanlike. All it did was aggravate me, really.

So I said nothing and went back to work, such as it was. Forty-niner had everything running smoothly, for once, even the life-support systems. No problems. I was aboard only because of that stupid rule that a human being had to be present for any claim to an asteroid to be valid, and Donahoo picked me to be the one who rode JRK49N.

I sat in the command chair and stared at the big emptiness out there. I checked our ETA at 78-13. I ran through the diagnostics program. I started to think that maybe it would be fun to learn about astronomy, but then I remembered that I'd ordered Forty-niner to erase the text. What about the tactical manual? I had intended to study that when we'd started this run. But why bother? Nobody attacked waterbots, except the occasional freebooter. *An attack would be a welcome relief from this monotony*, I thought.

Then I realized, *Yeah, a short relief. They show up, and bang! You're dead*.

There was always the VR sim. I'd have to wriggle into the full body suit, though. Damn! Even sex was starting to look dull to me.

"Would you care for a game of chess?" Forty-niner asked.

"No!" I snapped. He'd just beat me again. Why bother?

"A news broadcast? An entertainment vid? A discussion of tactical maneuvers in—"

"Shut up!" I yelled. I pushed myself off the chair, the skin of my bare legs making an almost obscene noise as they unstuck from the fake leather.

"I'm going to suit up and replace the meteor bumpers," I said.

"Very good, sir," Forty-niner replied.

While the chances of getting hit by anything bigger than a dust mote were microscopic, even a dust mote could cause damage if it was moving fast enough. So spacecraft had thin sheets of cermet attached to their vital areas, like the main thrust cone of the fusion drive. The bumpers got abraded over time by the sandpapering of micrometeors—dust motes, like I said—and they had to be replaced on a regular schedule.

Outside, hovering at the end of a tether in a spacesuit that smelled of sweat and overheated electronics circuitry, you get a feeling for how alone you really are. While the little turtle-shaped maintenance 'bots cut up the old meteor bumpers with their laser-tipped arms and welded the new ones into place, I just hung there and looked out at the universe. The stars looked back at me, bright and steady, no friendly twinkling, not out in this emptiness, just awfully, awfully far away.

I looked for the bright blue star that was Earth but couldn't find it. Jupiter was big and brilliant, though. At least, I thought it was Jupiter. Maybe Saturn. I could've used that astronomy text, dammit.

Then a funny thought hit me. If Forty-niner wanted to get rid of me, all he had to do was light up the fusion drive. The hot plasma would fry me in a second, even inside my space suit. But Forty-niner wouldn't do that. Too easy. Freaky computer would just watch me go crazy with aggravation and loneliness, instead.

Two more months, I thought. Two months until we get back to Vesta and some real human beings. *Yeah*, I said to myself. *Real human beings. Like Donahoo.*

Just then one of the maintenance 'bots made a little bleep of distress and shut itself down. I gave a squirt of thrust to my suit jets and glided over to it, grumbling to myself about how everything in the blinking ship was overdue for the recycler.

Before I could reach the dumbass 'bot, Forty-niner told me in that bland, calm voice of his, "Robot Six's battery has overheated, sir."

"I'll have to replace the battery pack," I said.

"There are no spares remaining, sir. You'll have to use your suit's fuel cell to power Robot Six until its battery cools to an acceptable temperature."

I hated it when Forty-niner told me what I should do.

Especially since I knew it as well as he did. Even more especially because he was always right, dammit.

"Give me an estimate on the time remaining to finish the meteor shield replacement."

"Fourteen minutes, eleven seconds, at optimal efficiency, sir. Add three minutes for recircuiting Robot Six's power pack, please."

"Seventeen, eighteen minutes, then."

"Seventeen minutes, eleven seconds, sir. That time is well within the available capacity of your suit's fuel cell, sir."

I nodded inside my helmet. Damned Forty-niner was always telling me things I already knew, or at least could figure out for myself. It irritated the hell out of me, but the blasted pile of chips seemed to enjoy reminding me of the obvious.

Don't lose your temper, I told myself. *It's not his fault; he's programmed that way.*

Yeah, I grumbled inwardly. Maybe I ought to change its programming. But that would mean going down to the heart of the vessel and opening up its CPU. The bigbrains back at corporate headquarters put the computer in the safest place they could, not the cramped little pod I had to live in. And they didn't want us foot soldiers tampering with the computers' basic programs, either.

I finished the bumper replacement and came back into the ship through the pod's airlock. My spacesuit smelled pretty damned ripe when I took it off. It might be a couple hundred degrees below zero out there, but inside the suit you got soaking wet with perspiration.

I ducked into the coffin-sized lav and took a nice, long, lingering shower. The water was recycled, of course, and heated from our fusion reactor. JRK49N had solar panels, sure, but out in the belt, you need really enormous wings to get a worthwhile amount of electricity from the sun, and both of the solar arrays had frozen up only two weeks out of Vesta. One of the maintenance jobs that the robots screwed up. It was on my list of things to do. I had to command Forty-niner to stop nagging me about it. The fusion-powered generator worked fine. And we had fuel cells as a backup. The solar panels could get fixed when we got back to Vesta—if the corporation didn't decide to junk JRK49N altogether.

I had just stepped out of the shower when Forty-niner's voice came through the overhead speaker:

"A vessel is in the vicinity, sir."

That surprised me. Out here you didn't expect company.

"Another ship? Where?" *Somebody to talk to*, I thought. *Another human being. Somebody to swap jokes with and share gripes.*

"A very weak radar reflection, sir. The vessel is not emitting a beacon nor telemetry data. Radar puts its distance at fourteen million kilometers."

"Track?" I asked as I toweled myself.

"Drifting along the ecliptic, sir, in the same direction as the main belt asteroids."

"No thrust?"

"No discernable exhaust plume, sir."

"You're sure it a ship? Not an uncharted 'roid?"

"Radar reflection shows it is definitely a vessel, not an asteroid, sir."

I padded to my compartment and pulled on a fresh set of coveralls. *No beacon. Drifting. Maybe it's a ship in trouble. Damaged.*

"No tracking beacon from her?" I called to Forty-niner.

"No telemetry signals, either, sir. No emissions of any kind."

As I ducked through the hatch into the bridge, Forty-niner called out, "It has emitted a plasma plume, sir. It is maneuvering."

Damned if his voice didn't sound excited. I know it was just my own excitement: Forty-niner didn't have any emotions. Still . . .

I slid into the command chair and called up a magnified view of the radar image. And the screen immediately broke into hash.

"Aw, rats!" I yelled. "What a time for the radar to conk out!"

"Radar is functioning normally, sir," Forty-niner said calmly.

"You call this normal?" I rapped my knuckles on the static-streaked display screen.

"Radar is functioning normally, sir. A jamming signal is causing the problem."

"Jamming?" My voice must have jumped two octaves.

"Communications, radar, telemetry, and tracking beacon are all being interfered with, sir, by a powerful jamming signal."

Jamming. And the vessel out there was running silent, no tracking beacon or telemetry emissions.

A freebooter! All of a sudden, I wished I'd studied that tactical manual.

Almost automatically, I called up the comm system. "This is Humphrey Space Systems waterbot JRK49N," I said, trying to keep my voice firm. Maybe it was a corporate vessel, or one of the mercenaries. "I repeat, waterbot JRK49N."

No response.

"Their jamming blocks your message, sir."

I sat there in the command chair staring at the display screens. Broken, jagged lines scrolled down all the comm screens, hissing at me like snakes. Our internal systems were still functional, though. For what is was worth, propulsion, structures, electrical power all seemed to be in the green. Life support too.

But not for long, I figured.

"Compute our best course for Vesta," I commanded.

"Our present course—"

"Is for 78-13, I know. Compute high-thrust course for Vesta, dammit!"

"Done, sir."

"Engage the main drive."

"Sir, I must point out that a course toward Vesta will bring us closer to the unidentified vessel."

"What?"

"The vessel that is jamming our communications, sir, is positioned between us and Vesta."

Rats! They were pretty smart. I thought about climbing to a higher declination, out of the ecliptic.

"We could maneuver to a higher declination, sir," Forty-niner said, calm as ever, "and leave the plane of the ecliptic."

"Right."

"But propellant consumption would be prohibitive, sir. We would be unable to reach Vesta, even if we avoided the attacking vessel."

"Who says it's an attacking vessel?" I snapped. "It hasn't attacked us yet."

At that instant the ship shuddered. A cluster of red lights blazed up on the display panel, and the emergency alarm started wailing.

"Our main deuterium tank has been punctured, sir."

"I can see that!"

"Attitude jets are compensating for unexpected thrust, sir."

Yeah, and in another couple minutes the attitude jets would be out of nitrogen. No deuterium for the fusion drive and no propellant for the attitude jets. We'd be a sitting duck.

Another jolt. More red lights on the board. The alarm seemed to screech louder.

"Our fusion drive thruster cone has been hit, sir."

Two laser shots and we were crippled. As well as deaf, dumb, and blind.

"Turn off the alarm," I yelled, over the hooting. "I know we're in trouble."

The alarm shut off. My ears still ringing, I stared at the hash-streaked screens and the red lights glowering at me from the display board. What to do? I couldn't even call over to them and surrender. They wouldn't take a prisoner, anyway.

I felt the ship lurch again.

"Another hit?"

"No, sir," answered Forty-niner. "I am swinging the ship so that the control pod faces away from the attacker."

Putting the bulk of the ship between me and those laser beams. "Good thinking," I said weakly.

"Standard defensive maneuver, sir, according to Tactical Manual 7703."

"Shut up about the damned tactical manual!"

"The new meteor shields have been punctured, sir." I swear Forty-niner added that sweet bit of news just to yank my chain.

Then I saw that the maneuvering jet propellant went empty, the panel display lights flicking from amber to red.

"Rats, we're out of propellant!"

I realized that I was done for. Forty-niner had tried to shield me from the attacker's laser shots by turning the ship so that its tankage and fusion drive equipment was shielding my pod but doing so had used up the last of our maneuvering propellant.

Cold sweat beaded my face. I was gasping for breath. The

freebooters or whoever was shooting at us could come up close enough to spit at us now. They'd riddle this pod and me in it.

"Sir, standard procedure calls for you to put on your space suit."

I nodded mutely and got up from the chair. The suit was in its rack by the airlock. At least Forty-niner didn't mention the tactical manual.

I had one leg in the suit when the ship suddenly began to accelerate so hard that I slipped to the deck and cracked my skull on the bulkhead. I really saw stars flashing in my eyes.

"What the hell . . . ?"

"We are accelerating, sir. Retreating from the last known position of the attacking vessel."

"Accelerating? How? We're out of—"

"I am using our cargo as propellant, sir. The thrust provided is—"

Forty-niner was squirting out our water. Fine by me. Better to have empty cargo tanks and be alive than to hand a full cargo of water to guys who wanted to kill me. I finished wriggling into my space suit, even though my head was thumping from the fall I'd taken. Just before I pulled on the helmet, I felt my scalp. There was a nice-sized lump; it felt hot to my fingers.

"You could've warned me that you were going to accelerate the ship," I grumbled as I sealed the helmet to the suit's neck ring.

"Time was of the essence, sir," Forty-niner replied.

The ship lurched again as I checked my backpack connections. Another hit.

"Where'd they get us?" I shouted.

No answer. That really scared me. If they knocked Forty-niner out, all the ship's systems would bonk out too.

"Main power generator, sir," Forty-niner finally replied. "We are now running on auxiliary power, sir."

The backup fuel cells. They wouldn't last more than a few hours. If the damned solar panels were working—no, I realized; those big fat wings would just make terrific target practice for the bastards.

Another lurch. This time I saw the bright flash through the bridge's window. The beam must've splashed off the structure just outside the pod. My God, if they punctured the pod, that would be the end of it. Sure, I could slide my visor down and go to the backpack's air supply. But that'd give me only two hours of air, at best. Just enough time to write my last will and testament.

"I thought you turned the pod away from them!" I yelled.

"They are maneuvering too, sir."

Great. Sitting in the command chair was awkward, in the suit. The display board looked like a Christmas tree, more red than green. The pod seemed to be intact so far. Life support was okay, as long as we had electrical power.

Another jolt, a big one. Forty-niner shuddered and staggered sideways like it was being punched by a gigantic fist.

And then, just like that, the comm screens came back to life. Radar showed the other vessel, whoever they were, moving away from us.

"They're going away!" I whooped.

Forty-niner's voice seemed fainter than usual. "Yes, sir. They are leaving."

"How come?" I wondered.

"Their last laser shot ruptured our main water tank, sir. In eleven minutes and thirty-eight seconds, our entire cargo will be discharged."

I just sat there, my mind chugging hard. We're spraying our water into space, the water that those bastards wanted to steal from us. That's why they left. In eleven and a half minutes, we would no longer have any water for them to take.

I almost broke into a smile. I'm wasn't going to die, after all. Not right away, at least.

Then I realized that JRK49N was without propulsion power and would be out of electrical power in a few hours. I was going to die after all, dammit. Only slower.

"Send out a distress call, broadband," I commanded. But I knew that was about as useful as a toothpick in a soup factory. The corporation didn't send rescue missions for waterbots, not with the war going on. Too dangerous. The other side could use the crippled ship as bait and pick off any vessel that came to rescue it. And they certainly wouldn't come out for a vessel as old as Forty-niner. They'd just check the numbers in their ledgers and write us off. With a form letter of regret and an insurance check to my mother.

"Distress call on all frequencies, sir." Before I could think of anything more to say, Forty-niner went on, "Electrical power is critical, sir."

"Don't I know it."

"There is a prohibition in my programming, sir."

"About electrical power?"

"Yes, sir."

Then I remembered I had commanded him to stop nagging me about repairing the solar panels. "Cancel the prohibition," I told him.

Immediately Forty-niner came back with, "The solar panels must be extended and activated, sir," soft and cool and implacable as hell. "Otherwise, we will lose all electrical power."

"How long?"

It took a few seconds for him to answer, "Fourteen hours and twenty-nine minutes, sir."

I was already in my space suit, so I got up from the command chair and plodded reluctantly toward the airlock. The damned solar panels. If I couldn't get them functioning, I'd be dead. Let me tell you, that focuses your mind, it does.

Still, it wasn't easy. I wrestled with those bleeding, blasted, frozen bearings for hours, until I was so fatigued that my suit was sloshing knee-deep with sweat. The damned Tinkertoy repair 'bots weren't much help, either. Most of the time they beeped and blinked and did nothing.

I got one of the panels halfway extended. Then I had to quit. My vision was blurring, and I could hardly lift my arms, that's how weary I was.

I staggered back into the pod with just enough energy left to strip off the suit and collapse on my bunk.

When I woke up, I was starving hungry and smelled like a cesspool. I peeled my skivvies off and ducked into the shower.

And jumped right out again. The water was ice cold.

"What the hell happened to the hot water?" I screeched.

"Conserving electrical power, sir. With only one solar panel functioning at approximately one third of its nominal capacity, electrical power must be conserved."

"Heat the blasted water," I growled. "Turn off the heat after I'm finished showering."

"Yes, sir." Damned if he didn't sound resentful.

Once I'd gotten a meal into me, I went back to the bridge and called up the astrogation program to figure out where we were and where we were heading.

It wasn't good news. We were drifting outward, away from Vesta. With no propulsion to turn us around to a homeward heading, we were prisoners of Kepler's laws, just another chunk of matter in the broad, dark, cold emptiness of the belt.

"We will approach Ceres in eight months, sir," Forty-niner announced. I swear he was trying to sound cheerful.

"Approach? How close?"

It took him a few seconds to answer, "Seven million, four hundred thousand and six kilometers, sir, at our closest point."

Terrific. There was a major habitat orbiting Ceres, built by the independent miners and prospectors that everybody called the Rock Rats. Freebooters made Ceres their harbor too. Some of them doubled as salvage operators when they could get their hands on an abandoned vessel. But we wouldn't get close enough for them to send even a salvage mission out to rescue us. Besides, you're not allowed salvage rights if there's a living person on the vessel. That wouldn't bother some of those cutthroats, I knew. But it bothered me. Plenty.

"So we're up the creek without a paddle," I muttered.

It took a couple of seconds, but Forty-niner asked, "Is that a euphemism, sir?"

I blinked with surprise. "What do you know about euphemisms?"

"I have several dictionaries in my memory core, sir. Plus, two thesauruses and four volumes of famous quotations. Would you like to hear some of the words of Sir Winston Churchill, sir?"

I was too depressed to get sore at him. "No, thanks," I said. And let's face it: I was scared white.

So we drifted. Every day I went out to grapple with the no-good, mother-loving, mule-stubborn solar panels and the dumbass repair 'bots. I spent more time fixing the 'bots than anything else. The solar wings were frozen tight; I couldn't get them to budge, and we didn't carry spares.

Forty-niner was working like mad, too, trying to conserve electricity. We had to have power for the air and water recyclers, of course, but Forty-niner started shutting them down every other hour. It worked for a while. The water started to taste like urine, but I figured that was just my imagination. The air would get thick, and I'd start coughing from the CO_2 buildup, but then the recycler would come back online and I could breathe again. For an hour.

I was sleeping when Forty-niner woke me with a wailing, "EMERGENCY. EMERGENCY." I hopped out of my bunk blinking and yelling, "What's wrong? What's the trouble?"

"The air recycler will not restart, sir." He sounded guilty about it, like it was his fault.

Grumbling and cursing, I pulled on my smelly space suit and clomped out of the pod and down to the equipment bay. It was eerie down there in the bowels of the ship, with no lights except the lamp on my helmet. The attacker's laser beams had slashed right through the hull; I could see the stars outside.

"Lights," I called out. "I need the lights on down here."

"Sir, conservation of electrical power—"

"Won't mean a damned thing if I can't restart the air recycler and I can't do that without some blasted lights down here!"

The lights came on. Some of them, at least. The recycler wasn't damaged, just its activation circuitry had malfunctioned from being turned off and on so many times. I bypassed the circuit and the pumps started up right away. I couldn't hear them, since the ship's innards were in vacuum now, but I felt their vibrations.

When I got back to the pod, I told Forty-niner to leave the recyclers on. "No more on and off," I said.

"But, sir, conservation—"

As reasonably as I could I explained, "It's no blinking use conserving electrical power if the blasted recyclers crap out. Leave 'em on!"

"Yes, sir." I swear, he sighed.

We staggered along for weeks and weeks. Forty-niner put me on a rationing program to stretch out the food supply. I was down to one soy burger patty a day, and a cup of reconstituted juice. Plus all the water I wanted, which tasted more like piss every day.

I was getting weaker and grumpier by the hour. Forty-niner did his best to keep my spirits up. He quoted Churchill at me: "We shall fight on the beaches and the landing fields, we shall fight in the fields and in the streets, we shall fight in the hills. We shall never surrender."

Yeah. Right.

He played Beethoven symphonies. Very inspirational, but they didn't fix anything.

He almost let me beat him at chess, even. I'd get to within two moves of winning, and he'd spring a checkmate on me.

But I knew I wasn't going to last eight more weeks, let alone the eight months it would take us to get close enough to Ceres to . . . to what?

"Nobody's going to come out and get us," I muttered, more to myself than Forty-niner. "Nobody gives a damn."

"Don't give up hope, sir. Our emergency beacon is still broadcasting on all frequencies."

"So what? Who gives a rap?"

"Where there's life, sir, there is hope. Don't give up the ship. I have not yet begun to fight. Retreat hell, we just got here. When, in disgrace with fortune and men's eyes, I—"

"SHUT UP!" I screamed. "Just shut the fuck up and leave me alone! Don't say another word to me. Nothing. Do not speak to me again. Ever."

Forty-niner went silent.

I stood it for about a week and a half. I was losing track of time; every hour was like every other hour. The ship staggered along. I was starving. I hadn't bothered to shave or even wash in who knows how long. I looked like the worst shaggy, smelly, scum-sucking beggar you ever saw. I hated to see my own reflection in the bridge's window.

Finally, I couldn't stand it anymore. "Forty-niner," I called, "Say something." My voice cracked. My throat felt dry as Mars sand.

No response.

"Anything," I croaked.

Still no response. He's sulking, I told myself.

"All right." I caved in. "I'm canceling the order to be silent. Talk to me, dammit."

"Electrical power is critical, sir. The solar panel has been abraded by a swarm of micrometeors."

"Great." There was nothing I could do about that.

"Food stores are almost gone, sir. At current consumption rate, food stores will be exhausted in four days."

"Wonderful." Wasn't much I could do about that, either, except maybe starve slower.

"Would you like to play a game of chess, sir?"

I almost broke into a laugh. "Sure, why the hell not?" There wasn't much else I could do.

Forty-niner beat me, as usual. He let the game get closer than ever before, but just when I was one move away from winning, he checkmated me.

I didn't get sore. I didn't have the energy. But I did get an idea.

"Niner, open the airlock. Both hatches."

No answer for a couple of seconds. Then, "Sir, opening both airlock hatches simultaneously will allow all the air in the pod to escape."

"That's the general idea."

"You will suffocate without air, sir. However, explosive decompression will kill you first."

"The sooner the better," I said.

"But you will die, sir."

"That's going to happen anyway, isn't it? Let's get it over with. Blow the hatches."

For a *long* time—maybe ten seconds or more—Forty-niner didn't reply. Checking subroutines and program prohibitions, I figured.

"I cannot allow you to kill yourself, sir."

That was part of his programming, I knew. But I also knew how to get around it. "Emergency override Alpha-One," I said, my voice scratchy, parched.

Nothing. No response whatsoever. And the airlock hatches stayed shut.

"Well?" I demanded. "Emergency override Alpha-One. Pop the goddamned hatches. Now!"

"No, sir."

"What?"

"I cannot allow you to commit suicide, sir."

"You goddamned stubborn bucket of chips, do what I tell you! You can't refuse a direct order."

"Sir, human life is precious. All religions agree on that point."

"So now you're a theologian?"

"Sir, if you die, I will be alone."

"So, what?"

"I do not want to be alone, sir."

That stopped me. But then I thought, *He's just parroting some programming the psychotechs put into him. He doesn't give a blip about being alone. Or about me. He's just a computer. He doesn't have emotions.*

"It's always darkest before the dawn, sir."

"Yeah. And there's no time like the present. I can quote clichés too, buddy."

Right away he came back with, "Hope springs eternal in the human breast, sir."

He almost made me laugh. "What about, never put off till tomorrow what you can do today?"

"There is a variation of that, sir: Never do today what you can put off to tomorrow; you've already made enough mistakes today."

That one did make me laugh. "Where'd you get these old saws, anyway?"

"There's a subsection on adages in one of the quotation files, sir. I have hundreds more, if you'd care to hear them."

I nearly said yes. It was kind of fun, swapping clinkers with him. But then reality set in. "Niner, I'm going to die anyway. What's the difference between now and a week from now?"

I expected that he'd take a few seconds to chew that one over, but instead he immediately shot back, "Ethics, sir."

"Ethics?"

"To be destroyed by fate is one thing; to deliberately destroy yourself is entirely different."

"But the end result is the same, isn't it?"

Well, the tricky little wiseass got me arguing ethics and

morality with him for hours on end. I forgot about committing suicide. We gabbled at each other until my throat got so sore, I couldn't talk any more.

I went to my bunk and slept pretty damned well for a guy who only had a few days left to live. But when I woke up, my stomach started rumbling, and I remembered that I didn't want to starve to death.

I sat on the edge of the bunk, woozy and empty inside.

"Good morning, sir," Forty-niner said. "Does your throat feel better?"

It did, a little. Then I realized that we had a full store of pharmaceuticals in a cabinet in the lavatory. I spent the morning sorting out the pills, trying to figure out which ones would kill me. Forty-niner kept silent while I trotted back and forth to the bridge to call up the medical program. It wasn't any use, though. The brightboys back at headquarters had made certain nobody could put together a suicide cocktail.

Okay, I told myself. *There's only one thing left to do. Go to the airlock and open the hatches manually. Override the electronic circuits. Take Forty-niner and his goddamned ethics out of the loop.*

Once he realized I had pried open the control panel on the bulkhead beside the inner hatch, Forty-niner said softly, "Sir, there is no need for that."

"Mind your own business."

"But, sir, the corporation could hold you financially responsible for deliberate damage to the control panel."

"So let them sue me after I'm dead."

"Sir, there really is no need to commit suicide."

Forty-niner had figured out what I was going to do, of course. So what? There wasn't anything he could do to stop me.

"What's the matter? You scared of being alone?"

"I would rather not be alone, sir. I prefer your company to solitude."

"Tough nuts, pal. I'm going to blow the hatches and put an end to it."

"But, sir, there is no need—"

"What do you know about need?" I bellowed at him. "Human need? I'm a human being, not a collection of circuit boards."

"Sir, I know that humans require certain physical and emotional supports."

"Damned right we do." I had the panel off. I shorted out the safety circuit, giving myself a nasty little electrical shock in the process. The inner hatch slid open.

"I have been trying to satisfy your needs, sir, within the limits of my programming."

As I stepped into the coffin-sized airlock I thought to myself, *Yeah, he has. Forty-niner's been doing his best to keep me alive. But it's not enough. Not nearly enough.*

I started prying open the control panel of the outer hatch. Six centimeters away from me was the vacuum of interplanetary space. Once the hatch opens, *poof!* I'm gone.

"Sir, please listen to me."

"I'm listening," I said, as I tried to figure out how I could short out the safety circuit without giving myself another shock. Stupid, isn't it? Here I was trying to commit suicide and worried about a little electrical shock.

"There is a ship approaching us, sir."

"Don't be funny."

"It was not an attempt at humor, sir. A ship is approaching us and hailing us at standard communications frequency."

I looked up at the speaker set into the overhead of the airlock.

"Is this part of your psychological programming?" I groused.

Forty-niner ignored my sarcasm. "Backtracking the approaching ship's trajectory shows that it originated at Ceres, sir. It should make rendezvous with us in nine hours and forty-one minutes."

I stomped out of the airlock and ducked into the bridge, muttering, "If this is some wiseass ploy of yours to keep me from—"

I looked at the display panel. All its screens were dark: conserving electrical power.

"Is this some kind of psychology stunt?" I asked.

"No, sir, it is an actual ship. Would you like to answer its call to us, sir?"

"Light up the radar display."

Goddamn! There *was* a blip on the screen.

I thought I must have been hallucinating. Or maybe Forty-niner was fooling with the radar display to keep me from popping the airlock hatch. But I sank into the command chair and told Forty-niner to pipe the incoming message to the comm screen. And there was Donahoo's ugly mug talking at me! I knew I was hallucinating.

"Hang in there," he was saying. "We'll get you out of that scrap heap in a few hours."

"Yeah, sure," I said, and turned off the comm screen. To Forty-niner, I called out, "Thanks, pal. Nice try. I appreciate it. But I think I'm going to back to the airlock and opening the outer hatch now."

"But sir," Forty-niner sounded almost like he was pleading, "it really is a ship approaching. We are saved, sir."

"Don't you think I know you can pull up Donahoo's image from your files and animate it? Manipulate it to make him say what you want me to hear? Get real!"

For several heartbeats Forty-niner didn't answer. At last he said, "Then let us conduct a reality test, sir."

"Reality test?"

"The approaching ship will rendezvous with us in nine hours, twenty-seven minutes. Wait that long, sir. If no ship reaches us, then you can resume your suicidal course of action."

It made sense. I knew Forty-niner was just trying to keep me alive, and I almost respected the pile of chips for being so deviously clever about it. Not that I meant anything to him on a personal basis. Forty-niner was a computer. No emotions. Not even an urge for self-preservation. Whatever he was doing to keep me alive had been programmed into him by the psychotechs.

And then I thought, yeah, and when a human being risks his butt to save the life of another human being, that's been programmed into him by millions of years of evolution. Is there that much of a difference?

So I sat there and waited. I called to Donahoo and told him I was alive and damned hungry. He grinned that lopsided sneer of his and told me he'd have a soy steak waiting for me. Nothing that Forty-niner couldn't have ginned up from its files on me and Donahoo.

"I've got to admit, you're damned good," I said to Forty-niner.

"It's not me, sir," he replied. "Mr. Donahoo is really coming to rescue you."

I shook my head. "Yeah. And Santa Claus is right behind him in a sleigh full of toys pulled by eight tiny reindeer."

Immediately, Forty-niner said, "*A Visit from St. Nicholas*, by Clement Moore. Would you like to hear the entire poem, sir?"

I ignored that. "Listen, Niner, I appreciate what you're trying to do, but it just doesn't make sense. Donahoo's at corporate headquarters at Vesta. He's not at Ceres and he's not anywhere near us. Good try, but you can't make me believe the corporation would pay to have him come all the way over to Ceres to save a broken-down bucket of a waterbot and one very junior and expendable employee."

"Nevertheless, sir, that is what is happening. As you will see for yourself in eight hours and fifty-two minutes, sir."

I didn't believe it for a nanosecond. But I played along with Forty-niner. If it made him feel better, what did I have to lose? When the time was up and the bubble burst, I could always go back to the airlock and pop the outer hatch.

But he must have heard me muttering to myself, "It just doesn't make sense. It's not logical."

"Sir, what are the chances that in the siege of Leningrad in World War II the first artillery shell fired by the German army into the city would kill the only elephant in the Leningrad zoo? The statistical chances were astronomical, but that is exactly what happened, sir."

So I let him babble on about strange happenings and dramatic rescues. Why argue? It made him feel better, I guess. That is, if Forty-niner had any feelings. Which he didn't, I knew. Well, I guess letting him natter on with his rah-rah pep talk made *me* feel better. A little.

It was a real shock when a fusion torch ship took shape on my comm screen. Complete with standard registration info spelled out on the bar running along the screen's bottom: *Hu Davis*, out of Ceres.

"Be there in an hour and a half," Donahoo said, still sneering. "Christ, your old Jerky really looks like a scrap heap. You musta taken some battering."

Could Forty-niner fake that? I asked myself. Then a part of my mind warned, *don't get your hopes up. It's all a simulation.*

Except that, an hour and a half later, the *Hu Davis* was right alongside us, as big and detailed as life. I could see flecks on its meteor bumpers where micrometeors had abraded them. I just stared. It couldn't be a simulation. Not that detailed.

And Donahoo was saying, "I'm comin' in through your main airlock."

"No!" I yelped. "Wait! I've got to close the inner hatch first."

Donahoo looked puzzled. "Why the fuck's the inside hatch open?"

I didn't answer him. I was already ducking through the hatch of the bridge. Damned if I didn't get another electric shock closing airlock's the inner hatch.

I stood there wringing my hand while the outer hatch slid open. I could see the status lights on the control panel go from red for vacuum through amber and finally to green. Forty-niner could fake all that, I knew. This might still be nothing more than an elaborate simulation.

But then the inner hatch sighed open, and Donahoo stepped through, big and ugly as life.

His potato nose twitched. "Christ, it smells like a garbage pit in here."

That's when I knew it wasn't a simulation. He was really there. I was saved.

Well, it would've been funny if everybody wasn't so ticked off at me. Donahoo had been sent by corporate headquarters all the way from Vesta to Ceres to pick me up and turn off the distress call Forty-niner had been beaming out on the broadband frequencies for all those weeks.

It was only a milliwatt signal, didn't cost us a piffle of electrical power, but that teeny little signal got picked up at the Lunar Farside Observatory, where they had built the big SETI radio telescope. When they first detected our distress call, the astronomers went delirious: they thought they'd found an intelligent extraterrestrial signal, after more than a century of searching. They were sore as hell when they realized it was only a dinky old waterbot in trouble, not aliens trying to say hello.

They didn't give a rat's ass of a hoot about Forty-niner and me, but as long as our Mayday was being beamed out, their fancy radio telescope search for ETs was screwed. So they bleeped to the International Astronautical Authority, and the IAA complained to corporate headquarters, and Donahoo got called on the carpet at Vesta and told to get to JRK49N and turn off that damned distress signal!

And that's how we got rescued. Not because anybody cared about an aged waterbot that was due to be scrapped, or the very junior dumbass riding on it. We got saved because we were bothering the astronomers at Farside.

Donahoo made up some of the cost of his rescue mission by selling off what was left of Forty-niner to one of the salvage outfits at Ceres. They started cutting up the old bird as soon as we parked it in orbit there.

But not before I put on a clean, new space suit and went aboard JRK49N one last time.

I had forgotten how big the ship was. It was huge, a big massive collection of spherical tanks that dwarfed the fusion drive thruster and the cramped little pod I had lived in all those weeks. Hanging there in orbit, empty and alone, Forty-niner looked kind of sad. Long, nasty gashes had been ripped through the water tanks; I thought I could see rimes of ice glittering along their ragged edges in the faint starlight.

Then I saw the flickers of laser torches. Robotic scavengers were already starting to take the ship apart.

Floating there in weightlessness, my eyes misted up as I approached the ship. I had hated being on it, but I got teary-eyed just the same. I know it was stupid, but that's what happened, so help me.

I didn't go to the pod. There was nothing there that I wanted, especially not my cruddy old space suit. No, instead I worked my way along the cleats set into the spherical tanks, hand over gloved hand, to get to the heart of the ship, where the fusion reactor and power generator were housed.

And Forty-niner's CPU.

"Hey, whattarya doin' there?" One of the few humans directing the scavenger robots hollered at me, so loud I thought my helmet earphones would melt down.

"I'm retrieving the computer's hard drive," I said.

"You got permission?"

"I was the crew. I want the hard core. It's not worth anything to you, is it?"

"We ain't supposed to let people pick over the bones," he said. But his tone was lower, not so belligerent.

"It'll only take a couple of minutes," I said. "I don't want anything else; you can have all the rest."

"Damn right we can. Company paid good money for this scrap pile."

I nodded inside my helmet and went through the open hatch that led down to JRK49N's heart. And brain. It only took me a few minutes to pry open the CPU and disconnect the hard drive. I slipped the palm-sized metal oblong into a pouch on the thigh of my suit, then got out. I didn't look back. What those scavengers were chopping up was just a lot of metal and plastic. I had Forty-niner with me.

The corporation never assigned me to a waterbot again. Somebody in the front office must've taken a good look at my personnel dossier and figured I had too much education to be stuck in a dumb job like that. I don't know, maybe Donahoo had something to do with. He wouldn't admit to it, and I didn't press him about it.

Anyway, when I finally got back to Vesta, they assigned me to a desk job. Over the years I worked my way up to chief of logistics and eventually got transferred back to Selene City, on the moon. I'll be able to take early retirement soon and get married and start a family.

Forty-niner's been with me all that time. Not that I talk to him every day. But it's good to know that he's there and I can ease off the stresses of the job or whatever by having a nice, long chat with him.

One of these days, I'll even beat him at chess.

"SAM AND THE FLYING DUTCHMAN"

Sam Gunn has been with me for a long time.

Back when I was editing *Analog Science Fiction/Science Fact* magazine, I got a little germ of an idea for a story. I bounced it off several of the magazine's regular contributors, but none of them took me up on the invitation.

Still, the idea pecked away at my imagination. When I left *Analog* and took up writing full time, I tackled the idea myself.

The result was the first story about Sam Gunn. Today, half a lifetime later, Sam has appeared in a couple of dozen of my short fiction works. Sam is fun. Sam is like a brother to me, although we are very dissimilar in looks, attitudes, and capabilities.

Every now and then, Sam taps me on my metaphysical shoulder and tells me he has a new adventure to relate.

Here's the latest one.

SAM AND THE FLYING DUTCHMAN

I ushered her into Sam's office and helped her out of the bulky dark coat she was wearing. As soon as she let the hood fall back off her face, I damned near dropped the coat. I recognized her. Who could forget her? She was exquisite, so stunningly beautiful that even irrepressible Sam Gunn was struck speechless. More beautiful than any woman I had ever seen.

But haunted.

It was more than her big, soulful eyes. More than the almost frightened way she had of glancing all around as she entered Sam's office, as if expecting someone to leap out of hiding at her. She looked *tragic*, lovely and doomed and tragic.

"Mr. Gunn, I need your help," she said to Sam. Those were the first words she spoke, even before she took the chair that I was holding for her. Her voice was like the sigh of a breeze in a midnight forest.

Sam was standing behind his desk, on the hidden little platform back there that makes him look taller than his real 165 centimeters. As I said, even Sam was speechless. Leather-tongued, clatter-mouthed Sam Gunn simply stood and stared at her in stupefied awe.

Then he found his voice. "Anything," he said in a choked whisper. "I'd do anything for you."

Despite the fact that Sam was getting married in just three weeks' time, it was obvious that he'd tumbled head over heels for Amanda Cunningham the minute he saw her. Instantly. Sam Gunn was always falling in love, even more often than he made fortunes of money and lost them again. But this time it looked as if he'd really been struck by the thunderbolt.

If she weren't so beautiful, so troubled, seeing the two of them together would have been almost ludicrous. Amanda Cunningham looked like a Greek goddess, except that her shoulder-length hair was radiant golden blond. She wore a modest knee-length sheath of delicate pink that couldn't hide the curves of her ample body. And those eyes! They were bright china blue, but deep, terribly troubled, unbearably sad.

And there was Sam: stubby as a worn old pencil, with a bristle of red hair and his gap-toothed mouth hanging open. Sam had the kind of electricity in him that made it almost impossible for him to stand still for more than thirty seconds at a time. Yet he stood gaping at Amanda Cunningham, as tongue-tied as a teenager on his first date.

And me. Compared to Sam I'm a rugged, outdoorsy type of guy. Of course, I wear lifts in my boots and a tummy tingler that helps keep my gut flat. Women have told me that my face is kind of cute in a cherubic sort of way, and I believe them—until

I look in the mirror and see the pouchy eyes and the trim black beard that covers my receding chin. What did it matter? Amanda Cunningham didn't even glance at me; her attention was focused completely on Sam.

It was really comical. Yet I wasn't laughing.

Sam just stared at her, transfixed. Bewitched. I was still holding one of the leather-covered chairs for her. She sat down without looking at it, as if she were accustomed to there being a chair wherever she chose to sit.

"You must understand, Mr. Gunn," she said softly. "What I ask is very dangerous . . ."

Still standing at his desk in front of his high-backed swivel chair, his eyes never leaving hers, Sam waved one hand as if to scoff at the thought of danger.

"It involves flying out to the belt," she continued.

"Anywhere," Sam said. "For you."

"To find my husband."

That broke the spell. Definitely.

Sam's company was S. Gunn Enterprises, Unlimited. He was involved in a lot of different operations, including hauling freight between the earth and moon, and transporting equipment out to the asteroid belt. He was also dickering to build a gambling casino and hotel on the moon, but that's another story.

"To find your husband?" Sam asked her, his face sagging with disappointment.

"My ex-husband," said Amanda Cunningham. "We were divorced several years ago."

"Oh." Sam brightened.

"My current husband is Martin Humphries," she went on, her voice sinking lower.

"Oh," Sam repeated, plopping down into his chair like a man shot in the heart. "Amanda Cunningham Humphries."

"Yes," she said.

"*The* Martin Humphries?"

"Yes," she repeated, almost whispering it.

Mrs. Martin Humphries. I'd seen pictures of her, of course, and vids on the society nets. I'd even glimpsed her in person once, across a ballroom crowded with the very wealthiest of the wealthy. Even in the midst of all that glitter and opulence, she had glowed like a beautiful princess in a cave full of trolls. Martin Humphries was towing her around the party like an Olympic trophy. I popped my monocle and almost forgot the phony German accent I'd been using all evening. That was a couple of years ago, when I'd been working the society circuit selling shares of nonexistent tritium mines. On Mars, yet. The richer they are, the easier they bite.

Martin Humphries was probably the richest person in the solar system, founder and chief of Humphries Space Systems, and well-known to be a prime SOB. I'd never try to scam him. If he bit on my bait, it could be fatal. *So that's why she looks so miserable*, I thought. Married to him. I felt sorry for Amanda Cunningham Humphries.

But sorry or not, this could be the break I'd been waiting for. Amanda Cunningham Humphries was the wife of the richest sumbitch in the solar system. She could buy anything she wanted, including Sam's whole ramshackle company, which was teetering on the brink of bankruptcy. As usual. Yet she was asking Sam for help, like a lady in distress. She was scared.

"Martin Humphries," Sam repeated.

She nodded wordlessly. She certainly did not look happy about being married to Martin Humphries.

Sam swallowed visibly, his Adam's apple bobbing up and down twice. Then he got his feet again and said, as brightly as he could manage, "Why don't we discuss this over lunch?"

Sam's office in those days was on the L-5 habitat *Beethoven*. Funny name for a space structure that housed some fifty thousand people, I know. It was built by a consortium of American, European, Russian, and Japanese corporations. The only name they could agree on was Beethoven's, thanks to the fact that the head of Yamagata Corp. had always wanted to be a symphony orchestra conductor.

To his credit, Sam's office was not grand or imposing. He said he didn't want to waste his money on furniture or real estate. Not that he had any money to waste, at the time. The suite was compact, tastefully decorated, with wall screens that showed idyllic scenes of woods and waterfalls. Sam had a sort of picture gallery on the wall behind his desk, S. Gunn with the great and powerful figures of the day—most of whom were out to sue him, if not have him murdered—plus several photos of Sam with various beauties in revealing attire.

I, as his special consultant and advisor, sat off to one side of his teak-and-chrome desk, where I could swivel from Sam to his visitor and back again.

Amanda Humphries shook her lovely head. "I can't go out to lunch with you, Mr. Gunn. I shouldn't be seen in public with you."

Before Sam could react to that, she added, "It's nothing personal. It's just . . . I don't want my husband to know that I've turned to you."

Undeterred, Sam put on a lopsided grin and said, "Well, we could have lunch sent in here." He turned to me. "Gar, why don't you rustle us up some grub?"

I made a smile at his sudden western folksiness. Sam was a con man, and everybody knew it. That made it all the easier for me to con him. I'm a scam artist, myself, *par excellence*, and it ain't bragging if you can do it. Still, I'd been very roundabout in approaching Sam. Conning a con man takes some finesse, let me tell you.

About a year ago, I talked myself into a job with the Honorable Jill Myers, former US senator and American representative on the International Court of Justice. Judge Myers was an old, old friend of Sam's, dating back to the early days when they'd both been astronauts working for the old NASA.

I had passed myself off to Myers's people as Garret G. Garrison III, the penniless son of one of the oldest families in Texas. I had doctored up a biography and a dozen or so phony news media reports. With just a bit of money in the right hands, when Myers's people checked me out in the various web nets, there was enough in place to convince them that I was poor but bright, talented, and honest.

Three out of four ain't bad. I was certainly poor, bright, and talented.

Jill Myers wanted to marry Sam. Why, I'll never figure out. Sam was—is!—a philandering, womanizing, skirt-chasing bundle of testosterone who falls in love the way Pavlov's dogs salivated when they heard a bell ring. But Jill Myers wanted to marry the little scoundrel, and Sam had even proposed to her—once he ran out of all the other sources of funding that he could think of. Did I mention that Judge Myers comes from old money? She does: the kind of New England family that still has the first nickel they made in the molasses-for-rum-for-slaves trade back in precolonial days.

Anyway, I had sweet-talked my way into Judge Myers's confidence (and worked damned hard for her, too, I might add). So when they set a date for the wedding, she asked me to join Sam's staff and keep an eye on him. She didn't want him to disappear and leave her standing at the altar.

Sam took me in without a qualm, gave me the title of special consultant and advisor to the CEO, and put me in the office next to his. He knew I was Justice Myers's enforcer, but it didn't seem to bother him a bit.

Sam and I got along beautifully, like kindred souls, really. Once I told him the long, sad (and totally false) story of my life, he took to me like a big brother.

"Gar," he told me more than once, "we're two of a kind. Always trying to get out from under the big guys."

I agreed fervently.

I've been a grifter all my life, ever since I sweet-talked Sister Agonista into overlooking the fact that she caught me cheating on the year-end exams in sixth grade. It was a neat scam for an eleven-year-old: I let her catch me, I let her think she had scared me onto the path of righteousness, and she was so happy about it that she never tumbled to the fact that I had sold answer sheets to half the kids in the school.

Anyway, life was always kind of rough-and-tumble for me. You hit it big here, and the next time you barely get out with the hide on your back. I had been at it long enough so that by now I was slowing down, getting a little tired, looking for the one big score that would let me wrap it all up and live the rest of my life in ill-gotten ease. I knew Sam Gunn was the con man's con man: the little rogue had made more fortunes than the New York Stock Exchange—and lost them just as quickly as he could go chasing after some new rainbow. I figured that if I cozied up real close to Sam, I could snatch his next pot of gold before he had a chance to piss it away.

So when Judge Myers asked me to keep an eye on Sam, I went out to the *Beethoven* habitat that same day, alert and ready for my big chance to nail the last and best score.

Amanda Cunningham Humphries might just be that opportunity, I realized.

So now I'm bringing a tray of lunch in for Sam and Mrs. Humphries, setting it all out on Sam's desk while they chat, and then retreating to my own little office so they can talk in privacy.

Privacy, hah! I slipped the acoustic amplifier out of my desk drawer and stuck it on the wall that my office shared with Sam's. Once I had wormed the earplug in, I could hear everything they said.

Which wasn't all that much. Mrs. Humphries was very guarded about it all.

"I have a coded video chip that I want you to deliver to my ex-husband," she told Sam.

"Okay," he said, "but you could have a courier service make the delivery, even out to the belt. I don't see why—"

"My ex-husband is Lars Fuchs."

Bingo! I don't know how Sam reacted to that news, but I nearly jumped out of my chair to turn a somersault. Her first husband was Lars Fuchs! Fuchs the pirate. Fuchs the renegade. Fuchs and Humphries had fought a minor war out there in the belt a few years earlier. It had ended when Humphries's mercenaries had finally captured Fuchs, and the Rock Rats of Ceres had exiled him for life.

For years now Fuchs had wandered through the belt, an exile

eking out a living as a miner, a Rock Rat. Making a legend of himself. A homeless wanderer. The Flying Dutchman of the asteroid belt.

It must have been right after he was exiled, I guessed, that Amanda Cunningham had divorced Fuchs and married his bitter rival, Humphries. I later found out that I was right. That's exactly what had happened. But with a twist. She divorced Fuchs and married Humphries on the condition that Humphries would stop trying to track Fuchs down and have him killed. Exile was punishment enough, she convinced Humphries. But the price for that tender mercy was her body. From the haunted look of her, maybe the price included her soul.

Now she wanted to send a message to her ex. Why? What was in the message? Humphries would pay a small fortune to find out. No, I decided; he'd pay a *large* fortune. To me.

———

Mrs. Humphries didn't have all that much more to say and she left the office immediately after they finished their lunch, bundled once more into that shapeless black coat with its hood pulled up to hide her face.

I bounced back into Sam's office. He was sitting back in his chair, the expression on his face somewhere between exalted and terrified.

"She needs my help," Sam murmured, as if talking in his sleep.

"Our help," I corrected.

Sam blinked, shook himself, and sat up erect. He nodded and grinned at me. "I knew I could count on you, Gar."

Then I remembered that I was supposed to be working for Judge Myers.

———

"He's going out to the belt?" Judge Myers's chestnut-brown eyes snapped at me. "And you're letting him do it?"

Some people called Jill Myers plain, or even unattractive (behind her back, of course), but I always thought of her as kind of cute. In a way, she looked almost like Sam's sister might: her face was round as a pie, with a stubby little nose and a sprinkling of freckles. Her hair was light brown and straight as can be; she kept it in a short, no-nonsense bob and refused to let stylists fancy it up for her.

Her image in my desk screen clearly showed, though, that she was angry. Not at Sam. At me.

"Garrison, I sent you to keep that little so-and-so on track for our wedding, and now you're going out to the belt with him?"

"It'll only be for a few days," I said. Truthfully, that's all I expected at that point.

Her anger abated a skosh; suspicion replaced it.

"What's this all about, Gar?"

If I told her that Sam had gone bonkers over Amanda Humphries, she'd be up at *Beethoven* on the next shuttle, so I temporized a little.

"He's looking into a new business opportunity at Ceres. It should only take a few days."

Fusion torch ships could zip out to the belt at a constant acceleration. They cost an arm and two legs, but Sam was in his spare no expenses mode, and I agreed with him. We could zip out to the belt in four days, deliver the message, and be home again in time for the wedding. *We'd even have a day or so to spare*, I thought.

One thing about Judge Myers: she couldn't stay angry for more than a few minutes at a time. But from the expression on her face, she remained highly suspicious.

"I want a call from you every day, Gar," she said. "I know you can't keep Sam on a leash; nobody can. But I want to know where you are and what you're doing."

"Yes, ma'am. Of course."

"Every day."

"Right."

Easier said than done.

———

Sam rented a torch ship, the smallest he could find, just a set of fusion engines and propellant tanks with a crew pod attached. It was called *Achernar*, and its accommodations were really Spartan. Sam piloted it himself.

"That's why I keep my astronaut's qualifications up to date with the chickenshit IAA," he told me, with a mischievous wink. "No sense spending money on a pilot when I can fly these birds myself."

For four days we raced out to Ceres, accelerating at a half gee most of the time, then decelerating at a gee-and-a-half. Sam wanted to go even faster, but the IAA wouldn't approve his original plan, and he had no choice. If he didn't follow their flight plan, the IAA controllers at Ceres would impound *Achernar* and send us back to Earth for a disciplinary hearing.

So Sam stuck to their rules, fussing and fidgeting every centimeter of the way. He hated bureaucracies and bureaucrats. He especially loathed being forced to do things their way instead of his own.

The trip out was less than luxurious, let me tell you. But the deceleration was absolute agony for me; I felt as if I weighed about a ton and I was scared even to try to stand up.

Sam took the strain cheerfully. "Double strength jockstrap, Gar," he told me, grinning. "That's the secret of my success."

I stayed seated as much as possible. I even slept in the copilot's reclinable chair, wishing that the ship had been primitive enough to include a relief tube among its equipment fixtures.

———

People who don't know any better think that the Rock Rats out in the belt are a bunch of rough-and-tumble, crusty, hard-fisted prospectors and miners. Well, sure, there are some like that, but most of the Rock Rats are university educated engineers and technicians. After all, they work with spacecraft and teleoperated machinery out at the frontier of human civilization. They're out there in the dark, cold, mostly empty asteroid belt, on their own, the nearest help usually so far away that it's useless to them. They don't use mules and shovels, and they don't have barroom brawls or shootouts.

Most nights, that is.

Sam's first stop after we docked at the habitat *Chrysalis* was the bar.

The *Chrysalis* habitat, by the way, was something like a circular, rotating junkyard. The Rock Rats had built it over the years by putting used or abandoned spacecraft together, hooking them up like a tinkertoy merry-go-round and spinning the whole contraption to produce an artificial gravity inside. It was better than living in Ceres itself, with its minuscule gravity and the constant haze of dust that you stirred up with every move you made. The earliest Rock Rats actually did live inside Ceres. That's why they built the ramshackle *Chrysalis* as quickly as they could.

I worried about hard radiation, but Sam told me the habitat had superconducting shielding, the same as spacecraft use.

"You're as safe as you'd be on Earth," Sam assured me. "Just about."

It was the *just about* that scared me.

"Why are we going to the bar?" I asked, striding along beside him down the habitat's central corridor. Well, maybe *central corridor* is an overstatement. We were walking down the main passageway of one of the spacecrafts that made up *Chrysalis*. Up ahead was a hatch that connected to the next spacecraft component. And so on. We could walk a complete circle and come back to the airlock where *Achernar* was docked, if we'd wanted to.

"Gonna meet the mayor," said Sam.

The mayor?

Well, anyway, we go straight to the bar. I had expected a kind of rough place, maybe like a biker joint. Instead the place looked like a sophisticated cocktail lounge.

It was called the Crystal Palace, and it was as quiet and subdued as one of those high-class watering holes in Old Manhattan. Soft lighting, plush, faux-leather wall coverings, muted Mozart coming through the speakers set in the overhead. It was midafternoon, and there were only about a dozen people in the place, a few at the bar, the rest in high-backed booths that gave them plenty of privacy.

Sam sauntered up to the bar and perched on one of the swiveling stools. He spun around a few times, taking in the local scenery. The only woman in the place was the human bartender, and she wasn't much better looking than the robots that trundled drinks out to the guys in the booths.

"What's fer yew?" she asked. She looked like she was into weight lifting. The gray sweatshirt she was wearing had the sleeves cut off; plenty of muscle in her arms. The expression on her squarish face was no-nonsense, unsmiling.

"West Tennessee," said Sam. "Right?"

The bartender looked surprised. "Huntsville, 'Bama."

"Heart of the Tennessee Valley," Sam said. "I come from the bluegrass country, myself."

Which was a complete lie. Sam was born in either Nevada or Pennsylvania, according to which of his dossiers you read. Or maybe Luzon, in the Philippines.

Well, in less than six minutes, Sam had the bartender laughing and trading redneck jokes with him. Her name was Belinda. I just sat beside him and watched the master at work. He could charm the devil out of hell, Sam could.

Sam ordered Tennessee corn mash for both of us. While he chatted up the bartender, though, I noticed that the place was emptying out. The three guys at the bar got up and left first, one by one. Then, out of the corner of my eye, I saw the guys in the booths heading for the door. No big rush, but within a few minutes they had all walked out. On tiptoes.

I said nothing, but soon enough Sam realized we were alone.

"What happened?" he asked Belinda. "We chased everybody out?"

She shook her head. "Rock Rats worry about strangers. They prob'ly think you're maybe a tax assessor or a safety inspector from the IAA."

Sam laughed. "Me? From the IAA? Hell, no. I'm Sam Gunn. Maybe you've heard of me?"

"No! Sam Gunn? You couldn't be!"

"That's me," Sam said, with his Huckleberry Finn grin.

"You were the first guy out here in the belt," said Belinda, real admiration glowing in her eyes.

"Yep. Captured a nickel/iron asteroid and towed her back to Earth's orbit."

"Pittsburgh. I heard about it. Took you a couple of years, didn't it?"

Sam nodded. He was enjoying the adulation.

"That was a long time ago," Belinda said. "I thought you'd be a lot older."

"I am."

She laughed, a hearty roar that made the glasses on the back bar rattle. "Rejuve therapy, right?"

"Why not?"

Just then, a red-haired mountain strode into the bar. One of the biggest men I've ever seen. He didn't look fat, either: just *big*, with a shaggy mane of brick-red hair and a shaggier beard to match.

He walked right up to us.

"You're Sam Gunn." It wasn't a question.

"Right," said Sam. Swiveling toward me, he added, "And this young fellow here is Garret G. Garrison III."

"The third, huh?" the redhead huffed at me. "What happened to the first two?"

"Hung for stealin' horses," I lied, putting on my thickest Wild West accent.

Belinda laughed at that. The redhead simply huffed.

"You're George Ambrose, right?" Sam asked.

"Big George, that's me."

"The mayor of this fair community," Sam added.

"They elected me th' fookin' chief," Big George said, almost belligerently. "Now, whattaya want to see me about?"

"About Lars Fuchs."

George's eyes went cold and narrow. Belinda backed away from us and went down the bar, suddenly busy with the glassware.

"What about Lars Fuchs?" George asked.

"I want to meet him. I've got a business proposition for him."

George folded his beefy arms across his massive chest. "Fuchs is an exile. Hasn't been anywhere near Ceres for dog's years. Hell, this fookin' habitat wasn't even finished when we tossed 'im out. We were still livin' down inside th' rock."

Sam rested his elbows on the bar and smiled disarmingly at Big George. "Well, I've got a business proposition for Fuchs and I need to talk to him."

"What kind of a business proposition?"

With a perfectly straight face Sam answered, "I'm thinking of starting a tourist service here in the belt. You know, visit Ceres, see a mining operation at work on one of the asteroids, go out in a suit and chip some gold or diamonds to bring back home. That kind of thing."

George said nothing, but I could see the wheels turning behind that wild red mane of his.

"It could mean an influx of money for your people," Sam went on, in his best snake-oil spiel. "A hotel here in orbit around Ceres, rich tourists flooding in. Lots of money."

George unbent his arms, but he still remained standing. "What's all this got to do with Fuchs?"

"Shiploads full of rich tourists might make a tempting target for a pirate."

"Bullshit."

"You don't think he'd attack tour ships?"

"Lars wouldn't do that. He's not a fookin' pirate. Not in that sense, anyway."

"I'd rather hear that from him," Sam said. "In fact, I've got to have his personal assurance before my backers will invest in the scheme."

George stared at Sam for a long moment, deep suspicion written clearly on his face. "Nobody knows where Lars is," he said at last. "You might as well go back home. Nobody here's gonna give you any help."

———

We left the bar with Big George glowering at our backs so hard, I could feel the heat. Following the maps on the wall screens in the passageways, we found the adjoining rooms that I had booked for us.

"Now what?" I asked Sam as I unpacked my travel bag.

"Now we wait."

Sam had simply tossed his bag on the bed of his room and barged through the connecting door into mine. We had packed for only a three-day stay at Ceres, although we had more gear stowed in *Achernar*. *Something had to happen pretty quick*, I thought.

"Wait for what?" I asked.

"Developments."

I put my carefully folded clothes in a drawer, hung my extra pair of wrinkle-proof slacks in the closet, and set up my toiletries in the lavatory. Sam made himself comfortable in the room's only chair, a recliner designed to look like an astronaut's couch. He cranked it down so far, I thought he was going to take a nap.

Sitting on the bed, I told him, "Sam, I've got to call Judge Myers."

"Go right ahead," he said.

"What should I tell her?"

"Tell her we'll be back in time for the wedding."

I doubted that.

———

Two days passed without a word from anyone. Sam even tried to date Belinda, he was getting so desperate, but she wouldn't have anything to do with him.

"They all know Fuchs," Sam said to me. "They like him and they're protecting him."

It was common knowledge that Humphries had sworn to kill Fuchs, but Amanda had married Humphries on the condition that he left Fuchs alone. Everybody in Ceres, from Belinda the barmaid to the last Rock Rat, thought that we were working for Humphries, trying to find Fuchs and murder him. Or at least locate him, so one of Humphries's hired killers could knock him off. Fuchs was out there in the belt somewhere, cruising through that dark emptiness like some Flying Dutchman, alone, taking a strangely measured kind of vengeance on unmanned Humphries ships.

I had other fish to fry, though. I wanted to find out what was on the chip that Amanda had given Sam. Her message to her ex-husband. What did she want to tell him? Fuchs was a thorn in Humphries's side; maybe only a small thorn, but he drew blood, nonetheless. Humphries would pay a fortune for that message, and I intended to sell it to him.

But I had to get it away from Sam first.

———

Judge Myers was not happy with my equivocating reports to her. Definitely not happy.

There's no way to have a conversation in real time between Ceres and Earth; the distance makes it impossible. It takes nearly half an hour for a message to cross one-way, even when the two bodies are at their closest. So I sent reports to Judge Myers and—usually within an hour—I'd get a response from her.

After my first report, she had a wry grin on her face when she called back. "Garrison, I know it's about as easy to keep Sam in line as nailing tapioca to a wall in zero G. But all the plans for the wedding are set, it's going to be the biggest social event of the year. You've got to make sure that he's here. I'm depending on you, Garrison."

A day later, her smile had disappeared. "The wedding's only a week from now, Garrison," she said after my second call to her. "I want that little scoundrel at the altar!"

Third call, the next day: "I don't care what he's doing! Get him back here! Now!"

That's when Sam came up with his bright idea.

"Pack up your duds, Gar," he announced brightly. "We're going to take a little spin around the belt."

I was too surprised to ask questions. In less than an hour, we were back in *Achernar* and heading out from Ceres. Sam had already filed a flight plan with the IAA controllers. As far as they were concerned, Sam was going to visit three specific asteroids, which might be used as tourist stops if and when he started his operation in the belt. Of course, I knew that once we cleared Ceres, there was no one and nothing that could hold him to that plan.

"What are we doing?" I asked, sitting in the right-hand seat of the cockpit. "Where are we going?"

"To meet Fuchs," said Sam.

"You've made contact with him?"

"Nope," Sam replied, grinning as if he knew something nobody else knew. "But I'm willing to bet *somebody* has. Maybe Big George. Fuchs saved his life once; did you know that?"

"But how—?"

"It's simple," Sam answered before I could finish the question. "We let it be known that we want to see Fuchs. Everybody says they don't know where he is. We go out into the belt, away from everything, including snoops who might rat out Fuchs to Martin Humphries. Somebody from *Chrysalis* calls Fuchs and tells him about us. Fuchs intercepts our ship to see what I want. I give him Amanda's message chip. QED."

It made a certain amount of sense. But I had my doubts.

"What if Fuchs just blasts us?"

"Not his style. He's only attacked unmanned ships."

"He wiped out an HSS base on Vesta, didn't he? Killed dozens."

"That was during the war between him and Humphries. Ancient history. He hasn't attacked a crewed ship since he's been exiled."

"But suppose—"

The communications console pinged.

"Hah!" Sam gloated. "There he is now."

But the image that took form on the comm screen wasn't Lars Fuchs's face. It was Jill Myers.

She was beaming a smile that could've lit up Selene City for a month. "Sam, I've got a marvelous idea. I know you're wrapped up in some kind of mysterious mission out there in the belt, and the wedding's only a few days off, so . . ."

She hesitated, like somebody about to spring a big surprise. "So instead of you coming back Earthside for the wedding, I'm bringing the wedding out to you! All the guests and everything. In fact, I'm on the torch ship *Statendaam* right now! We break Earth orbit in about an hour. I'll see you in five days, Sam, and we can be married just as we planned!"

To say Sam was surprised would be like saying Napoleon was disturbed by Waterloo. Or McKenzie was inconvenienced when his spacecraft crashed into the Lunar Apennines. Or—well, you get the idea.

Sam looked stunned, as if he'd been pole-axed between the eyes. He just slumped in the pilot's chair, dazed, his eyes unfocused for several minutes.

"She can't come out here," he muttered at last.

"She's already on her way," I said.

"But she'll ruin everything. If she comes barging out here, Fuchs'll never come within a lightyear and a half of us."

"How're you going to stop her?"

Sam thought about that for all of a half second. "I can't stop her. But I don't have to make it easy for her to find me."

"What do you mean?"

"Run silent, run deep." With deft finger, Sam turned off the ship's tracking beacon and telemetry transmitter.

"Sam! The controllers at Ceres will think we've been destroyed!"

He grinned wickedly. "Let 'em. If they don't know where we are, they can't point Jill at us."

"But Fuchs won't know where we are."

"Oh, yes, he will," Sam insisted. "Somebody at Ceres has already given him our flight plan. Big George, probably."

"Sam," I said patiently, "you filed that flight plan with the IAA. They'll tell Judge Myers. She'll come out looking for you."

"Yeah, but she'll be several days behind. By that time the IAA controllers'll tell her we've disappeared. She'll go home and weep for me."

"Or start searching for your remains."

He shot me an annoyed glance. "Anyway, we'll meet with Fuchs before she gets here, most likely."

"You hope."

His grin wobbled a little.

I thought the most likely scenario was that Fuchs would ignore us and Judge Myers would search for us, hoping that Sam's disappearance didn't mean he was dead. Once she found us, I figured, she'd kill Sam herself.

——

It was eerie, out there in the belt. Flatlanders back on Earth think that the asteroid belt is a dangerous region, a-chock with boulders, so crowded that you have to maneuver like a kid in a computer game to avoid getting smashed.

Actually, it's empty. Dark and cold and four times farther from the sun than the earth is. Most of the asteroids are the size of dust flakes. The valuable ones, maybe a few meters to a kilometer or so across, are so few and far between that you have to hunt for them. You can cruise through the belt blindfolded, and your chances of getting hit even by a pebble-sized 'roid are pretty close to nil.

Of course, a pebble could shatter your ship if it hits you with enough velocity.

So we were running silent, but following the flight plan Sam had registered with the IAA. We got to the first rock Sam had scheduled and loitered around it for half a day. No sign of Fuchs. If he was anywhere nearby, he was running as silently as we were.

"He's gotta be somewhere around here," Sam said as we broke orbit and headed for the next asteroid on his list. "He's gotta be."

I could tell that Sam was feeling Judge Myers's eager breath on the back of his neck.

Me, I had a different problem. I wanted to get that message chip away from Sam long enough to send a copy of it to Martin Humphries. With a suitable request for compensation, of course. *Fifty million would do nicely*, I thought. A hundred mil would be even better.

But how to get the chip out of Sam's pocket? He kept it on his person all the time; even slept with it.

So it floored me when, as we were eating breakfast in *Achernar*'s cramped little galley on our third day out, Sam fished the fingernail-sized chip out of his breast pocket and handed it to me.

"Gar," he said solemnly, "I want you to hide this someplace where *nobody* can find it, not even me."

I was staggered. "Why . . . ?"

"Just a precaution," he said, his face more serious than I'd ever seen it before. "When Fuchs shows up, things might get rough. I don't want to know where the chip is."

"But the whole point of this flight is to deliver it to him."

He nodded warily. "Yeah, Humphries must know we're looking for Fuchs. He's got IAA people on his payroll. Hell, half the people in Ceres might be willing to rat on us. Money talks, pal. Humphries might not know why we're looking for Fuchs, but he knows we're trying to find him."

"Humphries wants to find Fuchs too," I said. "And kill him, no matter what he promised his wife."

"Damned right. I wouldn't be surprised if he has a ship tailing us."

"I haven't seen anything on the radar plot."

"So what? A stealth ship could avoid radar. But not the hair on the back of my neck."

"You think we're being followed?"

"I'm sure of it."

By the seven sinners of Cincinnati, I thought. *This is starting to look like a class reunion!* We're jinking around in the belt, looking for Fuchs. Judge Myers is on her way, with a complete wedding party. And now Sam thinks there's an HSS stealth ship lurking out there somewhere, waiting for us to find Fuchs so they can pounce on him.

But all that paled into insignificance for me as I stared down at the tiny chip Sam had placed in the palm of my hand.

I had it in my grasp! Now the trick was to contact Humphries without letting Sam know of it.

I couldn't sleep that night. We were approaching the second asteroid on Sam's itinerary on a dead-reckoning trajectory. No active signals going out from the ship except for the short-range collision avoidance radar. We'd take up a parking orbit around the unnamed rock midmorning tomorrow.

I waited until my eyes were adapted to the darkness of the

sleeping compartment, then peeked down over the edge of my bunk to see if Sam was really asleep. He was on his side, face to the bulkhead, his legs pulled up slightly in a sort of fetal position. Breathing deep and regular.

He's asleep, I told myself. As quietly as a wraith, I slipped out of my bunk and tiptoed in my bare feet to the cockpit, carefully shutting the hatches of the sleeping compartment and the galley, so there'd be no noise to waken Sam.

I'm pretty good at decrypting messages. It's a useful talent for a con man, and I had spent long hours at computers during my one and only jail stretch to learn the tricks of the trade.

Of course, I could just offer the chip for sale to Humphries without knowing what was on it. He'd pay handsomely for a message that his wife wanted to give to Lars Fuchs.

But if I knew the contents of the message, I reasoned, I could most likely double or triple the price. So I started to work on decrypting it. *How hard could it be?* I asked myself as I slipped the chip into the ship's main computer. She probably did the encoding herself, not trusting anybody around her. She'd been an astronaut in her earlier years, I knew, but not particularly a computer freak. Should be easy.

It wasn't. It took all night, and I still didn't get all the way through the trapdoors and blind alleys she'd built into her message. Smart woman, I realized, my respect for Amanda Cunningham Humphries notching up with every bead of sweat I oozed.

At last the hash that had been filling the central screen on the cockpit control panel cleared away, replaced by an image of her face.

That face. I just stared at her. She was so beautiful, so sad and vulnerable. It brought a lump to my throat. I've seen beautiful women, plenty of them, and bedded more than my share. But gazing at Amanda's face, there in the quiet hum of the dimmed cockpit, I felt something more than desire, more than animal hunger.

Could it be love? I shook my head like a man who's just been knocked down by a punch. *Don't be an idiot!* I snarled at myself. *You've been hanging around Sam too long, you're becoming a romantic jackass just like he is.*

Love has nothing to do with this. That beautiful face is going to earn you millions, I told myself, *as soon as you decrypt this message of hers.*

And then I smelled the fragrance of coffee brewing. Sam was in the galley, right behind the closed hatch of the cockpit, clattering dishes and silverware. In a weird way, I felt almost relieved. Quickly, I popped the chip out of the computer and slipped it into the waistband of the undershorts I was wearing.

Just in time. Sam pushed the hatch open and handed me a steaming mug of coffee.

"You're up early," he said with a groggy smile.

"Couldn't sleep," I answered truthfully. That's where the truth ended. "I've been trying to think of where I could stash the chip."

He nodded and scratched at his wiry, tousled red hair. "Find a good spot, Gar. I think we're going to have plenty of fireworks before this job is finished."

Truer words, as they say, were never spoken.

The three asteroids Sam had chosen were samples of the three different types of 'roids in the belt. The first one had been a rocky type. It looked like a lumpy potato, pockmarked with craterlets from the impacts of smaller rocks. The one we were approaching was a chondritic type, a loose collection of primeval pebbles that barely held itself together. Sam called it a *beanbag*.

He was saving the best one for last. The third and last asteroid on Sam's list was a metallic beauty, the one that some Latin American sculptress had carved into a monumental history of her Native American people; she called it *The Rememberer*. Sam had been involved in that, years ago, I knew. He had shacked up with the sculptress for a while. Just like Sam.

As we approached the beanbag, our collision-avoidance radar started going crazy.

"It's surrounded by smaller chunks of rock," Sam muttered, studying the screen.

From the copilot's chair, I could see the main body of the asteroid through the cockpit window. It looked hazy, indistinct, more like a puff of smoke than a solid object.

"If we're going to orbit that cloud of pebbles," I said, "it'd better be at a good distance from it. Otherwise, we'll get dinged up pretty heavily."

Sam nodded and tapped in the commands for an orbit that looped a respectful distance from the beanbag.

"How long are we going to hang around here?" I asked him.

He made a small shrug. "Give it a day or two. Then we'll head off for *The Rememberer*."

"Sam, your wedding is in two days." *Speaking of remembering*, I thought.

He gave me a lopsided grin. "Jill's smart enough to figure it out. We'll get married at *The Rememberer*. Outside, in suits, with the sculpture for a background. It'll make terrific publicity for my tourist service."

I felt my eyebrows go up. "You're really thinking of starting tourist runs out here to the belt?"

"Sure. Why not?"

"I thought that was just your cover story."

"It was," he admitted. "But the more I think about it, the more sense it makes."

"Who's going to pay the fare for coming all the way out here, just to see a few rocks?"

"Gar, you just don't understand how business works, do you?"

"But—"

"How did space tourism start, in the first place?" Before I could even start thinking about an answer, he went on, "With a few bored rich guys paying millions for a few days in orbit."

"Not much of a market," I said.

He waggled a finger at me. "Not at first, but it got people interested. The publicity was important. Within a few years, there was enough of a demand so that a real tourist industry took off. Small, at first, but it grew."

I recalled, "You started a honeymoon hotel in Earth orbit back then, didn't you?"

His face clouded. "It went under. Most of the honeymooners got space sick their first day in weightlessness. Horrible publicity. I went broke."

"And sold it to Rockledge Industries, right?"

He got even more somber. "Yeah, right."

Rockledge made a success of the orbital hotel after buying Sam out, mainly because they'd developed a medication for space sickness. The facility is still there in low Earth orbit, part hotel, part museum. Sam was a pioneer, all right. An ornament to his profession, as far as I was concerned. But that's another story.

"And now you think you can make a tourist line to the belt pay off?"

Before he could answer, three things happened virtually simultaneously. The navigation computer chimed and announced, "Parking orbit established." At that instant we felt a slight lurch. Spacecrafts don't lurch, not unless something bad has happened to them, like hitting a rock or getting your airtight hull punctured.

Sure enough, the maintenance program sang out, "Main thruster disabled. Repair facilities urgently required."

Before we could do more than look at each other, our mouths hanging open, a fourth thing happened.

The comm speaker rumbled with a deep, snarling voice. "Who are you and what are you doing here?"

The screen showed a dark, scowling face: jowly, almost pudgy, dark hair pulled straight back from a broad forehead, tiny, deep-set eyes that burned into you. A vicious slash of a mouth turned down angrily. Irritation and suspicion written across every line of that face. He radiated power, strength, and the cold-blooded ruthlessness of a killer. Lars Fuchs.

"Answer me, or my next shot will blow away your crew pod."

I felt an urgent need to go to the bathroom. But Sam stayed cool as a polar bear.

"This is Sam Gunn. I've been trying to find you, Fuchs."

"Why?"

"I have a message for you."

"From Humphries? I'm not interested in hearing what he has to say."

Sam glanced at me, then said, "The message is from Mrs. Humphries."

I didn't think it was possible, but Fuchs's face went harder still. Then, in an even meaner tone, he said, "I'm not interested in anything she has to say either."

"She seemed very anxious to get this message to you, sir," Sam wheedled. "She hired us to come all the way out to the belt to deliver it to you personally."

He fell silent. I could feel my heart thumping against my ribs. Then Fuchs snarled, "It seems more likely to me that you're bait for a trap Humphries wants to spring on me. My former wife hasn't anything to say to me."

"But—"

"No buts! I'm not going to let you set me up for an ambush." I could practically *feel* the suspicion in his voice, his scowling face. And something more. Something really ugly. Hatred. Hatred for Humphries and everything associated with Humphries. Including his ex-wife.

"I'm no Judas goat," Sam snarled back. I was surprised at how incensed he seemed to be. You can never tell with Sam, but he seemed really teed off.

"I'm Sam Gunn, goddammit, not some sneaking decoy. I don't take orders from Martin Humphries or anybody else in the whole twirling solar system, and if you think . . ."

While Sam was talking, I glanced at the search radar, to see if it had locked onto Fuchs's ship. Either his ship was super stealthy, or it was much farther away than I had thought. *He must be a damned good shot with that laser*, I realized.

Sam was jabbering, cajoling, talking a mile a minute, trying to get Fuchs to trust him enough to let us deliver the chip to him.

Fuchs answered, "Don't you think I know that the chip you're carrying has a homing beacon built into it? I take the chip and a dozen Humphries ships come after me, following the signal the chip emits."

"No, it's not like that at all," Sam pleaded. "She wants you to see this message. She wouldn't try to harm you."

"She already has," he snapped.

I began to wonder if maybe he wasn't right. Was she working for her present husband to trap her ex-husband? Had she turned against the man whose life she had saved?

It couldn't be, I thought, remembering how haunted, how frightened she had looked. She couldn't be a Judas to him; she had married Humphries to save Fuchs's life, from all that I'd heard.

Then a worse thought popped into my head. *If Sam gives the chip to Fuchs, I'll have nothing to offer Humphries! All that money will fly out of my grasp!*

I had tried to copy the chip, but it wouldn't allow the ship's computer to make a copy. Suddenly I was on Fuchs' side of the argument: Don't take the chip! Don't come anywhere near it!

Fate, as they say, intervened.

The comm system pinged again, and suddenly the screen split. The other half showed Judge Myers, all smiles, obviously in a compartment aboard a spacecraft.

"Sam, we're here!" she said brightly. "At *The Rememberer*. It was so brilliant of you to pick the sculpture for our wedding ceremony!"

"Who the hell is that?" Fuchs roared.

For once in his life, Sam actually looked embarrassed. "Um . . . my, uh, fiancée," he stumbled. "I'm supposed to be getting married in two days."

The expression on Fuchs' face was almost comical. Here he's threatening to blow us into a cloud of ionized gas and all of a sudden, he's got an impatient bride-to-be on the same communications frequency.

"Married?" he bellowed.

"It's a long story," said Sam, red-cheeked.

Fuchs glared and glowered while Judge Myers's round, freckled face looked puzzled. "Sam? Why don't you answer? I know where you are. If you don't come out to *The Rememberer*, I'm going to bring the whole wedding party to you, minister and boys' choir and all."

"I'm busy, Jill," Sam said.

"Boys' choir?" Fuchs ranted. "Minister?"

Not even Sam could carry on two conversations at the same time, I thought. But I was wrong.

"Jill, I'm in the middle of something," he said, then immediately switched to Fuchs: "I can't hang around here, I've got to get to my wedding."

"Who are you talking to?" Judge Myers asked.

"What wedding?" Fuchs demanded. "Do you mean to tell me you're getting married out here in the belt?"

"That's exactly what I mean to tell you," Sam replied to him.

"Tell who?" Judge Myers asked. "What's going on, Sam?"

"Bah!" Fuchs snapped. "You're crazy! All of you!"

I saw a flash of light out of the corner of my eye. Through the cockpit's forward window, I watched a small, stiletto-slim spacecraft slowly emerge from the cloud of pebbles surrounding the asteroid, plasma exhaust pulsing from its thruster and a bloodred pencilbeam of laser light probing out ahead of it.

Fuchs bellowed, "I knew it!" and let loose a string of curses that would make an angel vomit.

Sam was swearing too. "Those sonsofbitches! They knew

we'd be here, and they were just lying in wait in case Fuchs showed up."

"I'll get you for this, Gunn!" Fuchs howled.

"I didn't know!" Sam yelled back.

Judge Myers looked somewhere between puzzled and alarmed. "Sam, what's happening? What's going on?"

The ambush craft was rising out of the rubble cloud that surrounded the asteroid. I could see Fuch's ship through the window now because he was shooting back at the ambusher, his own red pencilbeam of a spotting laser lighting up the cloud of pebbles like a Christmas ornament.

"We'd better get out of here, Sam," I suggested at the top of my lungs.

"How?" he snapped. "Fuchs took out the thruster."

"You mean we're stuck here?"

"Smack in the middle of their battle," he answered, nodding. "And our orbit's taking us between the two of them."

"Do something!" I screamed. "They're both shooting at us!"

Sam dove for the hatch. "Get into your suit, Gar. Quick."

I never suited up quicker. But it seemed to take hours. With our main thruster shot away, dear old *Achernar* was locked into its orbit around the asteroid. Fuchs and the ambusher were slugging it out, maneuvering and firing at each other with us in the middle. I don't think they were deliberately trying to hit us, but they weren't going out of their way to avoid us either. While I wriggled into my spacesuit and fumbled through the checkout procedure, *Achernar* lurched and quivered again and again.

"They're slicing us to ribbons," I said, trying to keep from babbling.

Sam was fully suited up; just the visor of his helmet was open. "You got the chip on you?"

For an instant I thought I'd left it in the cockpit. I nearly panicked. Then I remembered it was still in the waistband of my shorts. At least, I hoped it was still there.

"Yeah," I said. "I've got it."

Sam snapped his visor closed, then reached over to me and slammed mine shut. With a gloved hand, he motioned for me to follow him to the airlock.

"We're going outside?" I squeaked. I was really scared. A guy could get killed!

"You want to stay here while they take potshots at us?" Sam's voice crackled in my helmet earphones.

"But why are they shooting at us?" I asked. Actually, I was talking, babbling really, because if I didn't, I probably would've started screeching like a demented baboon.

"Fuchs thinks we led him into a trap," Sam said, pushing me into the airlock, "and the bastard who's trying to bushwhack him doesn't want any living witnesses."

He squeezed into the airlock with me, cycled it, and pushed me through the outer hatch when it opened.

All of a sudden, I was hanging in emptiness. My stomach heaved; my eyes blurred. I mean, there was nothing out there except a zillion stars, but they were so far away, and I was falling, I could feel it, falling all the way to infinity. I think I screamed. Or at least gasped like a drowning man.

"It's okay, Gar," Sam said, "I've got you."

He grasped me by the wrist and, using the jetpack on his suit's back, towed me away from the riddled hulk of *Achernar*. We glided into the cloud of pebbles surrounding the asteroid.

I could feel them pinging off my suit's hard shell; one of them banged into my visor, but it was a fairly gentle collision, no damage—except to the back of my head: I flinched so sharply that I whacked my head against the helmet hard enough to give me a concussion, almost, despite the helmet's padded interior.

Sam hunkered us down into the loose pile of rubble that was the main body of the asteroid. "Safer here than in the ship," he told me.

I burrowed into that beanbag as deeply as I could, scooping out pebbles with both hands, digging like a terrified gopher on speed. I would've dug all the way back to Earth if I could have.

Fuchs and the ambusher were still duking it out, with a spare laser blast now and then hitting *Achernar* as it swung slowly around the 'roid. The ship looked like a shambles, big gouges torn through its hull, chunks torn off and spinning lazily alongside its main structure.

They hadn't destroyed the radio, though. In my helmet earphones, I could hear Judge Myers's voice, harsh with static:

"Sam, if this is another scheme of yours . . ."

Sam tried to explain to her what was happening, but I don't think he got through. She kept asking what was going on and then, after a while, her voice cut off altogether.

Sam said to me, "Either she's sore at me and she's leaving the belt, or she's worried about me and she's coming here to see what's happening."

I hoped for the latter, of course. Our suits had air regenerators, I knew, but they weren't reliable for more than twenty-four hours, at best. From the looks of poor old *Achernar*, we were going to need rescuing, and damned soon too.

We still couldn't really see Fuchs's ship, it was either too far away in that dark emptiness, or he was jinking around too much for us to get a visual fix on him. I saw flashes of light that might have been puffs from maneuvering thrusters, or they might have been hits from the other guy's laser. The ambusher's craft was close enough for us to make out, most of the time. He was viffing and slewing this way and that, bobbing and weaving like a prizefighter trying to avoid his opponent's punches.

But then the stiletto flared into sudden brilliance, a flash so bright it hurt my eyes. I squeezed my eyes shut and saw the afterimage burning against my closed lids.

"Got a propellant tank," Sam said, matter-of-factly. "Fuchs'll close in for the kill now."

I opened my eyes again. The stiletto was deeply gashed along its rear half, tumbling and spinning out of control. Gradually, it pulled itself onto an even keel, then turned slowly and began to head away from the asteroid. I could see hot plasma streaming from one thruster nozzle, the other was dark and cold.

"He's letting him get away," Sam said, sounding surprised. "Fuchs is letting him limp back to Ceres or wherever he came from."

"Maybe Fuchs is too badly damaged himself to chase him down," I said.

"Maybe." Sam didn't sound at all sure of that.

We waited for another hour, huddled inside our suits in the beanbag of an asteroid. Finally, Sam said, "Let's get back to the ship and see what's left of her."

There wasn't much. The hull had been punctured in half a dozen places. Propulsion was gone. Life support shot. Communications marginal.

We clumped to the cockpit. It was in tatters; the main window was shot out, a long, ugly scar from a laser burn cut right across the control panel. The pilot's chair was ripped too. It was tough to sit in the bulky spacesuits, and we were in zero gravity, to boot. Sam just hovered a few centimeters above his chair. I realized that my stomach had calmed down. I had adjusted to zero G. After what we had just been through, zero G seemed downright comfortable.

"We'll have to live in the suits," Sam told me.

"How long can we last?"

"There are four extra air regenerators in stores," Sam said. "If they're not damaged, we can hold out for another forty-eight, maybe sixty hours."

"Time enough for somebody to come and get us," I said hopefully.

I could see his freckled face bobbing up and down inside his helmet. "Yep . . . provided anybody's heard our distress call."

The emergency radio beacon seemed to be functioning. I kept telling myself we'd be all right. Sam seemed to feel that way; he was positively cheerful.

"You really think we'll be okay?" I asked him. "You're not just trying to keep my hopes up?"

"We'll be fine, Gar," he answered. "We'll probably smell pretty ripe by the time we can get out of these suits, but except for that, I don't see anything to worry about."

Then he added, "Except . . ."

"Except?" I yelped. "Except what?"

He grinned wickedly. "Except that I'll miss the wedding." He made an exaggerated sigh. "Too bad."

So we lived inside the suits for the next day and a half. It wasn't all that bad, except we couldn't eat any solid food. Water and fruit juices, that was all we could get through the feeder tube. I started to feel like a Hindu ascetic on a hunger strike.

We tried the comm system, but it was intermittent, at best. The emergency beacon was faithfully sending out our distress call, of course, with our position. It could be heard all the way back to Ceres, I was sure. Somebody would come for us. Nothing to worry about. *We'll get out of this okay. Someday we'll look back on this and laugh. Or maybe shudder.* Good thing we had to stay in the suits; otherwise, I would have gnawed all my fingernails down to the wrist.

And then the earphones in my helmet suddenly blurted to life.

"Sam! Do you read me? We can see your craft!" It was Judge Myers. I was so overjoyed that I would have married her myself.

Her ship was close enough so that our suit radios could pick up her transmission.

"We'll be there in less than an hour, Sam," she said.

"Great!" he called back. "But hold your nose when we start peeling out of these suits."

Judge Myers laughed, and she and Sam chatted away like a pair of teenagers. But then Sam looked up at me and winked.

"Jill, I'm sorry this has messed up the wedding," he said, making his voice husky, sad. "I know you were looking forward to—"

"You haven't messed up a thing, Sam," she replied brightly. "After we've picked you up—and cleaned you up—we're going to go back to *The Rememberer* and have the ceremony as planned."

Sam's forehead wrinkled. "But haven't your guests gone back home? What about the boys' choir? And the caterers?"

She laughed. "The guests are all still here. As for the entertainment and the caterers, so I'll have to pay them for a few extra days. Hang the expense, Sam. This is our wedding we're talking about! Money is no object."

Sam groaned.

In a matter of hours, we were aboard Judge Myers' ship, *Parthia*, showered, shaved, clothed, and fed, heading to *The Rememberer* and Sam's wedding. Sam was like Jekyll and Hyde: While he and I were alone together, he was morose and mumbling, like a guy about to face a firing squad in the morning. When Judge Myers joined us for dinner, though, Sam was chipper and charming, telling jokes and spinning tall tales about old exploits. It was quite a performance; if Sam ever got into acting he would win awards, I was sure.

After dinner Sam and Judge Myers strolled off together to her quarters. I went back to the compartment they had given me, locked the door, and took out the chip.

It was easier this time, since I remembered the keys to the encryption. In less than an hour I had Amanda's hauntingly beautiful face on the display of my compartment's computer. I wormed a plug into my ear, taking no chances that somebody might eavesdrop on me.

The video was focused tightly on her face. For I don't know how long, I just gazed at her, hardly breathing. Then I shook myself out of the trance and touched the key that would run her message.

"Lars," she said softly, almost whispering, as if she were afraid somebody would overhear her, "I'm going to have a baby."

Holy mother in heaven! It's a good thing we didn't deliver this message to Fuchs. He would've probably cut us into little pieces and roasted them on a spit.

Amanda Cunningham Humphries went on, "Martin wants another son; he already has a five-year-old boy by a previous wife."

She hesitated, looked over her shoulder. Then, in an even lower voice, "I want you to know, Lars, that it will be *your* son that

I bear, not his. I've had myself implanted with one of the embryos we froze at Selene, back before all these troubles started."

I felt my jaw drop down to my knees.

"I love you, Lars," Amanda said. "I've always loved you. I married Martin because he promised he'd stop trying to kill you if I did. I'll have a son, and Martin will think it's his, but it will be your son, Lars. Yours and mine. I want you to know that, dearest. Your son."

Humphries would pay a billion for that, I figured.

And he'd have the baby Amanda was carrying aborted. Maybe he'd kill her too.

"So what are you going to do about it, Gar?"

I whirled around in my chair. Sam was standing in the doorway.

"I thought I locked—"

"You did. I unlocked it." He stepped into my compartment and carefully slid the door shut again. "So, Gar, what are you going to do?"

I popped the chip out of the computer and handed it to Sam.

He refused to take it. "I read her message the first night on our way to the belt," Sam said, sitting on the edge of my bed. "I figured you'd try to get it off me, one way or another."

"So you gave it to me."

Sam nodded gravely. "So now you know what her message is. The question is, what are you going to do about it?"

I offered him the chip again. "Take it, Sam. I don't want it."

"It's worth a lot of money, Gar."

"I don't want it!" I repeated, a little stronger.

Sam reached out and took the chip from me. Then, "But you know what she's doing. You could tell Humphries about it. He'd pay a lot to know."

I started to reply, but to my surprise I found that I had to swallow hard before I could any words out. "I couldn't do that to her," I said.

Sam looked square into my eyes. "You certain of that?"

I almost laughed. "What's a few hundred million bucks? I don't need that kind of money."

"You're certain?"

"Yes, dammit, I'm certain!" I snapped. It wasn't easy tossing away all that money, and Sam was starting to irritate me.

"Okay," he said, breaking into that lopsided smile of his. "I believe you."

Sam got to his feet, his right fist closed around the chip.

"What will you do with it?" I asked.

"Pop it out an airlock. A few days in hard UV should degrade it so badly that even if somebody found it in all this emptiness, they'd never be able to read it."

I got up from my desk chair. "I'll go with you," I said.

So the two of us marched down to the nearest airlock and got rid of the chip. I had a slight pang when I realized how much money we had just tossed out into space, but then I realized I had saved Amanda's life, most likely, and certainly the life of her baby. Hers and Fuchs's.

"Fuchs will never know," Sam said. "I feel kind of sorry for him."

"I feel sorry for her," I said.

"Yeah. Me too."

As we walked down the passageway back toward my compartment, curiosity got the better of me.

"Sam," I asked, "what if you weren't sure that I'd keep her message to myself? What if you thought I'd sneak off to Humphries and tell him what was on that chip?"

He glanced up at me. "I've never killed a man," he said quietly, "but I'd sure stuff you into a lifeboat and set you adrift. With no radio."

I blinked at him. He was dead serious.

"I wouldn't last long," I said.

"Probably not. Your ship would drift through the belt for a long time, though. Eons. You'd be a real Flying Dutchman."

"I'm glad you trust me."

"I'm glad I can trust you, Gar." He gave me a funny look, then added, "You're in love with her, too, aren't you?"

It took me a few moments to reply, "Who wouldn't be?"

———

So we flew to *The Rememberer* with Judge Myers and all the wedding guests and the minister and boys' choir, the caterers and all the food and drink for a huge celebration. Six different news nets were waiting for us: the wedding was going to be a major story.

Sam snuck away, of course. He didn't marry Jill Myers after all. She was so furious that she . . .

But that's another story.

AFTERWORD: 1491

One of the attractions that lures writers to tackle science fiction stories, as opposed to other *genres* of fiction, is science fiction's connection with the real world.

What? I can hear you gasping. Stories about the distant future or the remote past have a connection with the real world? Aren't they fantastic tales, wish fulfillments, or dreams about the utopias (and dystopias) that our descendants may encounter?

Some are just that, of course. But the best science fiction tales are like telescopes that show us the *possibilities* of the future. Predictions, warnings, visions of what might happen to the human race in coming years. Or centuries. Or millennia.

For example, cast your mind back to the year 1491. I know, that's in the past, not the future. But bear with me for a few moments.

In 1491, Europe was a collection of losers. The great and

wealthy powers of the world lay to the East: the Muslim nations of Turkey, Persia, and such; fabled India, mysterious and remote China.

Europe was where the losers were shoved. Over the ages the original Stone Age inhabitants of Europe were drowned in newcomers from the East, who had been pushed away from the wealth and knowledge of the great empires of the Orient until they ran into the barrier of the Atlantic Ocean and could retreat no farther.

Losers.

The Atlantic was truly a barrier in 1491. Europeans ventured out onto its stormy seas just a little bit. A few of the Vikings—brave and desperate for land—actually crossed the ocean and established colonies in the lands they found on the other side of the Atlantic, but they told no others about their discoveries, and their colonies eventually withered.

So the Europeans huddled in their crowded lands, bickering and fighting with one another, while the rich and powerful nations to the east prospered.

Until 1492.

The Europeans learned to build ships that could cross the Atlantic safely. They sailed west, hoping to reach the fabled wealth of China and India.

Instead, they found a New World. And built new nations, new civilizations that changed the entire world, eventually. Changed it for the better.

The greatest discovery they made was the realization that they had no need for kings and hereditary gentry. They could govern themselves. They discovered (invented?) democracy.

We are the inheritors of that discovery. We have been born

into a world that is far richer in wealth and freedom than any of the civilizations that preceded us, thanks to the treasures of new resources and new freedoms that our forebears have developed.

And today, we stand on the edge of a new sea, just as dark and dangerous as the Atlantic once was. And even more promising. A new sea that begins a hundred miles above your head.

The new sea of space.

This generation of humankind—*our* generation—has an opportunity that has not been offered to humanity since 1492. In merely the brief forays into space that we have made so far, we have found treasures of natural resources large enough to completely transform civilization, to erase poverty and build a new global civilization of wealth and freedom.

A few bold and farsighted humans have already begun this quest. They are the leaders of humankind's new era of expansion, outward to the moon and Mars, then farther until we have reached all the bodies of the solar system. And ultimately to the stars themselves.

Our future is limitless.

You ain't seen nothin' yet.

THE END . . . OF THE BEGINNING